WELL-HEELED

AN EMILY'S PLACE MYSTERY

BY ROZ SIEGEL

To my Grandchildren, Hallie, Evan, Willa, Josh and Eli—May you enjoy your own creativity in all the myriad forms it already exists—and invent new ones.

By Roz Siegel

Cover Design: Lisa Chovnick

ONE

A complete shoe was recently discovered in a cave in Armenia that is believed to be approximately 5500 years old.

Does the Angel of Death exist? And if so, does He wear shoes? Or, now that I think of it, does She wear shoes? And if so, what kind of shoes? Surely they would have to have soft soles so the victim wouldn't hear anyone coming.

These are the kinds of questions that occur to me at night, after I have put up the Closed sign on Emily's Place—the most successful discount shoe store on the whole Upper West Side if I must say so myself.

Would The Angel of Death wear high heels? Never! She would have to cover too much territory.

I tried to picture the Angel of Death, but I didn't get very far. And yet, there are some people who see her very clearly. Sophia Sarfatti, for example.

I was sure if I could see the shoes of the Angel of Death I would know everything about her.

You can tell a lot about a person from their shoes. Take Sophia Sarfatti, for example. Neat as a pin, all over, small, porcelain skin, deeply lined and powdered. Her hair dyed black and pulled back in a bun. Her shoes were always carefully polished but the soles! How she must drag her feet. Bruised, pitted, worn down paper-thin. Holes! There were holes in her soles.

Was there a metaphor hiding here somewhere?

Former English teacher that I am—did I mention the shoe store is a second career?—I couldn't resist a metaphor. Just thinking of poor Sophia's soul. Wounded, worn-out. Like a small bird that never learned to fly, she could dress her upper body but she could never lift her feet from the mire. A Jew, whose family had lived in Italy since the days of the Spanish Inquisition. Her whole family was killed by the Fascists in Italy during WWII.

You can read souls from soles.

Habits. You can learn the habits of people from their shoes too.

In my former life, living with the two-timing, low-down Larry The Loser, about whom the less said the better, I would go to fancy restaurants with friends who always insisted on changing their table.

It didn't matter what the restaurant, what the table. Harriet Klein, Marcia Jacobs, Hilda Perlmutter, would always ask for a different table.

So, it came as no surprise to me that certain customers, i.e. Rosa Gonzalez, Susan Nusbaum, and Felica Wong, always returned their shoes.

I must have sold three hundred pairs of shoes to Ida Rabinowitz but she only kept the last, because I could see, even though I am a little near-sighted, being a woman-of-a-certain-age, that she had worn them out in the street.

Complaints. There are some customers whose whole lives are filled with complaints—the shoes are too tight, too loose, too wide, too narrow; the color is wrong, faded, streaked; the strap is too tight, the strap is too loose; the bow fell off, the buckle is broken, the lining is lumpy, the heel is too high, the neck is too low, the toes are too pinched, the nails too exposed; the leather is stiff, the leather is soft; there's no support, there's too much slide.

And so, when Sophia Sarfatti, she of the worn down, worn out soles and shoes, who never made a complaint in her life and only just wants to be left alone to live her quiet, sad, little life in her small apartment in the brownstone across the street and down the block complained that "there was some problem, something lumpy" in her right shoe, I took the matter very seriously.

I had just finished my morning cup of coffee in the back room, and walked into the showroom to unlock the front door, when I saw her waiting on the doorstep.

Small—wrapped up in a worn black winter coat, although it was a balmy April morning—Sophia handed me a black patent-leather pump, size 7, right shoe.

"It don't feel good," she said, shaking her head. "I don't know. The left shoe is fine. But this one—the heel is—is bumpy. Lumpy. Something."

I took the shoe in one hand and Sophia with the other and helped her inside.

"No. Not today," she waved away my offer of a cup of coffee. "No time." Today she wouldn't even take a seat. "There are things I have to do," she said, "there is not much time left." And she pulled her lower eye-lid down with a finger and whispered, "Furbo! Furbo!"

So, Okay. I don't understand Italian words but I've learned a number of Italian symbols, such as fingers held in such a position as to indicate "horns" or a Cuckold. The eye-lid pull I've heard tell means "Shrewd" or "Sly" or "Sharp." As in "I know something you don't know."

Some of these gestures do not have an exact translation. It's enough to try to translate common Yiddish terms and gestures so when there is an Italian-Jew involved, you kind of had to be there and see it for yourself.

To make a long story short, Sophia was a little strange even on her good days, so I didn't think too much of what she said or did until much later.

"I'm sorry about the shoe," I said to her. It was manufactured in Italy by a small company, Periggi & Son, and this particular shoe I had bought a couple of weeks ago, in a shipment of "seconds."

I'm proud to say that in the four years I've been running Emily's Place it's gotten the reputation of being New York's

Supermarket for Shoes. Everything from a $5 discontinued sneaker to a $1200 pair of Prada shoes can be bought here—all at discount prices.

Naturally, in order to get the best prices for my customers, I've had to be very creative at finding independent contractors, new, undiscovered designers, and small, unknown vendors.

Also, I do a big business with the Chinese who have a genius for copying anything.

At Emily's Place you can buy a knock-off of a knock-off.

Wasn't it T.S. Eliot who said *an exact copy was better than an imitation*?

And of course, "Seconds" are a very important part of my business.

"Seconds" can be anything from a few left-over styles and sizes the Fifth Avenue Stores don't want, to a pair of shoes whose colors have faded; or have some defect in the sewing, or leather, or structure of the shoe itself.

It is usually understood that the greater the defect the lower the price, so my customers rarely complain.

So I wasn't entirely surprised when Sophia said there was some problem with the fit.

"Don't worry about it," I reassured her. "If I can't fix it I'll give you a credit for another pair of shoes."

Sophia sighed and handed me the mate. "So it don't get lost."

I took the shoes and put them on my work table in the back room to check them over after I closed up shop. When I came back out into the showroom I was surprised to see that Sophia was still there.

And a man had entered the store.

A very elegantly dressed gentleman with gray hair, a walking stick, and expensive Italian shoes.

Most of the men who come into Emily's Place are either cross-dressers, husbands or lovers of one of my customers. So a man alone was always a Special Occasion.

Suddenly out of nowhere, my store Manager, Merissa appeared. Almost six feet tall, dark as ebony, Merissa is drop-dead gorgeous.

Before I could even move my legs in his direction she was showing him to a seat and engaged in what looked like intimate, and most animated, conversation.

Suddenly Sophia let out a howl, as chilling as a dog run over by a truck, and uttered the words, "Fotinni Fatale," and fell to the floor.

Merissa, Mr. Elegant Gentleman and Moi arrived at Sophia's side at just about the same time and almost fell over each other lifting her frail body into the nearest chair.

Merissa untied a yellow silk scarf from her head and fanned Sophia, while I fetched her a glass of cold water.

Mr. Elegant Gentleman seemed entirely disconcerted.

"I can come back another day," he said, wringing his hands.

At this point, Sophia opened her eyes, and breathing heavily put her hand on her heart.

"I'll call a doctor," I offered.

"No! No!" Sophia grabbed my hand. "I'll be all right."

She stared at The Elegant Gentleman with horror in her eyes.

"How about Merissa here, takes you home?" I asked her, "What do you say?"

Sophia could not stop staring at The Elegant Gentleman. It was getting embarrassing. It was certainly not good for business.

I looked at Merissa and Merissa looked at me.

"Bien sur Merissa will take this lovely lady home. It is my pleasure," she said, turning on her fake French accent, and with that, she linked her arm around Sophia and started walking her to the door.

The Elegant Gentleman shook his head.

"Poverina" he said, "Poor woman."

"I think she will be all right," I tried to comfort him and turn the conversation around to the selling and buying of shoes. "How can I help you?"

Now the gentleman rallied. He smiled at me—a lovely smile displaying clean, straight, white teeth. He bowed and actually took my hand and lifted it to his lips.

"My name is Massimo Bellini," he said, in a slightly accented voice. And he looked directly into my eyes while he cradled my hand in his own.

Nice!

I mean, when was the last time a man kissed my hand?

"I have come to buy a pair of shoes for my girlfriend," he uttered at last, letting go of my hand.

I should have known he was too good to be alone.

"I am sure we can find a shoe to satisfy you and your friend." I told him

He held up his hand.

"My girlfriend is very particular. She has told me exactly the shoe she desires."

He took out a piece of paper from his vest pocket and read:

"Size 7, black patent leather, made by Periggi & Son, model # 84963."

I chuckled. "Such a coincidence!" I told him. "That is exactly the same shoe that I recently sold Sophia Sarfatti—the woman who swooned when she saw you."

Bellini's brown eyes opened wide.

"Certainly Sophia is not the first woman who has swooned when she sees you?"

Bellini was not amused by my attempt to flatter him.

Or perhaps it was the mention of Sophia that seemed to disconcert him.

He tucked the paper back in his pocket and glanced conspicuously at his watch—a Patek Phillippe in rose gold from the 1930's that I recognized immediately since one of my estranged husband's annoying habits was to buy himself outrageously over-priced vintage watches.

"That poor lady obviously mistook me for someone else," he said, shuffling his feet, "I am rather pressed for time, I'm afraid. If you would be so good as to look for the shoes—Size 7, I would be much obliged."

Shelving any thoughts of romance, I went into the store room and pulled out the last box of model #84963, size 7.

For a moment I wondered if I should warn him about a possible defect in the heel—but I decided to keep my mouth shut. Why put ideas into a customer's head that there will be a problem with a purchase? That much about business I had learned.

I handed Bellini the shoe box to him and his whole face lit up—before he even opened the box.

"Periggi & Son" he read the label happily, "Size 7."

I may be considered by many to be the Shoe Expert of the Western World—or at least of Upper Broadway—but I had never heard of Periggi & Son until a couple of months ago.

I watched Bellini with more and more interest. What could he possibly know about shoes that I didn't?

He opened the box and took out one of the shoes. Black Patent Leather, size 7.

Then he lifted the shoe to his nose, sniffed the leather, and then, he held it up to his ear.

And then he saw me staring at him.

He quickly replaced the shoe with the same guilty expression my estranged husband Larry the Loser used to wear when I caught him looking at pornography—and took out his wallet.

"Do you have any more like this, in this size? My friend, she has a sister. Also, she tells me this shoe is so comfortable, she wants two pair. I will buy whatever you have."

I glanced at the shoe. One customer said it was too uncomfortable to wear; another one says it is so comfortable she wants multiple pairs. Go figure! Edmund Wilson, the book critic once said, 'No two people read the same book.' I suppose it is equally true that 'No two women wear the same shoes.'

"I'm sorry," I told him. "This is my last pair."

He handed me $54 and didn't even wait for me to ring up a proper receipt or put the shoes in a bag—off he went.

An hour or so later, the gorgeous Merissa arrived back. After she admitted to me she really wasn't Haitian, I was annoyed at her phony French—but lately I'd decided it lent some class to Emily's Place. She was taking lessons to improve it. It certainly seemed to impress Bellini.

Since Sophia Sarfatti just lives around the block, I figured Merissa was not exactly rushing back. Indulgent employer that I am, I settled for a dirty look and said, as sweetly as possible, "How's Sophia?"

Merissa rolled her eyes. "Mon dieu! Cette Femme is not well, not well at all. She grabbed on to me like a cat hanging from the branch of a tree and say words over and over again, "A ghost! A ghost! I seen a ghost! Then she mumble all these other words, sound like Italian, and then some of those Jew words I hear from Sylvia Bloomberg, that sound like "Oy! Oy! Oy! And something with an M, "the mala…."

"The Molochamovis?"

"Yes," Merissa, smiled broadly. "That's it. She say that word over and over again."

I shivered. "It means The Angel of Death."

Merissa shook her head. " She sure act like she has seen him. So I put her to bed. Asked her if she had any medicine, help her relax, something, maybe for her heart. 'No,' she yell at me. 'I don't never take no medicine. Don't know what they put there in them pills.' Made her a cup of tea—that's what took so long—and come back to work."

We both looked out over the showroom which was filled with customers.

"I try to call a doctor, but she gets real upset. She say she will be fine. She don't need anything more. So I leave."

"Can't help someone, doesn't want help," I told her, "Try Chris Kennedy there in the corner. She's been waiting for fifteen minutes."

The rest of the day was pretty much of a blur. Things can get pretty busy at Emily's Place, especially when the new Spring Shoes come in.

Harriet Moskowitz kicked Antonia Morassini and tried to wrench the last pair of Gucci platform sandals out of her hands. Tiffany Brown wanted to return a pair of shoes she had already worn for a week. Hilda Mendez actually started to cry when I told her I was sold out of Jimmy Choo red satin stilettos. Two kids from the Brandeis High School sneaked a smoke in the store's bathroom setting off the smoke alarm so I didn't have any time to think about Sophia Sarfatti or the Angel of Death until closing time.

When the last customer had closed the door, and Merissa had helped me box and stack all the shoes lying around the showroom and gone home, I finally locked the front door, put up the CLOSED SIGN, and went into the backroom.

First thing I did was pour myself a cup of coffee. A cup of coffee is part of the tradition here at Emily's Place. I can't feed everyone in the neighborhood. I can't bring back Emma Levison's husband of forty-five years who died of a heart attack last week. I can't make Hallie Nussbaum—who's already had six miscarriages—pregnant. I can't find Dorothy Malone—who was fired after twenty-three years as a copyeditor and is six months behind in her rent—a job, but I can give everyone in the neighborhood a cup of coffee and a shoulder to lean on when they need it.

Also, I like coffee. One of the health magazines said it gave you cystic breasts so I tried to cut it out for a while but then I said, "the hell with it," and my breasts are doing just fine.

I walked over to my work table in the corner of the backroom. I've been selling shoes long enough to know what's wrong with a shoe, even if I can't fix it.

So I picked up Sophia's right shoe, black patent leather, size 7, Periggi & Son. First thing I did is run my hand over the smooth leather, inside and out.

Felt good. Surprisingly good.

Then I smelled it.

That's when I remembered that Massimo Bellini had smelled the shoe when I brought it out to him.

Now, most customers, especially men, will stare at a shoe presented to them. Then, they may stroke it—even cuddle it, depending on their sexual orientation—I've even seen someone "lick" it.

But only someone intimately involved with shoes will smell the leather.

What does Massimo Bellini know about shoes manufactured by Periggi & Son that Emily of Emily's Place does not? I have to say that my professional pride was at stake here.

Here was a company that produced a quality product, using high-end leather and I had just recently found out about it.

Accidently, if you will.

Frankie The Fox had offered me ten pair of Size 7, black patent leather shoes made by Periggi & Son for such a low price I could hardly refuse.

"Seconds," he said to me, as I peeled off a few bills. "There's more where that came from," he tossed over his shoulder as he walked out the door.

Did I mention that sometimes "Seconds" come with a murky history?

There are strict laws governing the movement of products from Europe and Asia across the seas into America. There are tariffs and fees and licenses all along the way. Just as there are strict laws, papers, fees, examinations and licenses governing the movement and entrance of immigrants into our country.

And yet, we all know, that undocumented immigrants appear in New York City.

Many of them find their way to the Upper West Side where they live with relatives or friends in spite of housing, fire, and immigration laws, and they manage to make a living without licenses and documents.

Just so with products. There are some that happen to "fall off the trucks." Or to put it another way, someone knew someone who knew someone who had a cousin who got his hands on a few pair of shoes that slipped the notice of the customs people, somewhere between Europe or Asia and the U.S. These shoes might be picked up by some of these same undocumented immigrants and find their way into shoe stores, or discount outlets all over the city.

And sometimes, they find their way into Emily's Place.

In these transactions my policy is like Bill Clinton's idea of dealing with gay men in the armed forces: "Don't ask, don't tell."

As far as I'm concerned, a few pair of shoes that fall off the truck now and then is a benefit to the whole neighborhood.

Frankie the Fox is a neighborhood kid who once had an expensive drug habit—now clean—just trying to make his way in the world.

Once upon-a-time, I gave Frankie a cup of coffee and a few dollars when he was really down and out, so now he figures, he owes me.

Every once in a while he hears of "a good deal" on a few pair of shoes and counts me in.

Try as I may, I can't feel guilty about cashing in every once in a while on a deal like this. It's good for Frankie, it's good for the customer and it's good for me.

If truth be told, not only am I not feeling guilty, I'm wondering how I can get my hands on more "seconds" from this interesting, new company.

After all, I've got to make a living, just like everybody else.

I ran my hand up and down the heel.

Solidly made. Two inches high, two inches thick. A really good, walking shoe.

I put my hand inside the shoe and ran my thumb over the top of the heel.

Felt perfectly fine to me.

But when I replaced it on the table, next to its mate, I could see that the heel was on crooked. The heights of the heels varied slightly. Something was wrong.

I reached for a tool, and carefully began to pull out the nails holding the heel onto the shoe.

With one final tug, the heel came free.

I stared dumbly down into a hollowed out center of the two inch heel.

It was filled to the top with shiny, white, stones.

Diamonds!

Instinctively I looked over my shoulder. I remembered that I had locked the door.

I bent over the table and carefully spilled out the diamonds.

Wow!

There must have been a couple of dozen, from little chips to full-cut diamonds in round, pear, and marquis-shapes.

Did I say I felt no guilt at dealing in a few shoes "that fell off the truck?"

This was a different situation all together! Even if I had to pay some fine or other for buying some items "without proper documentation," I'd chalk it up to just the cost of doing business. Small potatoes any way you look at it. But diamonds! Diamonds were serious. Even as I looked down upon the glittering pin points of light that danced in the air as if vibrating with a life of their own, I saw red lights of danger flashing in front of me.

I bit my lip.

What to do?

Had Frankie the Fox out-foxed me? Had he and some Mafia organization been using Emily's place as a clearing house for stolen goods?

Or was Frankie as much a dupe as I was in some scheme that was a lot larger than both of us?

I carefully picked up the diamonds and put them one by one back into the heel of the shoe. Damn! One of them rolled off the table and fell on the floor.

Did I mention that I have a really lovely carpet in Emily's Place? Blue-green like the sea. Plush, thick, so you can curl your toes in it. Makes everyone feel calm and happy as soon as they come in.

So here I am squatting down, running my hand up and down and all around. And squatting isn't easy for a woman of a certain age—strike that. Squatting is ok. It's getting up afterwards that's the problem.

I find the back of an earring I lost about a year ago, a couple of paper clips and finally—I find the thing—small and shiny like a star fallen out of heaven. Naturally, I put it in my pocket cause I need both hands to pull myself back up to a standing position.

When I finally got upright again, I stared down at the small pile of diamonds that remained on my work table.

I put my hand in my pocket and extracted the little stone. It was perfectly round and felt smooth and cold to the touch.

I held it up to the light. It seemed to cause the whole room to glow.

I have never owned a diamond.

When Larry and I got married, he was still in Law School. We didn't have a dime. When we finally got some money, there were other things to buy—a car—an apartment.

I had never thought much about diamonds, but I did now.

Who did these stones belong to? Mafia scum. People who lived off prostitution and drugs.

I looked over my shoulder—and then up at the ceiling.

Who could possibly know if one was missing?

The fact that it had rolled off the table and practically into my pocket seemed like The Hand of Providence. I mean, I wasn't a particularly religious person but I did believe there was Something Up There.

The long and short of it was I put the pretty little thing back into my pocket.

For sure the cops would keep a few samples before bringing the load to The Evidence Room.

The Cops!

What come to think of it, was I going to do with "this load" anyway?

For a minute I thought of calling Murphy the Cop, my some-time friend who I helped capture Goodie One Shoes.

But what would I say? It was now clear to me that these shoes that "fell off the truck" were stolen goods. People could be put in jail for dealing in stolen goods.

Not to mention the fact that people who rat on the Mafia tend to disappear off the face of the earth rather quickly.

No. I had to think of something else.

I called my estranged husband, Larry the Loser.

Larry might not excel as a husband, especially in the fidelity department, but he had been a Public Defender in the Bronx for ten years before turning his hand to wills and estates and had a great affinity for the criminal mind.

The phone rang four times before he picked it up.

"Yes." His voice was groggy and there was machine-gun fire in the background.

He probably fell asleep watching one of those World War II movies.

After twenty years of marriage I unfortunately knew all about his crumby little habits.

"It's me." I said.

I pictured him reaching for the rest of his half-finished scotch to give him the courage to talk to me. Our relationship has had its ups and downs. He still couldn't forgive me for leaving him—couldn't stand that there was no one around to pick up after him, find his glasses and keys. His Russian Borscht-guzzler hadn't proven to be talented in that area.

Also, he seemed afraid of me much of the time. Probably thought that one day I was going to demand a "real" divorce with money.

For all these reasons, he usually fortified himself with a stiff drink before dealing with me.

I could actually hear him swallow.

"So," he said at last. "To what do I owe the honor of this call?"

"I have a small problem I would like to share with you."

"Yeah," he said, "If you want to share it with me, it must be a big problem. The last time you asked for my help, a couple of people were murdered."

I ignored his remark in the spirit of cooperation that I was hoping for and tried to find some round-about manner of telling Larry about the diamonds without scaring him off.

"I found something that doesn't belong there in the heel of a shoe." I said at last.

There was a slight pause. He was taking another taste of scotch.

"And where did this shoe come from, may I ask—South America?"

"Don't be so smart," I told him. "My shoes don't come from South America. They come from Italy."

"That's even worse," said Larry the Loser. "If you're telling me you found some small packets of white powder in the heel of a shoe, count me out."

"Diamonds." I said. "I found diamonds." It felt good to know I could still surprise him, after all these years.

For this news he probably needed to pour himself another scotch.

I waited patiently, while bombs were being dropped on Germany—or possibly Italy—in the background.

"I'll be right over," he said, and hung up the phone.

"Wow!" said Larry the Loser when I poured out the diamonds on the table.

Exactly what I said when I saw them. Maybe there was a reason we were together for twenty years.

He picked up a few of them and cradled them in his hand.

"Haven't seen a stash like this since Monty-the-Mountain Esposito was arrested in 1986.

Where'd you get the shoes?"

"Neighborhood kid. Frankie the Fox."

"Italian kid?" Larry asked me.

I nodded.

"Do you have a bill of sale? Receipts? Customs clearance?"

I shrugged. "Kid said they fell off the truck."

Larry got up from the table and banged the chair on the floor.

"What is the matter with you?" he shouted. "Don't you know dealing in stolen goods is a crime?"

I sat down on the chair recently man-handled by Larry and stared calmly up at him.

"I was just trying to help this kid make a few bucks. He used to be a drug addict."

Larry shook his head.

"Yeah, and I bet his mother is dying of kidney failure and is paralyzed from a stroke."

"Could be," I said.

"You'd better hope she is. And those missing receipts we talked about? Didn't you have some water leak in here ? Could be they were lost in the flood."

"Absolutely." I told him. "Gone without a trace."

Larry opened his hand and slowly poured the diamonds back onto the table.

"How many did you put in your pocket," he asked me.

For a moment I was speechless.

"How could you think such a thing?" I challenged him.

"Don't forget I lived with you for twenty years."

I jumped up from my seat. "And you think I'm a thief?"

"Not a thief," he retreated. "Let's just say you are a person who can sometimes take advantage of a situation. I seem to remember some years ago when your bank made a slight error in your favor. I had a hell of a time convincing you to give the money back."

Now I really was angry.

"Those banks are the biggest thieves of all. They probably made hundreds of mistakes not in my favor." I sat down again. "As if you never broke the law!"

Larry cocked his head and smiled. "I never break the law. I might…bend the law from time to time…."

"Bend the law! More like "twist it into a pretzel. Call it whatever you want, but don't lecture me on morality!"

For a moment we faced each other, eyes flashing. We had been through this so many times before.

Larry the adulterer. Larry, whose Russian Kreplach was still working in his office.

How dare the kettle call the frying pan black!

And then we both turned away.

Larry took a deep breath.

"How many shoes fell off the truck?"

"I bought ten pair."

He looked down at the diamonds on the table.

"Could be there were diamonds in all ten pair—or only a few that were marked in some way. Where are the other pairs?"

I shook my head.

"There aren't any left. I'm sold out."

Larry ran his fingers through the few hairs left on his head.

"Whoever put those diamonds in the shoes will be coming back for them."

"I know." I said. "In fact, he might already have come."

I told Larry about the elegant Bellini and his interest in this particular shoe. He scowled.

"I wouldn't trust a man named after a drink from Harry's Bar." Then his face lit up.

"Remember Harry's Bar in Venice? Afterwards we rode in a gondolier and made love in our room overlooking the Grand Canal."

"I remember the gondolier," I told him. "That's about it."

"You're lying," he said to me. Then he shook his head and sighed.

"The Mafia people I know don't kiss lady's hands. There are other criminals. Anyway, you should be okay. The bad guys will only be interested in the shoes. Do you have a list of who you sold them to?"

I nodded.

"Lose it. Tell anyone else who comes looking you sold all the shoes to people off the street—for cash. They will understand that."

I nodded again. "What should we do with the diamonds?"

Larry shrugged. "That depends on who was sending them. If it is Mafia, I may be able to broker a deal with the D.A.'s office for whoever the fall guy is. But let me find out a little more about how these diamonds 'got lost.' If this is some kind of rival gang situation we might be better off just handing the stuff back to whoever says he lost it. For now, I'll keep the shoes and the diamonds and put them in the safe at home." Larry put his arm around my shoulder. "I wouldn't want either of us to be killed just when things are going so well between us."

Damn! I should have known Larry the Loser would want something in return for his help. Just because I slept with him on our anniversary doesn't mean I'm ready to lie down every time he does me a favor. I smiled politely. "What should I tell the customer who brought me the shoes?"

Larry looked out towards the show-room. "Why don't you just tell her you couldn't fix the pair she gave you so you have found her a better, more comfortable, more expensive pair to replace them."

He walked towards my desk and picked up a couple of shoe catalogues.

"Where's the bathroom?" he asked me.

I pointed to the door in the corner. "Sorry, "I told him, "I don't stock Playboy."

Larry walked right past me, and closed the door behind him.

Next thing I knew I heard the water going full force in the sink.

Larry emerged a couple of minutes later, sans catalogues and stood solidly in front of the door while I tried to push him away.

Behind the bathroom door the water splashed loudly and steadily. I could picture it sloshing over the rim of the sink and dripping down to the floor.

Larry folded his arms across his chest and stood his ground. “Your flood.” He told me, as water began slowly flowing out, under the door, and sinking into my sea-blue carpet.

“Be sure and call your insurance agent so there is a record,” he said at last as he moved away from the bathroom and picked up his jacket.

“Thanks a lot!” I yelled over my shoulder as I grabbed the towels off the rack and tried to stem the tide.

“My pleasure,” Larry called over his shoulder, and he walked out the door.

One of the things about Larry that really irritates me is that it is sometimes comforting to have him around.

I have chosen “to be a woman alone,” who is completely independent. But sometimes, though I hate to admit it, it felt good to have someone who understands you help solve your problems.

I looked at my watch. It was only 7:00 and Sophia just lived around the corner.

I picked out a pair of Ferragamo shoes in a similar style to the Periggi shoe, found a size 7 and wrapped them up.

I figured I’d visit with Sophia for a little while and see if she needed anything. Then I would head over to Zabar’s, one of the best gourmet food markets on Upper Broadway, and pick-up some exotically prepared chicken for dinner.

Sophia lived in a brownstone whose cracked front steps told the story of its tenants before you even reached the front door. Here was a corner of the West Side overlooked by the current mania for renovation.

A couple of young Hispanic women sat smoking on steps one and two. A tattered, homeless man was asleep on the third step. The top step was taken up by an immensely fat, gray-haired black lady known locally as SuperMama. Whether this was because she was the superintendent of the house, or because of her size, I was never quite sure.

"Got any shoes for me today?" SuperMama asked me, when I got close.

Today she was wearing a pair of pink bedroom slippers, Sears, circa, 1970.

"I'm going to look around, for you," I said, "Would that be size 9?"

"Now how you know that honey? Sure be nice to have a new pair of something to wear to church."

I made a mental note to check my sale racks for something suitable and opened the front door.

"Guess it's Miss Sarfatti you're wantin to see. Ain't seen her all day, since she come back with Merissa. I knock two, three times at her door but she don't answer."

I shrugged. "Don't think she was feeling well today. I'll just walk up and see if maybe she feels well enough for company."

SuperMama shook her head slowly from side to side.

"That woman too skinny. Some peoples—I don't tell no tales—but some peoples don't eat enough. Don't like to spend a dime. Miss Sarfatti. Just yesterday she so weak she almost fall down those stairs. The Senator—he skinny too but strong as an ox—grab her arm just in time. I say 'Miss Sarfatti—I going to the butcher today—I goin' get you a nice chicken. Cook it up just right for you, but she shake her head. 'It's these shoes', she say, 'They make me trip.' But I say she don't eat right. Lordy, Lordy."

"Well" I said to SuperMama, "Maybe not. But this time I think the problem really was the shoes. I brought her a new pair."

I pushed opened the front door, whose lock seemed permanently broken, and walked up the one flight of stairs to her apartment.

Inside, the halls looked clean. SuperMama was big enough to scare the kids so they didn't graffiti the walls. Nonetheless, there was a strong smell of urine. Guess the druggies who came and went weren't scared of anything.

When I got to her door I rang the bell.

There was no answer.

No surprise there. Sophia Sarfatti didn't open her door to just anyone.

I knocked on the door and called out loudly "It's me. Emily. I'm bringing you your shoes."

Still no answer. I knocked again a little harder and the door swung slightly open. This was a surprise. Sophia Sarfatti always kept her door securely locked. I was beginning to get a bad feeling in the pit of my stomach. I pushed the door open a little wider so I could look inside. The front room looked neat and tidy as usual.

I stuck my head in the door and called out loudly "Sophia! It's me Emily! I have your shoes!"

Not a sound.

Frail. Elderly—she must be well into her eighties and she clearly wasn't feeling well this morning. I felt more anxious than before. And a little guilty. Surely, I should have insisted on calling a doctor.

I walked into the living room. It was small and dark, like most of the rooms in these narrow brownstones. Just one window, facing the street—and that was in her bedroom.

The living room was crowded with large, dark pieces of furniture. Relics from another world, a different age. The room smelled of furniture polish. The floor was covered with a threadbare oriental carpet.

My alarm was suddenly replaced with a feeling of being a trespasser in another world. I walked across the carpet on my tiptoes.

The door to Sophia's bedroom was closed. I tapped softly. "Sophia," I called out gently.

There was still no answer. And then I pushed open the door.

Although I had opened the door to the bedroom with dread, there was Sophia, sitting up in bed, one hand clutched her glasses. A book she had been reading, even now as I looked at it, slipped slowly to the floor. Her head was cocked to one side as if she had fallen asleep, and I breathed a sigh of relief as I tip toed over to the bed.

It was only then that I saw her eyes were wide opened with a look of horror on her face that I had only seen once before—when she had encountered Bellini in my shop.

"Sophia!" I called out and clutched her shoulder—and then—as if she had been a balloon
that had suddenly lost its air, her whole body collapsed, with a "whoosh" and she tumbled off the bed.

"Sophia!" I bent over her, her eyes still fixed with horror on something across the room.

So intense was her gaze that I found myself turned fully around to follow its path—and there, standing in the doorway was a short dark man wearing a white shirt and a red bowtie .

"Ah Miss Emily, don't pay it no mind. You are a handsome-looking woman—she look like she done seen the devil himself—anyone come in sudden-like could have done the same thing."

"But I didn't…What are you talking about…it wasn't me she saw…"

"Don't touch nothing," he calmly addressed me. "Don't need no cops swarming all over SuperMama's house or Emily's Place neither look'in for something, anything to make trouble ."

He walked swiftly to the bed and bowed. "Alec Le Grand at your service," he said.

Then he took out a red handkerchief from his shirt pocket, held it in his hand and put his finger against Sophia's neck.

"Sure did like to play the ponies. Came round to get her bet. She gone," he said to me. Now we gone."

And then he gently took my arm and led me to the door.

"You and me," he said, "got a date with a trotter up in Yonkers and a horse don't wait for no man, or no woman neither. Besides, my honeypot don't like to be stood up."

I suppose I was in some sort of stupor because it took me that long to realize that I was practically being carried out the door by Merissa's current sweetheart, who, it was rumored all over the neighborhood, had a way with horses, only rivaled by his ability to sweep women off their feet.

When he got to the door he wiped off the doorknob with his red handkerchief.

"Wait!" I stopped short, and looked once more at the body of poor Sophia lying now at a strange, contorted position on the floor near her bed. "I saw something!" Was it a flicker of light across the window in her bedroom? A subtle change in the atmosphere of the room—some slight movement, like the flutter of an insect—There was something alive in that room!

Alec turned to look back, as I had done, and he shivered. "Ain't nothing there," he said to me, "'Cept maybe The Angel of Death, and I don't want to be meeting him."

And he swept me out of the room, through the hallway and through the front door.

"Good 'even Mam," Alec Le Grand tossed over his shoulder to SuperMama, still sitting rock still on the top step. "Ain't nobody here but us pigeons," he cooed as he slipped me down behind him. "A little bird did tell me you like GlintGold in the 4th."

SuperMama kept her eyes straight ahead, but her huge chest heaved. "That little Filly don't know what's good for her, goin' run her heart out one day for sure."

When I reached the bottom step and turned around, Alec Le Grand had vanished.

TWO

There is some evidence that anatomical changes in human feet beginning in the Middle Paleolithic period, with the appearance of narrow toes, was due to a heel-toe movement caused by the wearing of shoes.

So here I was at the bottom of the steps, my thoughts all awhirl. There was a dead woman upstairs who I just happened to visit—I shivered—just a few minutes it seemed to me, after she died—why was I sneaking around as if I had committed some crime? Besides, who knows if anyone had committed a crime? Sophia was an old lady after all, Hadn't SuperMama told me she had almost fallen down the stairs the day before? And while her shoe might be uncomfortable, it probably wouldn't account for a fall. She was certainly a little shaky in a number of ways when I had seen her this afternoon,

But even as I stood there, staring up at the mountainous figure of SuperMama, I had a feeling deep in the center of my gut, like when you've just eaten a rotten peanut that looked perfectly fine in the shell, that something was very wrong. Call it women's intuition, but I knew that Sophia had seen something really horrible right before she died.

I shivered again. Was there such a thing as The Angel of Death? And if so, was he still hanging around, dusting off his wings outside Sophia's bedroom window—on the top stoop—or perched right on the ample lap of SuperMama looking for another victim?

I shook myself. This was all utter nonsense. I didn't have to look for a supernatural explanation for Sophia's expression. I had seen it when she laid eyes on that dapper Signore Bellini.

If there was foul play at work in Sophia's death, I was sure it had something to do with Bellini and the diamonds hidden in the shoes.

Then I remembered that I had left the substitute pair of shoes I had brought for Sophia on the floor of her bedroom. Evidence aplenty that I had been there.

And besides, SuperMama had seen me go up to Sophia's room. We even had a long conversation.

No. Alec Le Grand might have his own reasons for wanting to keep his presence in Sophia's room a secret, but I certainly didn't.

On the other hand, I wasn't particularly interested in having the police poke around in my business either.

Maybe there was a perfectly normal way to act in a situation like this.

Unfortunately, I had lived in this neighborhood long enough to forget what would be "normal" in a situation like this. Despite the creeping gentrification on the Upper West Side, Broadway in the 90's and the surrounding streets were still like the Wild West. Here it was who you knew who made a difference, not a license or a certificate. And cops were never welcome. They represented authority and it was freedom from authority in one form or another, that most of the people living here had come for.

With some effort, I tried to get some perspective. If I still lived on Central Park West in a respectable apartment building with a respectable superintendent, and even a doorman and elevator man, I asked myself, what would I do?

It didn't take me more than a minute or two to figure it out. I would call Julio the elevator man and would ask him to call 911 and report an emergency. So I walked back up the stairs and greeted SuperMama once again.

"Hi, there," I called out.

"Hi your own self," SuperMama replied. "What you doin back here so soon. I just seen you leave."

So much for trying to sneak around SuperMama.

"I came back" I said, "because I'm a little worried about Sophia. She didn't look so good."

"Lordy, that lady never looked good since before you and me was born."

"True. true." I answered. I sat down beside her on the stoop. "But this time I really think she is pretty bad."

"Lordy, Lordy" SuperMama shook her leonine head slowly back and forth.

"In fact," I finally spit it out, "I think she's dead."

SuperMama stopped shaking and turned to me, her eyes wide.

"I knowed something bad were goin' to happen. I feels it in my bones." She grasped my hand. "What we goin do?"

"I think we need to call 911."

"No! No!" SuperMama suddenly pulled herself up to a standing position with an agility I can only call awesome.

"We can't have no cops here." She pulled me up next to her.

"Cops, Firemen, Ambulances, Sirens. Everyone in the neighborhood know she die in my house."

SuperMama raised her head to the sky. "No one want to rent that apartment-dead spirit hangin out. Last time Henry Hogsworth—Hoggy we calls him—was murdered in Apt.3C. It take two years'fore I find a tenant come from Russia and don't know nothing."

"Murdered!" I repeated. Was it possible that SuperMama had the same feeling I did about it? "But Sophia wasn't murdered. She just died of old age," I tested her.

SuperMama grunted. "Hah! There is plenty of old ladies live in this neighborhood. None of them act like that one. Something wrong with that one. That one don't die natural like."

Her eyes once more seemed to peer into the sky above us. "I seen the Angel!" she mumbled.

“What Angel?“ Then I didn’t imagine it! There was someone—or something—evil in that room. “What Angel?” I asked her again. “What did you see?”

“Listen to me!” She pulled me so close I could hear the heavy beating of her heart.

“I don’t see nothing. My eyes is bad. Everyone live here know that. If she dead, she dead. Ain’t no 911 Emergency squad goin’ bring her back to life. Seems to me you know some cop—I seen him around here with you before. Maybe that cop come quiet like. He sign some papers. I get a couple of friends—they carry her out the back.”

I was in no hurry to create a scene in the neighborhood myself—and I had to admit the idea of seeing Murphy again had some appeal. But he was Homicide and if I called him in I’d have to tell him why I thought it was murder—and that meant coming clean about the diamonds in the shoe, Bellini and the whole scene I had witnessed in the shop. Plus, I could be sure, eliciting some skull-numbing lectures about “merchandise that falls off a truck.”

For a moment I considered doing nothing. I could simply go back home and allow events to play out neighborhood style—a call to a shady undertaker, a white Xeroxed notice tied to a couple of straggly trees on the block announcing a service at Heidi’s Interfaith Chapel—a converted candy store on Broadway and 108th Street.

No. Sophia surely deserved something better than that. She had escaped from Mussolini’s Italy with just the clothes on her back. She had seen almost her entire family murdered by the fascists. Her death should have a certain dignity.

I stood tall next to SuperMama who still towered over me by at least a foot, and called Murphy on my cell.

Why, I wondered, as soon as I dialed his private number and heard his gruff ”Leave a message” recording did I want to involve myself again with this cop, who I don’t doubt for a minute would arrest me for jay-walking if he could?

For a moment I thought of my younger sister Shana—younger but no longer young—and the long list of losers she had touted about, a testimony to both her naiveté and her ever-lasting optimism. I, who was neither naive nor optimistic, still seemed to be drawn to Murphy even though I didn't like cops. And I was pretty sure, he didn't like Jewish smart-ass shoe-store owners either. We were not exactly made for each other.

Murphy! A cop who was unfriendly even on his answering machine!

After we had put Goodie One Shoes away for life, Murphy did fulfill his promise to "stay in touch," at least that was what he called meeting me at Dunkin Donuts a couple of mornings before work. To Murphy, keeping in touch obviously didn't mean an actual touch of any kind. Nevertheless, maybe it was the challenge, maybe it was the need to argue with somebody now that Larry the Loser wasn't around very much, but whatever it was, Murphy's couldn't care less attitude managed to turn me on.

Did I lie to Murphy when I told him over the phone that one of my customers had been murdered? I didn't think so. In fact the more I thought of the horrified expression on Sophia's face, the more certain I was that I was telling the truth.

I waited for Murphy in the dark living room outside Sophia's bedroom.

These brownstones that lined so many of the streets on the Upper West Side dated from the late 1800's. Most had been built for the wealthy—single family homes with carved marble fireplaces, curved mahogany staircases, stained glass windows, wainscoting.

Built side by side, and sharing a common wall, they ranged from fourteen feet wide to twenty feet wide and went back to small private gardens. The rooms however, were dark since there were windows only on the street and garden side and one walked through one room after another—railroad flats they used to call them. And when the wealthy moved to the more modern buildings on Central Park West, with central heating, elevators and large picture windows, these brownstones became home to generation after generation of new immigrants, and in more recent years to 'single room occupancies'—single rooms doing the service of a whole apartment for the indigent, the alcoholics, the welfare mothers.

But some, dilapidated now, the hallways dark and dingy, were cut up into small apartments where, if you didn't mind walking up a few flights of stairs, you could still find a sanctuary filled with an odd assortment of people—misplaced and marooned aging hippies from the West coast, Italian, Irish, Indian, Iranian, Russian, African-American and more—aspiring and/or retired actors, writers and musicians, bookies, fences, and assorted luftmenchen—the flotsam and jetsam of this whole country. All of them living in more or less harmony on the Upper West side. Until something happened to disturb the equilibrium.

Something like murder.

I had left the outside door half open and the light from the single, naked bulb in the hallway shined in.

I sat down on the sofa. A poof of dust rose from the cushions. They were dark and stiff—covered by what looked like an old pink chenille bed spread. Sophia had been saving the wear and tear on these cushions—my own mother in Brooklyn had done the same, but for what and for whom?

What kind of life did Sophia have? How many friends were still alive? Was it true that she didn't eat enough?

I rose and turned on a light on a small lamp in the corner of the room. There was a photo on the table of two girls—one tall, and older, maybe sixteen or seventeen, the other shorter, younger, perhaps ten or eleven. I looked closer. There was a marked similarity in the large, dark eyes, the heads of dark curly hair.

Sisters? Was one of them Sophia?

And then there was the whine of a police siren outside and the screech of brakes.

If SuperMama thought she could keep anything secret in this neighborhood she needed to think again.

Heavy footsteps and then the door pushed open wide and there was Murphy himself with another detective much younger by his side.

"Too long no see." Murphy said, extending his hand. "What is it with you and dead bodies? I'd have thought running a shoe store was a safe, quiet way to earn a living."

I had thought so too, when I quit working as a college English teacher and decided to resurrect my father's old family business on Upper Broadway in Manhattan as a second career.

"Not another woman murdered with a shoe?" he asked, looking straight into my eyes. Was it my imagination or did he hold on to my hand a tad more than courtesy demanded?

"See for yourself," I said and I stepped aside to let Murphy and the other detective into the bedroom.

I sat back down on the sofa while they explored the scene of the crime.

"Did you touch anything?" Murphy called out.

"Only the doorknob and the body," I answered him.

Then he slammed the bedroom door in a distinctly unfriendly manner and I didn't hear much more until a car came with a couple of more policeman and they carried out a body bag.

Murphy finally came out of the bedroom and sat down heavily next to me on the couch.

He had gained a little weight in the six months since I had seen him last, but his eyes were as blue as ever before. I could see a line of sweat had formed on his upper lip.

"No air in these damn buildings," he muttered.

I handed him a tissue from my purse, but he didn't say 'Thank you."

"First of all," he asked me, "how'd you know she was dead?"

"She looked dead," I told him. "She was all white and when I touched her she tumbled over on to the floor."

He pursed his lips and fingered the tissue. "Could have had a stroke—been catatonic."

I exhaled slowly. Of course the truth was I knew she was dead because Alec Le Grand had felt for a pulse and pronounced her dead. And there was something in Alec's manner that told me he knew a dead body when he saw one. The last thing I wanted to do was to involve him. He was so paranoid about cops as it were, trying to sneak me out of the building—who knows what skeletons he was trying to hide? Besides, in this situation at least, I was pretty sure he was an innocent bystander. Sophia was dead before either of us arrived at her door.

"I took her pulse." I lied.

"And?"

"There wasn't any."

Murphy seemed to mull this over for a few minutes. I could see he was trying to blame me for something, just like old times, but wasn't yet quite sure what.

"What made you think it was murder? There aren't any signs of forced entry. No trauma to the body that I can see. No blood." He shook his head. "Seems like a heart attack to me." He paused. "Cept for that expression on her face." Murphy crossed himself. "Like she had seen the Devil himself.!"

"Yes! Yes!" I jumped up. "Her expression. Call him the Devil if you want to—Sophia called him The Angel of Death. And she should know. Her whole family was killed by Mussolini's fascists."

And then I told Murphy about Sophia's meeting with the dapper Italian guy Bellini, and how she had almost fainted with shock and terror when she saw him. But Murphy wasn't too impressed by my story.

"So an old lady who has flashbacks to round-ups in Fascist Italy, sees some older guy with an Italian accent and has a stroke. Can't arrest a guy for that."

It was hot in the room and Murphy was not feeling friendly. However much I might yearn for his company, this was surely not the right approach. I was already beginning to feel guilty about getting him involved in this.

Murphy scowled at me. "You know calling Homicide for something like this could be a felony—like turning in a false alarm to the fire department. Why didn't you call 9ll?"

That, of course, was too long a story to tell Murphy, so instead, I told him about the Angel of Death.

It was so vague and so quick that even now I couldn't be sure I had actually seen something. Maybe like SuperMama, I felt it, but the more I thought about it, the more certain I was that there was someone—or something evil in that room right before I entered it.

"Someone had been in to see her. I know it Murphy." I turned toward him. "There was this…flicker…a shadow.. that crossed in front of the window and then it was gone!."

"Then you're telling me the perpetrator, killer, visitor, whatever he was—was still in the apartment?"

Now I was stumped. And scared. If there was someone in the apartment—someone who had, in fact, murdered Sophia, I could have been in great danger. But where would he have hidden?

Murphy shook his head. "There's surely no one else here now," he said. 'We looked in the closet. The window is locked shut. How could he have gotten away?"

"I left the apartment for a few minutes," I blurted out, " and then I came back."

"I see. You were so upset after finding your old friend murdered that you went for a walk—maybe had a sandwich—getting up your courage to call me."

No! No!" What was it with this cop, always putting me on the defensive? "I was scared. I didn't want to get involved. But then I felt badly about just leaving Sophia like that, so I came back."

"And in between times, your 'killer' escaped."

Murphy spread the fingers of his hands and flexed them. I had seen this motion before. Strong fingers. Longing for a neck to wring.

"Tell me more about this 'shadow'," Murphy commanded.

I closed my eyes. I could see the flicker, a subtle change in the light, a scent in the air, camphor! The rustle of wings. "Henry James wrote a story called "The Jolly Corner," I began.

"Oh Henry James, is it," Murphy countered. "With Dreiser you had a chance I could follow you, but Henry James is out of my league."

I knew immediately I had made a tactical mistake. We had shared a joke about seduction with a steak from Dreiser's Sister Carrie when I helped him catch Goodie One Shoes. Murphy had a literary side that was surprising in a cop, but I could see I had gone too far. Showing Murphy up was not the way to make friends. But, like a train in motion, once started, I couldn't stop running my mouth.

'There's this story and the main character goes back to his childhood house and he senses some other presence there. He keeps coming back and each time he almost catches…something…a flicker of light…a heart-beat…a sigh… and then, finally, one night he turns around quickly and finds it and…."

"And….And what?"

I had at least captured Murphy's attention.

"He comes upon an apparition of himself, a haggard, horrible image of what his life would have been if he had stayed at home and gone into trade."

Murphy nodded. "Right," he said. "Personally, I think I'd look a lot better today if I 'had gone into trade' instead of the homicide business. But what does any of this have to do with a possible murderer lurking in the bedroom?"

"Because, it doesn't really matter if the figure is real or not. There are no 'real' ghosts. What he sees is a projection of his own imagination—real because it reflects what Hawthorne would call, 'the truth of the human heart'."

Murphy breathed heavily. "And so what you 'saw' might not be real but only some figment of your own imagination?'

I nodded. Somehow none of this was coming out the way I meant.

"It was real to me." I said lamely. "There was a real evil presence in that room."

Murphy took my arm and sat me back down on the couch. He stood over me, blocking out the light from the small lamp in the corner.

"Well, me lovely, it's like this. I believe there's a pot of gold at the end of the rainbow with a little green leprechaun just itching to give it to me—but I'm not spending that money yet—no matter what Henry James and Nathaniel Hawthorne said." He bent a little closer to me. I could sense a change in the atmosphere between us. Suddenly, this was personal. 'There is something you're not telling me," he said. "What is it?"

Damn! How come the men in my life seem to be able to detect every little "detour" I might make in the stories I tell them?

And so at last, I blurted out the whole story of the diamonds in Sophia's *s*hoe.

"Diamonds!" Murphy uttered under his breath and sat down beside me once again on the sofa.

"Now at least we have a motive for murder. But we still may not have a murder. We'll know more when my boys finish up their work. So…" He looked me in the eye. "These shoes filled with diamonds. Where are they now?"

This is what I was afraid of. Whatever I tell that cop he wants more. And the thing about Murphy that made me nuts was that subtleties about 'right' and 'wrong' eluded him.

Something was either a felony or it was nothing. Someone was either a criminal, or he was not. Trying to explain the advantages to an entire neighborhood of shoes that fell off a truck would be like trying to describe a sunset to someone who was colorblind.

I was sure Murphy was not going to like my answer.

"I gave it to a friend for safe-keeping."

"God help your friends," Murphy spit out, looking at the ceiling. "They have a tendency to turn up dead. Name?"

I folded my arms across my chest and shook my head. "I'd rather not say."

Murphy brought his big hand down so heavily on the coffee table that two lace doilies slid to the floor.

"Did you know," he said to me, his face getting very red, "that trafficking in stolen property is a felony?"

"Here a felony, there a felony, everywhere a felony." I pushed back at him. His attempt to intimidate me was beginning to get me mad. "I was married to a lawyer long enough to know this. So far we don't have a murder and we don't have a felony. We don't even have a crime. An old customer brought me her shoe to fix. So far as I'm concerned those diamonds belong to Sophia. Maybe she just forgot where she put them. Has anyone reported them stolen?" I must say I enjoyed getting Murphy's goat. Sometimes I think I'd rather have a good argument than sex.

Before Murphy could utter another word, one of his detectives opened the bedroom door and nodded. Murphy composed his features and rose with dignity from the sofa.

"Perhaps you will be good enough," Murphy began, "to take a look around the bedroom and tell me if anything looks strange or out of place. If we all try hard enough," he continued pleasantly, "I'm sure we'll find a felony somewhere."

Sophia's bed had been stripped but other than that everything looked pretty much as I had last seen it. The bag with the Ferragamo replacement shoes I had brought were still at the side of the bed. Standing there I felt my anger fade away and my heart filled with sadness—for a life so filled with misery and misfortune and an ending that promised an uneasy spirit.

Even Murphy's flinty mood seemed to soften.

"Take a look inside the closet," he suggested. "Maybe you'll notice something we overlooked."

I pulled open the door a couple of inches and reluctantly peeked inside. A bedroom closet was so personal. It felt like a violation. I took a deep breath, opened the door wide.

An odor of camphor wafted out into the room. Camphor! That was the smell I remembered. Had the murderer hidden in the closet? Or was that the aroma of the Angel of Death?

Inside the closet the clothing was all encased in plastic, sent to the cleaner and returned but never worn again. A few hangers contained garment bags. A life encased in plastic!

Everything hidden from view!

On the shelf above were old fashioned hat boxes—Orbachs, Kleins. Once big department stores and now, like Sophia herself, defunct.

And then I saw the shoes.

Sophia had three rows of them, mostly black and brown, but in contrast to everything else, the shoes were tossed about every which way; one shoe on top of another, a heel sticking out from a toe. The few pair that stood next to each other were mismatched.

What did it mean? Was Sophia becoming so confused she could no longer pick out the pairs of her shoes? Or did someone quickly search her closet looking for a particular pair of shoes that were no longer there?

"The shoes!" I uttered, and then I fell to my knees and started groping wildly around the floor of the closet, my tears falling fast and silently down my face as if restoring order amongst Sophia's shoes would restore order in the whole rotten universe.

"It's okay," Murphy said, gently, bending over me. I felt his hand on my shoulder. "You don't have to do this."

"Yes, I do," I said, and I did.

My meltdown seemed to clear the air between Murphy and me. He became…solicitous would be too strong a word…but let's say, more friendly.

It was Murphy's contention that whoever caused Sophia's death made a mess of her closet searching for the shoes with the diamond-filled heels. It made sense, because everything else in the apartment was as neat as a pin. If Sophia was too confused to put a matched pair of blue Chanel sandals together, how could she stash her two piece navy suit with beige blouse to go with it in the same garment bag?

Murphy helped me to my feet and sat next to me on the bare bed.

He took out his little notebook and a pen from his breast pocket.

"Which vendor sold you the shoes?" he asked me.

"Freddie the Fox," I told him.

He raised one eyebrow. "Is that a manufacturer or a distributor?"

"That's just Freddie the Fox." I repeated.

Murphy put down his pen. "You have custom forms and receipts of purchase?" he asked me.

I shook my head. "Lost in a flood," I told him.

"And this flood, it happened when?"

"Yesterday." I shook my head. "Bad luck."

Murphy stared at me for a minute. "And I suppose the address of this Freddie the Fox has also been lost in the flood?"

"Actually," I was happy to report, "he lives with his mother."

"Ah!" Murphy lifted his pen, "And she is blind, deaf and dumb?"

I smiled. "So you know her?"

Murphy closed up his pen and put his little pad back in his pocket.

He took a deep breath. And then another. He reminded me of my friend Debra Karpatkin who was determined to give birth without anesthesia.

"Do send me her address when you have a chance. Shall we see who might still be left on the front stoop who may have something tell us?" Murphy said at last. And he pulled me, rather roughly, up from the bed and pushed me towards the door.

The only one left on the steps was SuperMama. She sat still as a mountain, eyes, front, her breath slow and even. Everyone else, I imagined, disappeared as soon as they heard the cop car.

Murphy gave her a big smile and extended his hand.

"I understand you are the Superintendent of this building. Wonderful stonework," he motioned to the cracked carvings of arrow heads and feathers under the first floor windows. 'You must be proud to work in such a fine house."

SuperMama turned her big head slowly to face him. "Finest people in the neighborhood live in my house," she chuckled. "Could have fooled me though. Most of them be deadbeats, 'cept Missy Sophia and now she be dead."

Murphy sat down next to SuperMama on the step.

"Did you like Miss Sophia?"

SuperMama shrugged. "She nice enough for someone don't hardly ever say nothing to nobody. She think she too good for people on this block. Lordy! Lordy!" SuperMama bent forward and back. "Lordy! Lordy! Her time done come. The Angel of Death, he come for her sure."

Murphy perked up at this news. "Who came for her," he asked. "Who did you see?"

"Hah! SuperMama stopped rocking. "I ain't seen nobody, but I knows when someone is taken. I feels it here," she patted her left breast.

"But you were sitting here, all day," Murphy protested. "Surely you saw people come and go."

"I sits here all right, but I don't see so good."

She turned towards Murphy and pulled down the lid of her right eye. "It's the diabeties. Doctor say I got to be careful of my sugar. I try. But I too busy here—got to keep the hallways clean—kids hear me comin' they runs away fast. But my eyes," SuperMama shook her head. "I don't see good but I still can work. Got to feed my girl Sammy. No one take care of SuperMama and Sammy 'cept me."

"And Sammy?" Murphy asked. "Was Sammy here this afternoon?"

SuperMama grunted. "My Sammy? She in school. Go to Brandeis High School over there down 84th street. Sammy smart as a whip. She don't sit on no stoop and smoke weed. She in school. Sure she help me sometimes at night. Then I can hardly see nothing—but daytime she in school."

It was all true, what SuperMama said. At least the part about her daughter Samantha. A tall beauty who wanted to be a nurse someday. As for her not seeing anyone—I had a feeling that SuperMama's blindness was like Hamlet's madness—North, North West. When it pleased her, she didn't miss an ant crossing a crack in the sidewalk.

"Any other ways in and out of the building, besides this door?"

SuperMama chuckled. "Tito Suarez, 2B. He done climbed in the window, swinging over from 440 next door., night he got drunk and locked himself out; Dana Brown—she come in one morning, 'bout 3:AM, broke the window in 3A and climb down to 2A. Also there be a basement filled with cartoons and trash me and Sammy ain't yet had time to deal with that's got a door, goes out to the alleyway."

She swayed back and forth. "Lordy, Lordy, now we got to separate the bottles and the papers' fore they takes 'em on the truck"

Murphy stood up. It was clear he wasn't going to get much more out of SuperMama. He passed his hand over his face. His skin looked pale in the dwindling light.

We were saying our good byes when a tall, thin figure emerged from the shadows.

"Signora Emily," he said to me, and bowed slightly.

He was dressed as usual in a dark blue suit and striped tie, his white shirt partially covered by a dark gray vest. Known throughout the neighborhood as "The Senator" because of his formal dress and bearing, he had come here from Italy, many years ago. His face, pitted and deeply lined, seemed to capture the shadows of the early evening, making him appear even older than he was.

I quickly introduced him to Murphy while SuperMama merely shifted her enormous thighs and stared straight ahead.

He waved a paper bag in front of her. "I brought some chocolates for Signorina Sarfatti—I know she likes them—and a deck of cards."

He chuckled. "Signorina Sarfatti, she loves to take my pennies when we play Bridge."

"Lordy, Lordy" SuperMama said, "She done passed away."

This news hit The Senator like a physical blow and he staggered, trembling dangerously close to the edge of the stairs until Murphy pulled him back to safety. Together we helped him to a seat next to SuperMama on the stairs. I could feel the sharp edges of his bones through the threadbare material of his suit.

"Poverina! Poverina!" he mumbled, shifting his paperbag from one hand to the other.

"I told her she needed to see the Doctoré for her heart. She promised me…."

"The Ace of Spades," SuperMama said. "She done drawn the Ace of Spades."

Then SuperMama laid a heavy arm on the Senator and rose to a standing position.

"Can I help?" The Senator looked up at the three of us. "The body? Funeral arrangements?"

"Don't need no help now," SuperMama said, and she turned her back and slowly walked inside the building.

"How well did you know Mrs. Sarfatti?" Murphy asked.

"Quarant anni—forty years. Roma. We were at school together…." His voice trailed off and he buried his face in his arms.

At last Murphy gave him his hand and pulled him to a standing position.

"I'll see you home," Murphy offered.

"No! No need!" The Senator did his best to straighten up. He smoothed his tie and ran his fingers over his vest. He took out a handkerchief from his trouser pocket and wiped his face.

"My time has not yet come." And he slowly descended the stairs and disappeared into the night.

THREE

In the mid-18th Century, shoes were made for either the right or left foot. Called "straights" the shoes were shaped by the wearer's foot simply by wearing it.

Murphy didn't offer me a ride home which was fine with me. He obviously regarded me as a person fully able to negotiate the neighborhood alone at night. Even though I was a woman of a certain age, regarded by some to be past my prime, I could still walk the streets of the Upper West Side without an armed escort.

That understood between us, we said our goodbyes and Murphy promised to give me a full coroner's report as soon as possible.

When I finally got home around 9:00 and put my key in the door, I heard a familiar click from across the hall and the welcoming squawk of Henry, Angelina's gray parrot. My neighbor Angelina spent a good deal of her time with her eye glued to her peephole, a habit that possibly saved my life in my encounter with Goodie One Shoes. Between Angelina and her bird, not even the Angel of Death could sneak in undetected.

Now she emerged, fully decked out in a lime green kimono, black silk pants and red platform shoes about three inches high.

"Great shoes!" I told her.

"Thanks Dolly. Wore them in the 1962 revival of *The Streetcar Named Desire*."

"Let me guess—you were Blanche DuBois, no?"

"Not quite, Dolly" Angelina chucked, "more like I walked from Stage Right to Stage Left two or three times." She raised her right leg and gave it a kick. At eighty plus years old, Angelina still had a chorus-girl's body.

Kicking was one thing, walking another—especially at 9:00 at night, after my friend downed a nightcap or two. Angelina wobbled over to me and leaned on my arm, while Henry fluttered about.

"Heard about Sophia," she said. "I'm sorry."

"How could you hear about it? It just happened!" I knew news traveled fast in this neighborhood but this was ridiculous.

"A little birdie told me,' she replied, winking at Henry. "Also Jose just delivered her newspaper to me because he knew she wouldn't be needing it. You liked her, didn't you?"

"Yes," I said. "Didn't you?"

She hesitated. "Never talk bad about the dead. How about a cup of tea—I've got half a lasagna left over too."

I suddenly remembered I hadn't eaten dinner and that sounded a lot better than a tuna-fish sandwich which was about all I had around at the moment. Besides, Angelina always cheered me up—not to mention she made the best lasagna this side of the Atlantic.

Henry perched on one battered kitchen chair and Angelina and I went to work on the lasagna. And, of course, who can eat lasagna without a bottle—or two—of wine? So pretty soon we were both feeling a lot better.

"Here's to Sophia," I said and we raised yet another glass to my old friend. I touched Angelina's glass and looked her in the eye.

"You said you didn't like her."

"No. You asked me if I liked her and I didn't answer Dolly."

She sighed. "Sophia Sarfatti....Sophia Sarfatti. The Sarfattis were too good for the Grossi's. They were rich. Aristocrats, living like Lords in Milan, and my family? Came from Sicily. I myself grew up in the South Bronx. We didn't have much to say to one another."

"Milan?" I repeated. "The Senator. He said he went to school with Sophia in Rome."

Angelina laughed. "The Senator! A peasant from Palermo, more likely—but Sophia? No. The Sarfattis came from Milan. And the Northern Italians always looked down on the Southern ones. I'm surprised Sophia even said hello to him. One of her cousins, Margherita, was a mistress of Mussolini for years. She was famous. I still remember my mother talking about her. In those days there were a lot of rich Jews in Northern Italy—called themselves Socialists. Kind of like your old friends on Central Park West. Socialists with money! Thought Mussolini was going to save the country. "

I poured myself another glass of wine. I had never really heard Sophia's full story. All I knew was that her whole family had been wiped out.

"If her cousin was Mussolini's mistress, the family would have had connections—enough to keep them safe—but they were all killed."

Angelina nodded. 'Sure, Dolly—but the way I heard it, while Mussolini was popular, the Sarfatti's were okay. But when the Germans began to put on pressure, Mussolini passed some half-baked racial laws most people ignored. You know Italians. They would rather eat than fight, and following orders isn't exactly their strongest suit. "

Angelina poured herself the remains of bottle number two. "I heard things only got bad for the Jews after Mussolini was killed and the Nazi's took over. Even then, people could pay their way out sometimes. It depended on the greed of the person in charge….."

I stopped her. "Fotinni Fatale! That's the name Sophia called out when she saw that Italian guy Bellini in my store!"

Angelina shook her head. "Never heard of that one. Maybe The Senator can tell you—if you can believe a word he tells you. He was real friendly to me once upon a time." She winked at me. "But I couldn't cotton to him. Not my type. Much too skinny. And Henry didn't like him at all."

At the sound of his name, Henry who had been pecking at the left-over noodles in Sophia's plate, fluttered around the table squawking out something that sounded very much like "Nevermore, Nevermore!"

"Nevermore?" I questioned Angelina. "Does he think he is Edgar Allan Poe's Raven?"

"Can't rightly say what Henry thinks," Angelina said philosophically, "but he likes my lasagna and that makes him a better man than The Senator."

And with that parting thought, I stumbled back into my own apartment and fell immediately asleep.

I woke up the next morning with a headache and a heavy heart. It was raining and my little window facing the back garden was too drenched with run-off from the higher floors to afford much visibility to the outside world. The only good thing was that it was Merissa's day to open Emily's Place and I could stay in bed for another hour or two.

I lay in bed and stared at my ceiling. The overhead boards creaked and I could hear the shower running. I found it rather comforting.

I was not close friends with Sophia Sarfatti but there was something about her that had found its way into my heart. She had been my first customer, and in her own quiet way, made me feel welcome when I had opened the shop. She never bought a lot of shoes, but she stopped in every few days to say hello. What SuperMama and Angelina took for snobbery, I was sure was simply shyness. She had never been completely at home in America.

What had happened to Sophia in those few hours between the time Merissa brought her home and I arrived at her apartment?

Like SuperMama, "I feels" more than "I sees." That a well-dressed Italian man should come into Emily's Place looking for the very shoes Sophia had bought—that those shoes should be filled with diamonds—and that Sophia would turn up dead, was too much of a coincidence. All anyone had to do was to connect the dots to know Sophia was murdered. Why was obvious. How and by whom was the real mystery?

I had lived in this neighborhood long enough to know nothing here was a coincidence. People were too connected to each other for anything purely random to occur. It was like living in a giant terrarium. Move out the spiders and the flies will proliferate. Kill the fish and the algae will take over the water. A murder in this neighborhood subtly changed all the relationships.

Doors that once were open would suddenly be closed. Eyes that met yours now shifted their focus to the horizon. Conversations roamed on the periphery of information. It was as if the entire neighborhood pulled down their shades and rolled up their awnings.

No coincidences. That got me thinking about Alec le Grand. What was he really doing at Sophia's door, just minutes after she died?

And how much did SuperMama really know about who came and went while she sat solidly on the stoop? And how did those diamonds get into those shoes? What does Freddie the Fox know about that?

I decided I had better call Freddie before Murphy got to him and scared him out of his wits. I had given Murphy Freddie's mother's address but the truth was no one ever really knew where Freddie hung out. Freddie found you when he wanted you. Other than that, he handled his business over the phone.

"Yeah?" Freddie answered on the first ring.

"It's Emily."

Freddie's tone changed immediately. "How'd you do with those shoes? Pretty good right? I told you, they'd sell. Real quality. There's more if you want 'em."

"I love them. Sold every pair," I told him. "But those shoes are too hot to touch."

"What you talkin' bout? Those shoes are cool. Friend of a friend got a good deal, is all. No one worries about a few pair of shoes gone missing."

I hesitated. It was pretty clear to me Freddie didn't know what was in the shoes—although maybe this "friend of a friend" knew.

"Someone is going to worry about these shoes, big time. The heels are filled with diamonds."

"What are you talking about?"

"Diamonds. One of my customers complained about the shoe. Said it was bumpy, lumpy, something not right. When I took off the heel, I found it was filled with diamonds."

Heavy breathing and then "Holy shit!" Freddie said. "I've got to get those shoes. Give them back. All of them. Something is going on. Nobody said nothing to me! I got to get those shoes!"

"The shoes were all sold, people off the street—I have no idea who—and the pair I got back, I had to hand over to the police" I lied. "you'd better have a good story about where you got them."

"Yeah right." Freddie said. "like the cops would listen to anything I said. It's not the cops who worry me anyway. It's the guys who put the diamonds in the shoes. Isn't anyone I know can get their hands on diamonds 'cept the Mafia—Russian or Italian—and either way, I'm a goner."

"Wait a minute," I said to him, "Maybe we can get the police to protect you if you lead us to the real criminal."

Freddie grunted. "The police can't even find a parking space in this neighborhood, and Freddie the Fox ain't a stool-pigeon."

'Listen." I said to him. "I think there's some Italian connection here but it may not be Mafia—something having to do with Mussolini and World War II. You've got to tell me where you got the shoes!"

But Freddie had hung up. Mussolini and World War II were things he might have heard about from the old people—or maybe seen on T.V. They had nothing to do with the world he lived in. I figured he was probably half way to Mexico by now.

I had just put the phone down when it rang again.

"Just take care of it—didn't I tell you already!" I immediately recognized the dulcet tones of my estranged husband Larry the Loser, giving orders to some poor underling at his office, while attempting to cover the phone with one hand so I wouldn't hear.

"Hi there!" he said finally, remembering that he had actually called me. "How are you this morning?"

"I'm not sure," I said, "That will depend in part on what you have to tell me."

"How about we talk about it over dinner. You're losing weight. Since you left me I bet you've hardly had a square meal."

"I do very well, thank you," I answered him. "Why don't you just tell me what you called to tell me and go back to yelling at your staff." One of the problems with dealing with The Loser is that he always wants something in return. The concept of altruism is something that entirely passed him by.

"I'm too busy to argue with you, this morning," he answered. "If you want to be poor, skinny, and miserable, that is your choice. I, on the other hand, have spent a good deal of yesterday afternoon calling my contacts in the community and my Mafia sources tell me it isn't them, but the idea is a good one and they want in."

Was this good news or bad? It was hard for me to tell. I was not in immediate danger of being rubbed out, but, on the other hand, the enemy was even more invisible. At least with the Mafia you knew who you were dealing with.

"What do you think we should do now?" I asked him. Years spent prosecuting criminals had taught Larry much about the criminal mind.

"What is this 'We' business? I'm just an innocent by-stander. But I would say the best thing is to lay low. Anyone comes looking for the shoes, you tell them you gave them to the Salvation Army 'cause your customer didn't want them. The others you sold to people for cash on the street—you don't have a clue who they are. And when this blows over, you might even be able to give the diamonds back to your old lady."

"I don't think so," I said. "She's dead."

I don't often come up with things that can leave Larry speechless, but this did. I heard his chair shuffle and a door slam shut. "What did you say?" he whispered into the phone.

"She died last night. I found her when I went to bring her a new pair of shoes. The police think she had a heart-attack but I'm sure someone did her in. I'm still waiting for the coroner's report."

"Do me a favor," Larry said, "Next time you need help, call someone else." And he hung up on me.

Two hang-ups and I hadn't even gotten out of bed yet. This was not going to be one of my better days.

I dragged myself into the kitchen and made myself a cup of coffee. I didn't think this situation was going to "blow over" anytime soon. Anyone who loses that many diamonds is not going to just walk away. I had visions of hoodlums in ski masks invading central headquarters of The Salvation Army—not to mention Emily's Place. I had to get to them before they got to me.

I looked at the clock on the wall. It was time to get dressed and get myself over to Emily's Place. I pulled on the pair of black pants I had worn the other day and put my hand in the pocket. I had almost forgotten about the little round diamond that still lay there. I held it up to the light. Where had it been? What secrets did it hold? It seemed now to burn my hand—heated by the fires of Hell. Why had I taken it?

I closed my fingers around it. I surely couldn't wear it. In this neighborhood? It would be noticed in an instant. Jose my newspaper delivery guy would tell Alec le Grand and within twenty minutes everyone on Upper Broadway would wonder where it had come from.

I put the stone back into my pocket. For the time being, at least, I was stuck with it.

The new spring shoes were beginning to come in, plus another small shipment from Freddie-the-Fox. I wanted to make sure there was nothing wrong with those shoes before I put them on the floor, so I stashed them in the back closet until I had some time to give them a good going-over. I have to say the store was so crowded I could hardly get through the door—and this on a rainy Friday afternoon in a poor neighborhood, during a recession.

I admit to feeling proud. Life is hard for Teressa Valdes. Her husband drinks and her son was arrested last week for stealing a car. Nevertheless, a new, discounted pair of three inch red sandals could make her smile. Same for Helena Viscounti whose only daughter has Lupus. And Yulia Lubiniska, who fell down a broke a hip—even though she's in a wheelchair and can't walk, she loves a nice, new pair of shoes.

So was I an asset to this neighborhood or what?

It's times like these that I felt really proud of myself and what I do. It's not rocket science but it does a lot of good for a lot of people. So here I was, basking in the pleasure of my accomplishments, running back and forth between Mildred Stein and Andrea Lutz, both of whom have asked me for the same pair of shoes—and there is only one pair left—wondering how to avoid bloodshed—when someone taps me on the shoulder.

It is Sammy, SuperMama's teenage daughter. Tall, light-skinned, with green eyes and long, curly hair, she had already been approached by one of the big modeling agencies to do some work for them.

Now she pulled my arm. "Emily. Please. I've got to talk to you."

I decided on the instant to tell both Mildred Stein and Andrea Lutz that we have run out of Size 8, gold Chanel platform pumps, and I led Sammy to the back of the store where the coffee pot gave out a lovely aroma.

"What's up?" I asked her, pouring both of us a cup, and knowing already it had something to do with poor Sophia Sarfatti.

Sammy sat down and covered her face with her hands.

"I didn't mean to do anything wrong," she said at last, "Giancarlo said it would be ok 'cause she was dead."

She opened her backpack and took out a small rectangular candy box. Inside the box was a photograph, a duplicate of the one framed of two young girls I had already seen in Sophia's apartment—and a gold colored brass button with the blue threads still attached.

"I don't understand," I said to her, "Where did this come from?"

She reached into her pocket and took out a safety deposit box key.

"I swear," she said, "there was nothing else in there!"

"Where did you get the key?" I asked her.

She covered her eyes again, and lowered her head. This time, when she took away her hands, her eyes were full of tears.

"I used to read to Sophia. Two, three times a week. Ever since I was little, she was nice to me. Mama didn't like it. I don't know why. Sophia didn't have any kids. She didn't seem to have anyone—so I guess she was lonely. When I was little, she would give me these special chocolates from Italy—Baci. I always loved them. She taught me some Italian words too. She even gave me a doll. Old doll, brought it all the way from Italy. Never had a doll like that in my whole life. When I got older she told me about her sister."

More tears. I waited. Sophia had once said something to me about a sister who had been killed by the Fascists in Italy but I never knew the whole story.

"She told me that there was this policeman in Italy, who would give visas to the Jews and let them out of the country if they paid him. Sophia's father had money and he gave the money to this policeman, but when the family came to the railroad station to get the train for Switzerland, he wouldn't let them board. She was little, at the time, only about ten; her sister was eighteen and she tried to argue with the policeman. He pushed her away and she grabbed hold of his sleeve and wouldn't let go—and then—- and then they shot her—and her father and mother flung themselves on the body and, and…it seemed that everyone was running in different directions and Sophia was little and she grabbed what was in her sister's hand—a button from the uniform of the policeman—and she ran away and hid while the soldiers took away her mother and father. She never saw any of them again."

I pulled a couple of tissues out of my purse—there's a good reason women usually carry a stash—and handed one to Sammy. She was a good girl—Sammy—a real flower growing in a cement garden. At this point, both of us were crying and we hugged each other for a few minutes and waited for all this emotion to pass. Then she continued:

"Sophia ran back to a cousin's house and eventually they found some other policeman to pay and they got to Belgium, and then France, and finally to the U.S."

"So what did you do wrong?" I asked her.

She took a deep breath. "The night Sophia died, she was really upset. She was calling out things in Italian that I couldn't understand. Finally she took out this key from her night table drawer and she told me to give it to you."

"To me?" This was a surprise. I thought we were friends, but we were never that close.

"She told me, 'Miss Emily will know what to do with it. Give it to Miss Emily."

Sammy shook her head. "But when she died, I got so scared I didn't know what to do. Mama started talking about The Angel of Death, and maybe she was murdered and then I really got scared—so I called Giancarlo."

Giancarlo was a neighborhood guy about thirty, a sometime jazz musician, who it was rumored, had some low-level relationship with the Mafia. He had somehow managed to impress Sammy, who had twice as many brains at eighteen than he would ever have, and now they hung out together. Giancarlo was bad news but since he was hardly smart enough to do much harm, no one paid him too much mind.

"And what wisdom did you glean from Giancarlo?" I asked her.

"Giancarlo said we should investigate the safety deposit box ourselves. I was the closest kin to her and Jews always have money."

She turned to me and grabbed my arm. "He said, Jews have money and maybe she had stashed some away somewhere, cause she never spent very much and she had no family. I swear! There was nothing else in the box. It was just that I was so scared. I didn't know what to do!"

I took the small box from Sammy and ran my fingers over the button. It had tarnished but was clearly the button of some policeman or soldier. It had to be the very button her sister had torn from the uniform of the official who would be the murderer of her family. Clearly, Sophia had made some connection between Bellini, the deportation of the Jews and the death of her sister. But Bellini, who looked to be about fifty would have been too young to have been a policeman in Fascist Italy. And what about the diamonds?

There were lots of things that still didn't make much sense to me, and thinking about them just made my head hurt. And the noise level from the showroom told me that a couple of other customers were fighting over the last pair of shoes. I would have to think more about this later. It was time I went back to work.

I gave Sammy a hug, thanked her for the key and the box. Did Sammy find the secret stash of wealth she hoped for in the safety deposit box? I had no way of knowing. I still had the diamond I had stashed in the pocket of my black slacks, filched from the treasure in Sophia's shoe. It is hard to resist temptation. So far as I knew, Sophia had no kin, so who could blame Sammy for helping herself—maybe using it to go to Nursing School? Sophia herself would probably have approved of that.

I was just about to return to the floor when the phone rang.

"Murphy here," he said. No good afternoon, Hello, how are you. Murphy was a no frills kind of guy.

"Emily here," I responded.

"Thought you might be interested in the coroner's report. Sarfatti didn't actually die of a heart attack. She died of a stroke. Seems like she took a serious overdose of Coumadin."

"What?"

"It's a common blood thinner. Given to people at risk for a blood clot in the brain. Problem is if you take too much, you can bleed out, into your brain."

"So it's murder?"

"Could be. Or it could just be Sarfatti lost track of how much she was taking. Do you have any idea who her doctor was?"

"I don't think she had much faith in doctors."

"Well, she got the medicine from somewhere. Somebody had to write a prescription. Unless the Coumadin fell off the same truck as the shoes you've been selling. I'll be in touch."

I hung up the phone and stared into space for a few minutes, trying to remember if Sophia had ever mentioned any clinic or doctor she was seeing. It was odd because lots of elderly people talk about their health all the time and spend many of their days going from one doctor to another. But Sophia was different. If she got sick she would rub her chest with camphor or drink her special herbal tea.

I shivered. I had known this woman for four years—but clearly, I didn't know her at all.

The noise from the showroom swirled around me as I stared into space. This was no time for day-dreaming. Nevertheless, the image of Sophia, hunched over her dead sister, refused to let go of me.

I turned on the computer and typed the name Fotinni Fatale into the search engine. And there before me was a photo that was a dead-ringer for Bellini. Under the photo were the words, "Massimo Fotinni. Nicknamed, Fotinni Fatale. Former Police Chief in Milan. Sought as a war criminal for hundreds of deportations of Jews, gypsies, and homosexuals from 1943-44. Never Apprehended.

FOUR

Like any other item of dress, shoes since the fourteenth century displayed the wearer's wealth and status to her peers. Fine leathers and shoes with elaborate decoration were reserved for the upper classes.

The rest of yesterday at Emily's Place made me long for the peace and quiet of my old life as a college English teacher where my biggest concerns were tenure—which I never got—and getting my students grades in on time.

The good thing was that I was pulled back into the present which meant dealing with Hannah Goldsmith who hadn't bought a pair of shoes since 1950 but insisted on trying on every pair in the store and Tamara Johnson who I caught carrying out a pair of shoes without paying. Altogether better than thinking about poor Sophia Sarfatti and the murder of her entire family.

By the time Merissa and I closed up shop I had no more energy left to worry about anything. I fell into a lovely, dreamless sleep and awoke to find the sun shining brightly.

This was a good thing because today I had to prepare for one of the most important events in the neighborhood: Big Bingo—to take place tomorrow, Sunday.

I loved Big Bingo. It was a charitable event set up to benefit the PTA of PS 96 on 100th Street and Amsterdam Avenue. It was always lots of fun for everyone in the neighborhood, and proof that you didn't have to be rich to have a good time on Upper Broadway. Last year it had rained, which did put a damper, if you'll pardon my pun, on the event, so this year I rented the store next to Emily's Place which had been empty for several months, just in case we needed some cover. Merissa and I had swept the place out, and, I admit to some ulterior motive there.

We got to look at the place close-up. Business had been so good, I was actually thinking of expanding.

For today though, all I was expanding was some empty display tables I was moving into the space for a couple of the vendors to use, and a small rack of second-hand shoes for my own booth.

The plan was for Merissa and me to meet early, do our set-up and then open Emily's Place by noon. That way I wouldn't lose much of Saturday, the busiest day in the week, and I could always keep the store open a couple of hours later if I wanted to.

I gulped down my usual cup of coffee, put on some jeans, and headed out to the shop.

And that was when I knew today was going to be more difficult than yesterday.

The door to Emily's Place was wide open and swinging now in the breeze on a broken hinge.

Someone had broken in during the night. And the alarm had not gone off.

I suppose I should have known better than to run down the block and throw myself inside. Without even a weapon in my hand to confront who might still be there. But no. Instinct took over. I had no children and now Emily's Place and the shoes in it were family. I was ready to defend them.

I was lucky. There was no one inside. Neither the perpetrator nor any passersby to whom any open door was an invitation to enter. Fortunately, this was a neighborhood that slept late on Saturday. I was greeted by an eerie silence. My mannequins, Sadie and Mary, always so elegantly done up in the latest vintage clothes and rhinestone shoes were obscenely positioned with their legs spread apart and their heads obscured by shoe boxes. At least they hadn't been stolen. I embraced poor Sadie and dragged her to an upright position. I pulled on Mary's arm until I managed to put her in a seated position and then I modestly crossed her legs. Mary had a reputation to protect. People didn't expect much from Sadie.

Then I turned my attention to the shoes. Dozens of shoes were thrown this way and that, the boxes strewn all over the floor. I bent down and started trying to sort them out.

"Hope you don't keep a lot of cash on hand, Miss Emily" said a voice behind me and I whirled around to find Alec Le Grand, standing in the doorway.

This time I knew he had not come to collect a bet.

I picked up a red Chanel shoe with a three inch heel and stood up. "What the hell are you doing here?" I challenged.

"Now, Now, Miss Emily. I just passing by. Getting ready to set up my booth for Big Bingo. Merissa—she goin' meet me here in about three minutes."

Alec Le Grand always set up a roulette wheel, and ran the Bingo games that were usually the hit of the fair. He looked at his watch. Then he glanced over my head to the store room beyond.

I put down the shoe.

"Why don't we take a look in the back room," he suggested. He picked up the shoe I had just put down and moved in front of me.

In the storeroom things were in a bigger mess than in the show-room. Someone had gone through most of the boxes and tossed the shoes every which way. I picked up a gold Jimmy Choo platform, and then reached for a black satin Weitzman pump—now scuffed and dusty and nestled them in my arms. Whoever broke in, didn't take the shoes. And, luckily, I never kept cash in the store. Merissa and I took turns each night depositing it in the bank.

And then I saw my computer had been turned on.

I walked over to the table and stared at the glowing screen. Whoever had turned it on had somehow gotten my password and had opened my accounts. I had thrown away my paper receipts for the shoes Freddie the Fox had procured for me—but I had forgotten completely about the computer record. A list of four names, addresses and phone numbers now stared me in the face.

Sophia Sarfatti was the first name and address.

The second name and address was my sister's.

My heart lurched. I plopped down on the chair. Thieves were getting much too sophisticated for me. Now you had to be able to hack into a computer as well as pick a lock.

I pressed the print button and printed out the names and addresses of the four customers. The other six people, including Bellini himself, had paid cash and there was no record. I had recorded my sister who paid me nothing at all because I needed to show something to the IRS. Thus, I thought to myself, is my honesty rewarded. My sister Shana could get into trouble just by crossing the street. And now, me, her older sister and protector against all evil, had put her directly in the path of a possible murderer.

"Don't touch nothin'" Alec Le Grand was giving me the same advice he gave me at Sophia Sarfatti's apartment. But, again, it was too late.

I felt his breath on the back of my neck as he looked over my shoulder on to the computer.

"Don't worry 'bout this, Miss Emily. Merissa and me don't let nothing happen to you and yours."

I clicked the off button on the computer and turned to face him.

"I don't need any help." I told him.

"Sure do, Miss Emily. Everyone need help lives in this world. But now maybe you call the police, come and do their work. Got to shut up the place too," he said, "'fore word get out that Miss Emily shoes are free to the neighborhood."

That at least, was advice I knew enough to heed. I called 911 and reported a break-in. I did not call Detective Paul Murphy. This was not, thank God, a homicide.

And then, I went next door to prepare for Big Bingo.

"Hey there!" Murphy the cop, called out of the window as he screeched the squad car to a halt in front of Emily's Place.

Merissa and I sat together on the island in the middle of Broadway and surveyed the scene.

“Don’t know what it is ‘bout that cop. Always show up when no one want to see him.” Merissa said, wiping the perspiration off her forehead. Between getting the shoes back in the boxes, carrying Mary and Sadie around, straightening up and moving the tables next door, we both felt pretty done in, and it was only 11:00 AM

“That’s what cops are for,” I agreed, “keep you on your toes.”

It was a surprise to see him. If he was annoyed I had called him in to investigate the possibly ordinary death of Sophia Sarfatti, what was he doing investigating a break-in at a shoe store? Besides, my “What is Life without Choice?” tee shirt, from the last march on Washington D.C. in support of Roe Vs. Wade in 1984, was covered with dirt, and I hadn’t washed my hair last night.

But the truth was I was very happy to see Murphy. \Whether or not Sophia had been murdered, I felt my sister and the other two people whose names were on that computer record were in danger, and the broad, muscular body of Murphy the Cop was comforting.

I left Merissa to rest on the bench and crossed Broadway to find out what was what.

“Hey, there,” I greeted Murphy, “What brings you to this part of town?”

Murphy smiled broadly. “Never did think I needed an excuse to visit an old friend, especially one who seems to attract trouble like orphans to a soup bowl.”

“I never much liked Oliver Twist,” I answered.

“No. But you seem to know as many unsavory “businessmen” as he did.”

It was clear he felt more comfortable with Dickens than James. I smiled and waited for him to tell me the real reason for his visit. Alec, Merissa and I had managed to tie the door shut with a piece of rope. Murphy took a pen knife out of his pocket and slit the tie in one stroke.

“An old Boy Scout trick” he explained, “should be a requirement of all on the NYPD ‘stead of college.”

He led me through the broken door of Emily's Place to a seat inside the show-room. He looked around and grunted.

"I won't even ask if you touched anything."

"Good. Then I won't have to tell you any lies. I hope to open for business in a couple of hours."

He raised his eye-brows and made a face. "Don't think so. This break-in may be connected to the Sarfatti case, so my men need some private time alone on the premises. You were right about the Sarfatti woman. Looking more and more like murder. It seems there was enough Coumadin in her herbal tea to cause a horse to hemorrhage."

Herbal tea! Sophia loved her herbal tea. Drank it instead of taking medicine. Claimed it was medicine. "But wouldn't she have tasted it?"

Murphy shook his head. "No. It's actually tasteless and colorless. We didn't find any bottles or anything that looked like it came from a legitimate pharmacy—a couple of bottles of calcium and Vitamin D From this place NATURE'S SECRET, up on 104th Street. Seems to attract a lot of nuts. But they don't sell Coumadin. We checked it out."

"What about the herbal tea?"

"Yeah! They sell that. All loose leaves. Small…easy to mix something else into it. Clerk remembered Sarfatti. She was a good customer." Murphy sat back on the chair and looked at me. "Ever have tea with her?"

"Yes. We were friends. Lots of times." I shivered. Did Sophia routinely mix Coumadin with her herbal tea? Was this Coumadin even now coursing through the veins in my brain? All of a sudden I began to feel a little faint.

"When was the last time you had tea together?" Murphy persisted.

I couldn't really remember. I knew it wasn't the day she died. And then I remembered. Merissa had mentioned she had made Sophia a cup of tea to calm her down because she was so upset when she left the shop after seeing Bellini. Merissa! I got up from the chair and walked to the door of the shop. Merissa still sat on the island in the middle of Broadway, staring at the traffic.

"How soon can I open the shop?" I asked Murphy.

"Couple of days. You're going to be closed tomorrow anyway for, what's it called? Big Bust?"

"Big Bingo." I corrected him. "Who told you about that?"

"I know a lot more than you think I know," he said, smiling. "What did the crooks get away with?"

"Nothing that I noticed. We don't keep cash. I'm sure whoever it was wanted the shoes. They hacked into my computer. I had lost the receipts but the names and addresses were recorded."

Murphy scowled. "That's not good news. I need copies of those names and addresses. We don't know who we are dealing with and all I need are a few more murders to round out the season."

I gave Murphy my print-out and he scanned it quickly. It only took him a minute to find my sister's name.

"Better talk to your sister so she doesn't freak out. I have the feeling she is the type who freaks out easily. Know anyone else on this list?

"Beverly Bernstein. She's a teacher at P.S. 96. Gives puppet shows in Riverside Park."

"Talk to her too. I'm kind of in a funny place right now. Until we can prove the old lady was murdered, I'm not officially on the case. There's just so much I can do in my spare time—to protect my friends."

His blue eyes seemed to twinkle. Was he flirting with me or what?

"See if you can get the shoes back without telling them why. Galina Kaplanskaya. Where'd you get her from?"

"Walked in off the street. I've seen her around but I don't know anything about her."

"I'll try to talk to her." Murphy took one more look around and adjusted his belt which I believe held his gun, but I didn't want to ask. I had already spent many sleepless hours wondering what was under his uniform. "Anything else you want to tell me?"

I suddenly remembered the safety deposit box, the photo and the brass button, but I had the feeling it wasn't the right time to discuss it. I didn't relish the idea of telling Murphy about Sammy and her boyfriend Giancarlo—and the possible theft of who knows what else that might have been in the safety deposit box. That safety deposit box was now somehow connected in my own mind with my taking the little diamond from the stash in Sophia's heel—surely something I had no intention of sharing with Murphy, the cop. Besides, I was still digesting the phrase "There's just so much I can do in my spare time—to protect my friends." Did this actually mean that Murphy had enough feelings for me that he wanted to protect me and mine?

I had a great deal more I would like to tell him but not right now. I shook my head.

"Better dress your mannequins before you get a ticket for indecency," he said to me. "I'll be in touch.

I really don't know why my sister Shana decided to move back to Brooklyn when it had been my life's ambition to leave that borough, but here she was, in a run-down building filled with Russian immigrants, a couple of blocks from the Brighton Beach subway stop.

The elevator was broken and there was a smell of cabbage in the hall, but the hallways had been scrubbed clean of graffiti and all, in all, it wasn't too bad a place for an aging hippy.

She was waiting for me at the top of the stairs.

"I'm so glad to see you," she said, falling into my outstretched arms.

I inhaled the sweet smell of her golden hair, which I noted, no matter what troubles Shana endured, remained lush and sparkling.

Shana had put on years without gaining weight, her bright, golden hair had no silver threads, her skin remained unlined and her mind and spirit belonged to the 60's even though she was born a generation later. Like Dorian Gray, no matter what experiences she had in life, her appearance mirrored nothing. Now in her mid-forties, she continued to go braless, eat peculiar vegetarian or, worse yet, phony food that masqueraded as beef or chicken but was really something like chickpeas and tofu mashed up together, and downs handfuls of peculiar capsules that she believed will ward off everything from the common cold to cancer.

I gave her the once-over. "Your eyes are bloodshot. Were you out late last night?"

Shana turned her head away. "You know," she said to me, "you are getting more like our mother every year."

I was nothing like my mother but I let it pass. I had come to warn my sister, not to argue with her.

"How is Colin?"

"The Welsh guy? He went back home. I'm with Mohammad now."

"A Muslim? What are you crazy? You'll be murdered in your bed!" I walked into the kitchen and plopped down on a shabby, wooden chair.

"He's Persian," Shana said. "I forgive you for being prejudiced. It's how you were brought up."

I got up and walked over to the window hoping to get a glimpse of the sea. Some image of tranquility to hang on to. I saw only dirty laundry hung out to dry. The only water around was a slow drip from the faucet in the sink, and water in the toilet that continued to run.

"Shana," I wanted to shake her but I control myself, "I need to talk to you about the last pair of shoes I gave you."

Shana looked confused. "Those black ones?" she asked after a few minutes, "the ones with the little heels?"

I nodded.

"Would you like some tea?" Shana asked me and took down a canister from the shelf above the sink.

"No!" I had had enough herbal tea to last me a lifetime.

"I'll have some cold water," I told her.

She ran the water for a few minutes and then handed me a cracked ceramic cup full of water. I made a mental note to buy Shana some glasses.

"What about them?" she asked, "They weren't very comfortable."

"That's just it," I told her, "My other customers complained too, so I am trying to collect them all and return them to the manufacturer."

Shana filled a dented metal tea kettle with some water and put it on the stove to heat.

"They're gone," she said," I think I left them in a taxi with my backpack."

"You left your backpack in a taxi? Were your keys in it? Did you change your lock?"

Shana poured her tea. "I'm working on it," she said. "my wallet was in there too."

'Did you cancel your cards?"

"What cards?" she asked me. I had forgotten that there were very few banks, however corrupt or incompetent who would offer Shana a credit card.

I put my hand on my own wallet and extracted a couple of $50 bills. I put them on the table, under a napkin. I wasn't sure if Shana's having lost the shoes was a good thing or not. On the one hand, it was a very good excuse if anyone came looking for them. On the other hand, the heels probably held a fortune in diamonds, which would never find their way back to their rightful owners unless the shoes were recovered. And what if whoever had stored those diamonds refused to believe her? While I was mulling these things over, Shana suddenly put her hand over mine and said,

"I have a small problem."

Could things get any worse? I suppose they could. I braced myself for more bad news.

"One of my clients is dying." She blurted out. "Tanya Solowitz."

I was not too surprised by this news, since my sister called herself a "Healer" and many of her clients had incurable diseases. "Russian?"

She nodded. "She says it's my fault. She says because of me she didn't go to Sloan Kettering and have her breast cut off." Her tea cup rattled and she put it down on the table. "I tried my best," she said. Her eyes filled with tears. "She had gone to Puerto Rico to some shaman."

I closed my eyes and pictured a middle-aged woman in an empty lot, surrounded by a number of dancing Hispanics, chanting loudly while sprinkling chicken blood over her head. I got up and put my arms around her. Shana's methods were better than that. At least I hoped so. I actually knew very little about what she did but had always concluded that her remedies, like everything else Shana did would be entertaining but not very effective. As far as I was concerned this Tanya person—being one of those sneaky, underhanded and always desperate Russians—probably just made up the whole deal as a way to get money.

"She's not dead yet," I told her, "She might not have cancer—she might not have anything wrong with her at all. Anyhow, I think it would be very hard to prove that anything you did made her worse. And no one prevented her from going to Sloan Kettering. It's a free country."

Shana sighed. "She sent me a lawyer's letter and a summons. They say I am practicing medicine without a license. I don't know what to do. Do you think that Larry…?"

No matter how hard I try to get away from Larry The Loser, he keeps intruding back into my life.

I shrugged. "He's still your brother-in-law. You can call him if you want."

Shana hugged me. "You're sure you don't want any tea? It's Black Tea from Southern China."

I shook my head. "Do you remember the name of the cab company where you lost your backpack?"

"It was a gypsy cab. The driver's name was Vladimir."

Right. Try looking for Vladimir in Brighton Beach.

"You'll tell me if anyone returns your back-pack? You'll change your lock?"

Shana nodded her head.

I was just beginning to relax a little bit, when I heard a strange scraping noise coming from close to the sink. Crawling slowly towards us was the biggest water bug I had ever seen.

I jumped up from the table and screamed. "Oh my God! Oh my God! Kill it! Kill it!"

I have to admit that I would rather deal with a serial killer in a dark alley way than a horrible water bug like the one now walking towards me over the kitchen floor.

"I will do no such thing," Shana shouted, backing up to the door next to me, 'And neither will you."

I took off my shoe, ready to smash it but Shana grabbed my hand.

"You can't kill it! I'm a Buddhist! I believe in reincarnation. It could be our mother!"

"You are not a Buddhist!" I screamed, "You are Jewish, and that is not our Mother!"

I knew that my sister Shana was a little weird, but living with a giant water bug was clearly beyond anything I could imagine.

"What about that book you like so much, by Kafka? The main character was a giant cockroach!"

"That was literature. Not Life!" I yelled.

I grabbed my purse, put back on my shoe and headed out the door as fast as I could make it, leaving Shana to come to terms with her Buddhist feelings and her new six-legged roommate.

"No," Beverly declared, "I don't want to exchange the shoes."

I had tracked down Beverly Bernstein, a kindergarten teacher and good customer, to try to get back the stolen shoes. This was a tricky proposition because I had to come up with a good reason to reclaim the shoes. Shana, God bless her, was not reasonable enough to care about my motives for doing things, but other people would surely want to know why the owner of a shoe store would take the time and trouble to make a home visit in order to fetch a pair of shoes marked distinctly, "FINAL SALE."

I mumbled something about some defect in the shoe that had inadvertently been shipped to Emily's Place and offered her a pair of designer shoes instead. Most people would have jumped at it. "But these are Stuart Weitzman. They sell for $300 in Saks!"

Beverly shook her head. "Weitzman, Schmeitzman! I don't buy labels. I would be ashamed to wear designer shoes when so many children—in our own neighborhood—can hardly afford any kind of shoes."

She stared at me accusingly. "I understand that selling to women of that kind is part of your business, but don't confuse me with them. I would never go to Saks. I like to keep the money in the neighborhood—as you know. Do you think I am one of those women who need to wear a label to feel good about themselves? To give themselves an identity? No! I am perfectly happy wearing these, what did you say they were? Peregee something? Perfect."

She was sitting cross-legged on the living room floor of her apartment, barefoot, cutting shapes out of colored paper, and she shook the scissors at me. "Why do you want them back anyway? I don't get it."

"It's a factory recall. There's something wrong with the way the shoes are made. They aren't safe."

She twisted one of the shapes and pieced it with a large needle.

"Unsafe? What? Are they going to explode?"

"No. It's just....The heel isn't stable. It might buckle when you are crossing the street or something."

Beverly brandished the scissors at me again. "I never heard of unsafe shoes. There are unsafe cribs; there are toys with lead in them. But unsafe shoes? There's something not right about this. A sale is a sale. This is America. If the company wants the shoes back, it must be because they are going to resell them to someone else for more money. And you—-I always thought you were an independent. Why are you taking orders from some cockamamie corporation that probably uses child labor?"

Why is it that everyone on the Upper West Side has an attitude? Everybody gives you an argument. I was surprised that Beverly had such an edge though. After all, she was a Kindergarten teacher. She gave lovely puppet shows in Riverside Park for free. Kindergarten teachers are kind and sweet, and gentle right? I pictured her as a female Mr. Rogers. She had never given me any trouble when she shopped at Emily's Place. And we had worked together quite nicely on last year's Big Bingo.

Maybe I was the trouble. And she was responding to something she sensed was untrustworthy about me—at least about how I was presenting the shoe recall. The truth was that I really wasn't much good at lying. It was so much easier to just blurt out the truth. And lies required an act of imagination that evaded me most of the time.

I decided to throw in the towel and go for the truth—or at least part of the truth.

"Actually," I sat down on the floor next to Beverly, "I have reason to believe those shoes have been stolen."

"Ah Hah!" she said, squeezing out some paste and spilling green and yellow sprinkles on top of them.

"Well you and I know I paid good money for them, so now they are mine. Hot shoes! That is kind of exciting don't you think?"

No. Actually I did not think this was very exciting. I picked up a line of red cut-out dolls and unrolled them. Dangerous is the word I would use. But how to get Beverly to think so too?

"Diamonds. There may be diamonds in the heels," I blurted out.

Beverly's clever fingers became suddenly motionless.

"Diamonds, you say."

I could see the wheels turning in Beverly's head but I wasn't sure where they were headed. The hand that was cutting out a blue square started moving again. When it was finished, Beverly put down the scissors and stared at me for a minute.

"Let's check them out." She got up from the floor and disappeared into her bedroom. A couple of minutes later, she threw the pair of shoes at my feet.

I walked over to her work table—a bunch of tools set out on her coffee table and found something I thought would work to pry off the heels. Within minutes I was able to detach one of the heels. Out spilled a bunch of red, blue and yellow stones.

Beverly dropped down beside me, her eyes wide.

I took hold of the left shoe and removed the heel. Nothing in that one.

Beverly looked disappointed. "Diamonds?" she asked

I shook my head. "Maybe each pair of shoes has different jewels."

Together we stared down at the pile of glittering stones.

Beverly picked up a handful and held them up to the light. They looked particularly brilliant lying on top of the colored shapes and sparkles.

"Do you think they are real?" she asked me.

I nodded. 'Why would anyone take the trouble to hide them like this if they weren't?"

Now Beverly beamed. "Sapphires! Rubies! Citrines!"

She picked up a handful and put them in her pocket.

In a way it was comforting to me that I was not the only person to give in to temptation.

But I had a duty to perform.

"Wait! You can't do that! These stones and shoes are stolen goods! The police are tracking them. Besides, whoever put the stones in there is going to come back for them. You'll be in danger!"

I told her about Sophia Sarfatti, and how she had turned up dead. Beverly chewed on her bottom lip and stared at me. She didn't know Sophia Sarfatti and her fate didn't seem to move her. Then her face broke out into a broad smile. She raised her hands to the ceiling. "Think what we could do with these stones, Emily. Here I am cutting out paper dolls for Big Bingo, to try to raise a few dollars. "

She picked up one blue stone and held it up. "We could build a real community center for all the kids to hang out. We could fund a half-way house for abused women. We could set up a drug-free program for addicts. We could…."

I held up my hand. "But you don't know who is going to come after you, Beverly. Think! This might be Mafia money—or even worse—it might be jewelry stolen from the Jews during WWII by the Fascists and the Nazis."

But Beverly was now in the throes of a fantasy bigger than anything I could throw at her. She went into the bedroom and came back with a small, leather pouch. She emptied her pocket into the pouch and filled it with the rest of the stones. "Jewelry stolen from the Jews during WWII, you say? Reparations! Then these jewels are mine by right. My grandfather skied across the Alps to get away from the Nazi's. They took everything he had. His home. His art collection. Killed his whole family. I'll hide them. I'll tell those bastards I threw away the shoes because they hurt my feet."

I was beginning to feel desperate. This was not the way I thought things would turn out.

"But they could hurt you—torture you—and make you tell where you hid them."

Beverly folded her arms across her chest and stared at me.

"My grandfather ate snow for four days. He caught rabbits with his bare hands and ate them raw. The Bernsteins never give in to Fascists!"

Is it possible for a person to catch a rabbit with their bare hands? The eating snow part I could credit, but I had an uneasy feeling about the rabbits. In fact, I was beginning to have an uneasy feeling about Beverly in general. She had never told me she was the child of survivors. Had she just decided to make it up as an excuse to keep the stones? Was it possible that she was part of the chain that was to launder this money and she knew all along exactly what was in the heel of that shoe?

Now she grabbed my hand. "Emily, who knows about these shoes besides us?"

"Freddie the Fox who sold them to me; whoever put the stones in there and the Police."

"Freddie's ok. He'll never squeal. The Police. If they thought a law had been broken they would be questioning me instead of you. If no one has reported these stones missing, there is no crime. They are just fishing—and using you to fish."

I didn't think this was quite true. Especially if it turned out that Sophia had been murdered. If she were murdered, the jewels in the shoes would have to be considered as a motive. But at this point, I really couldn't argue with her.

No one could say for sure that the diamonds didn't belong to Sophia Sarfatti. Or that these sapphires, rubies and citrines didn't belong to Beverly Bernstein.

And if no one reported anything missing, how could the police confiscate the jewels that Beverly Bernstein had found in her shoes?

"You can tell the police I threw away the shoes—or that there was nothing in the heels. As long as our stories agree, no one will be the wiser. In fact, "she looked me in the eye," Even if you decide to tell the police that you did find jewels in my shoes, I will deny it. There would be no way they could prove which one of us was lying. Besides, we can always bring forth the jewels if it turns out there was some robbery—some real people still alive waiting for the return of their jewels. In the meantime, I will hide them so no one will find them. And for all your trouble, I'll be happy to let you have a few jewels for the charity of your choice. Agreed?"

She put out her hand but I withheld my own. I believed Sophia Sarfatti had been murdered by whoever had put those stones in the shoes and I was sure some terrible crimes had resulted in their theft. But until I had some proof there was no point in arguing.

"I'll give it some thought," I told her. "In the meantime, don't open your door unless you know who has come calling."

I got up and walked toward the door. I didn't seem to be doing much of a job recovering the stolen stones, or protecting the people who might be in danger of holding them. On the other hand, it seemed to me that Beverly could take care of herself. Shana was another story .

At any rate, tomorrow was Big Bingo and I had other things on my mind.

FIVE

During the Industrial Revolution, advances in mechanization meant that members of the middle class could now afford lovely footwear such as riding boots, opera boots, dress pumps and carpet slippers.

"All bets down!—hey little lady—no more shiftin around—let it lay." Alec le Grand spun the wheel, and gave a thumbs up to Patty Murphy, when the little round ball landed in #7. With a flourish, Alec swept all the chips over to her side of the table.

"Bonjour Mon Petite jeune Fils," Merissa beamed at Patty. "Alors!" she produced a small red silk purse and helped Patty put in all her chips.

As usual, Alec's booth was doing the most business at this year's Big Bingo. The fact that he also had a poker game going on behind the curtain holding up the roulette wheel was nobody's business. I had been watching for a while and I noticed that when any of the kids put down their chips, the number never came up in the little green section that read 000, so someone always won something.

I hoped that Murphy the Cop didn't notice. Luckily, he seemed too pleased that his little daughter Patty was having such a good time. Strictly speaking, honesty might not be the strongest suit in this neighborhood but loyalty and generosity could be counted upon.

I was surprised that Murphy had turned up. I hadn't invited him, but I had to admit it felt good to have him around. Dare I think it was the pleasure of my company he sought? Probably not.

It was more likely his Sunday to take care of his daughter and he figured he might as well hang out here where there would be someone to help him.

He wore a tailored blue blazer—too dressy for this part of town but better than a trench coat. I filled him in about my visits to both Shana and Beverly.

Murphy shook his head. "Vladimir!" He didn't even bother to write it down in his little book.

"Your sister I can understand. We will probably never see those shoes again which could be a good thing, at least for her. But this Beverly person, I thought you told me she was a kindergarten teacher."

I shrugged. "The difference between a pit bull and a kindergarten teacher on the Upper West Side is that the teacher wears lipstick. Have you been able to prove that Sophia Sarfatti was murdered yet?"

Murphy pulled out a pack of cigarettes from his pants pocket, stared at the pack for a minute or two, and then replaced it.

"We found another set of prints on those mismatched shoes. Someone besides you and the old lady were moving them around. Trouble is, they don't match any known criminal."

"Wait a minute! What about foreign criminals? What about this Fotinni Fatale person that Sophia claims she saw? I looked him up on the internet. He really exists. He's a war criminal who was never captured. Surely someone has copies of his prints!"

Murphy's blue eyes sparkled. "Holy Mary, Mother of God. How did I ever solve a case without your advice? The NYPD also can operate a computer. And, through the ancient magic of the Druids we can actually access international files. The prints don't match."

Damn! There had to be something we were overlooking.

"We did find some prints on the tea cup," Murphy said. 'They belong to your friend Merissa."

No surprise there. "She told me she made Sophia a cup of tea to calm her down."

"It worked so well, rigor mortis set in." Murphy said. This time he did extract a cigarette. He stared at it and then crumpled it up and threw it on the sidewalk.

I grabbed his arm. "You're not telling me Merissa is a suspect?" We had already gone through this once before, with the Goodie One Shoes murder. Murphy ought to know better.

"If Sophia was murdered, the murder weapon was in the Coumadin in that tea cup. Who put the Coumadin in the tea cup is still an open question. How come Merissa didn't drink any of the tea?"

That Murphy disliked Merissa was a given—He could never forgive her for all those lies about her background. "Once a liar, always a liar," he had quoted to me more than once. He was not a man who understood subtleties when it came to human nature. But that he would once again try to pin a murder on her was getting me mad!

"Merissa is not a tea drinker! It's that simple!"

"Nothing you are involved in is simple," Murphy said, putting his big hand over mine.

"You called me, remember? If we consider the Sarfatti case a murder, we need a suspect. No murder, no suspect. You can't have it both ways."

"But why try to hang it on Merissa? She had no motive."

"Maybe she thought the old lady had a fortune under her mattress."

"Yeah—right," I muttered under my breath "Those Jews always have money."

"You said it, not me" Murphy chuckled. "Never let it be said the NYPD is a supporter of stereotypes."

I could have started a discussion about "profiling" but I thought better of it.

"There were lots of people who had access to that tea canister. What about SuperMama? Or the Senator?" I looked over the crowd. "What about Alec le Grand? He was in the building collecting bets; What about Sammy—she read to Sophia every evening…." I covered my mouth with my hand.

"Thanks," Murphy said, "I can use a few more suspects. I was actually hoping to run into Freddie The Fox—the man whose address you gave me. Seems a little out of date. His mother had palpitations as soon as she saw me and I spent the whole morning trying to revive her. According to her, Freddie hasn't been around since his confirmation at St. Ignatius when he was twelve."

I shrugged. "People in this neighborhood move around a lot. I haven't seen him yet. He usually shows up at this thing."

The trouble with Murphy was that he couldn't tell the difference between a suspect and a neighbor—and I had just fingered a couple of friends. I had deliberately refrained from telling Murphy about what Sammy and her boyfriend Giancarlo had done with the safety deposit box, because I knew he would over-react. And, of course, if it turned out Sophia hadn't been murdered, I didn't need to share it with him at all.

Murphy took my arm. "Truth is, I think you're right about the old lady being murdered. I got my own intuition. Someone wiped the fingerprints off the book she was reading—that's not the act of an innocent visitor. That old lady never knew those stones were in those shoes. If she had, why bring the shoes to you complaining they didn't fit right? There's a bunch of things here that don't add up, but unless I got some real proof, there's not much I can do. And if the Feds get wind of it—I'm out of here!" Murphy shook his head. "All I need is a bunch of guys in trench coats and crew cuts babbling about War Criminals to send me over the edge."

I didn't feel it necessary at this point to remind Murphy that there probably was a War Criminal mixed up in this somewhere. The first order of business was to prove a murder had been committed.

"The Coumadin—did you find a prescription anywhere?"

Murphy shook his head. "No. That's another problem. For Coumadin, the blood thinning medication, you need a prescription—but for Warfarin—the generic—that's rat poison. Anyone could have gotten it at any hardware store."

"And your lab can't tell the difference?"

Murphy snorted. "It's not that easy. The stuff had already been mixed into the tea leaves—and the tea leaves were mixed with a bunch of herbs, plus a few twigs and saw-dust. No agency oversees those "natural remedies"; they contain all sorts of crap. Who knows where that old lady got them."

At least she didn't get them from Shana. She lived too far away.

"Murder will out" I said.

"Ah—Murphy smiled at me. "I know that's Shakespeare—not sure which play, but it's Shakespeare. Shakespeare even a cop can understand. He understood human nature and human nature doesn't change. That "Jolly Corner" story, though, that's a different kettle of fish."

"'Murder will out' is from Macbeth. There's ghosts in that story too."

"I don't believe in ghosts. And I'm not so sure 'murder will out' any more. It requires a conscience and I don't see much evidence of conscience in my line of work."

I edged a little closer to Murphy. He didn't move away. He had remembered what I had said about the Henry James story. He had even read it.

"I think you do believe in ghosts," I told him. "I saw you cross yourself when you mentioned the Angel of Death at Sophia's apartment."

"Habit." he replied. "I went to Catholic School."

Together we looked over the crowd—men and women, boys and girls of all ages and skin shades—even a few stray cats had wandered in.

"Got a pretty good crowd here. Anyone here you think I should know?"

No sooner did those words come out of Murphy's mouth when I saw a vaguely familiar figure emerge from behind the curtain in Alec le Grand's booth. A well-dressed older man with a cane. Could it be? Massimo Bellini? The Italian who had sent Sophia into some kind of nervous fit when she saw him in my store? What was he doing in this neighborhood again? And what did he have to do with Alec le Grand?

Bellini must have seen me at the same time as I saw him, because he ducked back behind the curtain as quickly as possible. I wasn't about to blow the whistle on Alec's poker game—so I had no choice but to keep my mouth shut. As a matter of fact, I felt it my duty to distract Murphy from this particular situation.

I gently turned him around and directed his attention to the opposite side of the store.

The front of the store was taken over by Angelina Grossi's fortune-telling booth. She was decked out in one of her vintage kimonos—fuchsia with a huge gold dragon—four inch orange mules and a yellow silk bandanna wrapped around her hair, seated happily in front of a large glass ball—and making up stories for everyone in the neighborhood. Henry was perched on her shoulder, adding a few squawks to each prediction.

My sister Shana had set up a small table and a couple of chairs and was reading people's auras. Thank God she had left Muhammad and her six legged cockroach at home in Brighton Beach. And commanding the entire front of the store was Beverly Bernstein and her puppet theater.

A sign reading THE MERCHANT OF VENICE IN 15 MINUTES was taped to the top of her booth, and kids were already beginning to gather.

Harold Shapiro, my window-dresser, had dragged my mannequins Sadie and Mary to the corner of the street. Sadie sat on the water hydrant with Mary on her lap. "It's fab—just fab—for advertising!" he insisted, and was giving fashion advice to whoever stopped by to admire their outfits—ratty rabbit fur jackets, leopard printed mini-skirts, and red platform shoes. Next to him on the table were a bunch of shoes I couldn't sell last year marked down for $25.

Merissa, dressed for the occasion like an African Queen, (except for her shoes—three inch gold Jimmy Choos) long, black and white print robe, miles of coral and white beads around her neck, and a turban of orange silk, ran back and forth between my booth, and the Roulette wheel, a mesmerized Patty following her close behind.

SuperMama had stationed herself out in the street as well. A monumental form in a flowing flowered housecoat—making sure none of the more disreputable players in the area tried to steal her platters of fried chicken and apple pie without paying.

Nelson Nini, known affectionately as "Nancy" around the neighborhood was selling cheap costume jewelry. Irina Kaminsky, was selling phony antiques; Tiffany Jefferson was braiding hair; Jesus Gomez was rolling handmade cigars. Jimmy "Dandy" Daily was twisting balloons into shapes of animals.

And at a small table next to SuperMama, was seated her daughter Sammy and her boyfriend Giancarlo. They were doing magic tricks.

Before I had a chance to answer Murphy, I heard a loud commotion coming from inside the store.

"What do you know about anything?" Beverly Bernstein shouted out

"I know this play…this play bad for children!"

Murphy grabbed my arm and pulled me back in that direction. A tall, heavy-set man with wild gray hair was standing in front of Beverly. His chin was thrust forward as if he were about to bite her.

"Just a minute! Just a minute here!" I moved quickly in between the two warring parties. I figured he wouldn't hit a woman, whereas with Murphy, whose big hands were already resting on his hidden gun tucked under his jacket, we could easily have mayhem.

"That, that…that…Russian Gangster…has accused me of Anti-Semitism" Beverly sputtered.

I looked from one to another. "What are you talking about?"

The Russian guy pointed to the sign over her puppet theater. THE MERCHANT OF VENICE.

"That play…she give that play…that Shylock is bad. A Jew who sell his daughter for money. Kids think Jews are bad. Love money more than daughters."

Beverly stamped her foot. "What do you know? The kids always love my play. And Shylock isn't Jewish!"

"Wait a minute! "I looked at Beverly. This Russian guy had a point. "Shylock is Jewish."

"Shakespeare's Shylock is Jewish. Beverly Bernstein's Shylock is not." She pointed to her sign. In small letters it said, "by Beverly Bernstein."

"So what is your Shylock?" The Russian demanded to know.

We looked around at the rainbow of faces that now surrounded us. "Yeah what?" yelled out Jose Ramirez my newspaper delivery guy—"Did you make him Puerto Rican?"

"Could be one of them Arab dudes!" someone piped up from the crowd.

"Or one of them Indians from Bangladesh you gets on the phone when you complains about the service." Someone else chimed in.

The crowd was really getting into it now.

"Long as it ain't no Home Boy!"

"Maybe it be one of them Homosexuals!"

Beverly Bernstein stared at the crowd and put her hands on her hips.

I wondered how she—and the Big Bingo Association—of which I was President—were going to get out of this one.

"My Shylock is a Martian," she called out. "He's green!"

The crowd burst into applause.

I caught Murphy on the edge of the crowd shaking his head.

And then my sister Shana pushed her way to the front of the crowd. She put her hand on the Big Russian's arm.

"This is Vladimir!" She announced brightly. "He's a friend of mine!"

The crowd burst out again in applause.

I didn't know how much money Big Bingo would be able to contribute to the neighborhood kids, but we were way ahead in entertainment.

Shana gave Vladimir an affectionate tap on the behind as he wandered off in the direction of the roulette wheel, and smiled at me.

"Vladimir. The Gypsy Cab driver. He found your shoes?"

She nodded. I could see in the way her eyes followed his retreating figure that Muhammad was gone and forgotten.

"He's Jewish." She said to me. "He killed the water bug with a broom."

"Where are the shoes?" I asked her

"I'm wearing them," she answered. "Didn't you notice?"

I wasn't sure if this was good news or not, but it seemed unlikely that anyone could attack Shana and de-shoe her in front of the whole neighborhood, so I figured she was safe for a while.

I pushed through the crowd towards Murphy. He was holding tight to Patty's hand.

She grinned up at me and put a very sticky hand into mine.

"Look at my hair! That lady over there did it. She said it was corn rows."

Patty's pretty blond curls were now braided tightly in little rows and standing up from her head like a halo.

"Gorgeous!" I said, squeezing her hand. "I bet you'll be the only one at The St. Catherine's School with a hairdo like that."

Murphy scowled. "Looks like Topsy from Uncle Tom's Cabin. What will her mother say?"

"We don't care what mommy says, do we?" Patty answered, and Murphy didn't have a reply to that one.

"Oh look! Look! Magic tricks!" Patty pulled away from both of us and ran towards one of the tables.

Of all the assorted types now happily enjoying themselves at Big Bingo, one of the strangest couples were seated now a few feet away, doing magic tricks to a crowd of little kids; Sammy, the tall, lovely daughter of SuperMama, and her current boyfriend, Giancarlo.

I still couldn't figure this one out.

I never did get to have children of my own—Larry the Loser and me never seemed to get around to it and now it's too late—so I guess I'm especially drawn to some of the young people around the neighborhood. Sammy was one of them. Beautiful, intelligent, poised, with a kind of natural elegance, she stood out like a lily in a cactus garden. She didn't seem to belong in the shabby brownstone she grew up in. She didn't seem to belong to SuperMama. She certainly didn't seem to belong with Giancarlo.

She had helped me out from time to time in Emily's Place. I knew she wanted to go to college and study to be a nurse. Both Merissa and I had encouraged her and gave her extra work whenever we could.

I had hinted at helping her out with the tuition, in return for running some errands from time to time for Emily's Place. Of course, if she found the treasure she was looking for in Sophia's safety deposit box, she might have that one covered. But that is where my real influence ended. I could only scowl when she brought up Giancarlo's name. He was supposed to be a Jazz musician but I didn't think he worked very much at anything. He had the reputation in the neighborhood of being a lower-level Mafia runner of some sort. But nothing much I said about Giancarlo seemed to penetrate the spell he had woven around her.

If he were handsome, at least, I might understand it. But he looked like the gangster he was reputed to be. He was at least as tall, if not quite as wide as SuperMama, and his bulging muscles shown through his tee shirt which featured a large white skull on a black background. The back of his thick neck sported a tattoo of a snarling bear. The sun glowed off the top of his shaved head and a set of heavy keys and chains dangled from his jean pocket. On his feet, he wore a pair of red sneakers. Central casting could not have come up with a more suitable goon. What was a nice girl like Sammy doing with a creep like Giancarlo?

But there they both were, Sammy tall and elegant in a white blouse and freshly washed jeans, collecting tickets from a bunch of kids spell-bound by Giancarlo's sleight of hand.

He approached us with a wide grin and I instinctively recoiled—back into Murphy's chest—while Giancarlo pulled a red scarf from out of my ear.

"Hey!" I called out as Murphy put his hands around my waist to steady me. "How did you do that?"

But both Sammy and Giancarlo were too pleased with themselves to comment and all the kids who were watching, started pushing and shoving. "Me! Me! They all called out, as Giancarlo calmly proceeded to take a rose from Murphy's breast pocket and place it in my hands. This was as surprising to me as if a gorilla had baked me a soufflé and gently handed me a spoon.

Patty was utterly delighted and gave me a big hug when I handed her the rose.

It seemed possible that I had misjudged Giancarlo. That he was a goon, I still firmly believed. But it was possible that he was more talented than I had imagined.

While his thighs and forearms were as thick as tree trunks, his fingers were long and slender. For the first time I could believe he was a musician—the piano player he was supposed to be.

If Murphy's hands were executioners hands, large, with short, strong fingers, that I had seen flex with longing to squeeze the life out of somebody, Giancarlo's hands were small for his body, his fingers long and graceful. They danced through the air like acrobats, forming elongated circles, caressing invisible objects. That those fingers could pick a lock in the blink of an eye I had no doubt. But it was when his phone rang—he had one of those smart phones that can do just about anything except cook dinner—it occurred to me that he was probably as good with a computer as with any device that gave up its secrets with the right touch.

Murphy seemed to be as surprised as I was by the strange incongruity of Sammy and Giancarlo and I introduced him to them both. "Hey," He asked Giancarlo, "How did you do that?"

Giancarlo smiled. "You owe me two tickets." He said, putting out his hand.

Murphy put his hand in his pocket. "Guess I'm all out. Gave 'em to my little girl here."

We both turned around. Patty was gone!

Murphy looked at me and I looked at him. Not having any kids myself, I never knew they could move so fast. Murphy seemed completely stunned.

"You go that way; I'll go this way," I told him. "She couldn't have gotten far. Is she allowed to cross the street by herself?"

"I don't know. Don't think she would do that. "

I heard his breathing change. He reached into his other pocket and took out a container of pills. He popped one into his mouth and swallowed it without water.

"We can make an announcement!" Sammy said, and she set off towards a small table on the sidewalk under a banner that read: HEAD-QUARTERS. Lying on top of the table was a bullhorn.

Of course! This had happened before. Lots of times. I should have remembered.

"Patty—come to HEAD-QUARTERS. Anyone see a little blond girl—hair in corn-rows—wearing a red tee shirt—come to HEADQUARTERS. Murphy grabbed the bull-horn and climbed on top of the table: PATTY—WE NEED YOU.COME TO HEADQUARTERS, NOW!

I climbed up next to him. "What about her phone? Can you call her on her phone?"

"Her mother took it away—didn't want her 'communicating' with me too often. I got her another but we left it home."

PATRICIA MURPHY—COME TO HEADQUARTERS NOW! Murphy shouted over the bullhorn.

"Wait! I think I see her!" I yelled. "She's with Nancy!"

At this point Murphy too could see Patty pushing through the crowd and holding on to a tall man wearing a baseball cap.

"Thanks God!" Murphy said " There's my girl but I don't see any Nancy."

"Nancy is a man.

" It figures. Sammy is a girl; Nancy is a guy."

He jumped down from the table, leaving me to climb down by myself, while he hugged Patty and confronted Nancy—Nelson Nini, "Nancy" was a jeweler by trade—some said he was a fence for some of the locals. Nancy grinned. Despite his name, there was nothing gay about him. He looked like he needed a shave and his navy tee shirt had a couple of holes in it. The tips of his fingers and around his nails seemed permanently stained by some dark chemicals. Around his neck were three gold chains.

Around Patty's neck was a thick gold-colored chain from which hung a large P encrusted with rhinestones. "I know this must be Patty," Nancy said, "'cause she picked out a P to wear on her chain." Nancy chuckled. "Got a bunch of Bling down in China Town you could never find on 47th Street!"

"Thanks." Murphy said. "Really appreciate it." He put his hand in his pocket and took out a $20 dollar bill.

Nancy shook his head. "Hey man. It's my pleasure. Anyone here would do the same. Maybe next time I get a parking ticket, you can do me a favor."He turned and walked away.

"How did he know I was a Cop?" Murphy asked me.

I shrugged. 'Could be your uniform."

"What?" Murphy tugged on his blazer. "You think I'm not dressed right?"

I smiled. "I think you look just fine."

Murphy turned towards Patty and scowled."Didn't I teach you never to talk to strangers?"

Patty giggled. "He's not a stranger. I met him at the Roulette Game. "

Murphy shook his head. "I don't know if this neighborhood is the right place for my little girl."

"Right," I told him. "Like cops move in the best company. And anyway, Patty is having a great time."

"Right," Patty said, and she gave me five.

Then we heard another bull-horn, from inside the store. "THE PUPPET SHOW IS ABOUT TO BEGIN!"

Murphy, Patty and I joined hands, and headed back to the store

But standing directly in front of us and blocking our way was a tall, thin, man with a small mustache—The Senator. The Senator bowed politely to us and reached for Patty's hand, which he attempted draw up to his lips.

"Ah…such a beautiful signorina."

Patty looked up at him and pulled back her hand.

"I too have a gift for the little beauty," And he handed Patty a small, plastic container filled with a pale yellow substance.

She held it in one hand and turned her face away.

In an instant Murphy had grabbed the container, as if it held some poison. "I thank you," he said to The Senator, "But Patty has had entirely too much to eat already."

The Senator smiled and shook his head. "Oh No, Signore. Not to eat, to rub on her skin and make her even more beautiful. It is aloe. It comes from the cactus plant. I first found it many years ago in Arizona. The American Indians use it for burns."

"Thank you kindly," Murphy said, putting the container in his pocket. "Are you coming to the puppet show?"

The Senator shook his head. "Sadly, I cannot stay. I have many old friends who wait for my visits. Sophia Sarfatti—I miss her so. It was a heart attack? One hears so many peculiar things."

Murphy raised one eye-brow, like an antenna suddenly looking for signals. "What did you hear?" he asked.

The Senator shrugged. "SuperMama speaks of The Angel of Death."

"Oh," Murphy smiled. "We are still doing tests to ascertain the cause of death. But I suppose the Angel of Death gets us all sooner or later."

"Let us hope it is much later for all of us," The Senator said, and he bowed again, and disappeared into the crowd.

"I want a Shylike Puppet." Patty declared after the puppet show. Not only had Beverly made Shylock into a green Martian—

with big ears instead of a big nose—she had changed his name as well.

"I think you'll have to make your own," I told her, "Like Beverly Bernstein. Maybe—just maybe—next time you visit, I can help you put something together."

I figured all I needed was an old green sock, some stuffing and a few buttons and I could conjure up something. Maybe I had an ulterior motive, as in trying to attract her dad, but the truth is, I really liked the kid. She was spunky, and lively, and wide-eyed with curiosity. Plus, I wasn't her mother so I didn't have to deal with any of the bad stuff, like discipline.

Patty pulled on Murphy's arm and whispered something in his ear.

"Well, now," he turned to look at me, "here's something else maybe Mrs. Levine can help you with."

Patty looked a little embarrassed, but I figured I probably knew the problem.

"Need a bathroom?" I asked her.

She nodded.

There were a couple of portable toilets set up on the side of the street but there were lines of kids already waiting. And I could only imagine what they looked and smiled like inside.

"How about we just go next door to Emily's Place. I have a nice, new bathroom I'm sure will be fine."

Since Larry the Loser had destroyed my bathroom in his "flood," I had repainted the bathroom a soft, powder-blue, and put in a couple of new royal blue towels. Not a lot of money, and it gave the place a fresh, nice look.

I had had just enough time to have the lock replaced since the break-in and I slipped the new key into the lock.

Damn! It seemed jammed. The mechanism was probably stiff because it hadn't been used. I tried again to turn the lock and then Murphy gave it a final twist and the door swung open.

It was cool and somehow bleak inside. My two colorful mannequins, Sadie and Mary, a couple of display tables, and a bunch of shoes had been moved out to the street for the fair.

But there was something else that I was feeling. Call it intuition again. There was something wrong—a musky smell—a chilly dampness that was out of place on such a sunny day. The scent of damp earth—the smell of the grave.

I turned on the lights but the shadows lingered. Nonsense, I told myself, but the feeling of dread persisted. I walked slowly back towards the storeroom where the bathroom was located.

"I hope you like my new bathroom," I said to Patty, and I pushed open the door.

A dark shape sat on the toilet seat, his head hanging at an odd angle.

There was blood splattered all around my newly painted wall.

I shut the door quickly. The shock of what I saw was like a punch in the stomach.

I grabbed on to the nearest thing, which happened to be Murphy.

"Oops! I forgot, the toilet is stopped up!" I cried out. That might be the understatement of the year.

I pulled Patty aside. "Maybe your dad could give it a look. Men are good with this sort of problem."

I pushed Murphy towards the door of the bathroom. "In the meantime, I just live around the block. I'll take Patty to the bathroom in my apartment. I know that one works!"

And I led Patty quickly out of the store.

Whether Murphy would ever forgive me for suggesting he had a talent for fixing toilets, I didn't know. But one thing I did know. That dead body propped up on my toilet seat was Freddie The Fox.

SIX

The first rubber heels, that out-lasted leather ones, was invented by an Irish American in 1899.

"One bullet to the head sure spoiled your new paint job" Murphy told me the next morning as he helped me climb over the police tape surrounding Emily's Place.

First a flood and now a blood bath—never knew a toilet in a shoe store could produce so much drama. Thanks for taking my daughter to the bathroom."

Murphy's the only person I know who can say 'Thank You' in a manner that insults the recipient. Fortunately, I am smart enough to avoid taking the bait. I don't have much experience with little kids but I certainly bonded with Patty over a stuffed toilet.

She regaled me with "Doody" stories, in which her father, Murphy, The Cop, played a starring role, particularly in saving the family vast sums of money that might have gone to a plumber. Picturing Murphy in a sweaty tee shirt with a plunger in his hands was not the most romantic image but once she got started Patty was having too good a time to stop. Fortunately, she never realized the extent of the drama that had taken place in my own toilet at Emily's Place, and when Murphy came to fetch her, about four hours later, his navy blue blazer didn't even have a crease.

It was only after they left that the full force of Freddie's murder hit me. He had grown up the son of a single mother who worked as a waitress in Niko's Greek restaurant, dropped out of school when he was about sixteen and already a heroin addict, piled up a record of arrests for small thefts. One enlightened judge offered him a rehab program instead of jail time and this seemed to turn him around. At least as far as the drugs were concerned. His propensity for taking things that didn't belong to him, apparently never quite made it through rehab.

His mom did her best. I didn't lie when I said Freddie lived with her…when he stayed anywhere for more than a few days, and the neighborhood lent him a hand when they could. Taking care of someone like Freddie-the-Fox really would take a village and Upper Broadway had too many Freddies to pay enough attention to this one.

I thought I was doing Freddie a favor when I bought the shoes "that fell off the truck" but now it seemed to me I had just hastened his end. I tried to tell myself he would have sold those shoes to someone else if I hadn't bought them, but I kept picturing his mother's face, her bleached blond hair flat and straggly, her make-up smeared—her final surrender to putting on a good face—looking at the remains of the boy she had brought into the world. It was with this final thought that I stumbled into bed and cried myself to sleep.

The next morning, I took an ivy plant that was sitting near my bedroom window and planted it in the little backyard behind the brownstone. I mumbled the prayer for bread in Hebrew—the only Hebrew I knew, added a couple of pebbles around the leaves, and hoped that Freddie's soul would find its way to the great beyond. Then I set off for Emily's Place.

One of the things I've noticed about the New York City Police Department is that the idea of "fitting in" to a neighborhood seems never to have occurred to them. Oh yes, they have learned that it is helpful to have a few African-American cops in an all-black neighborhood, but that's about as far as it goes. In my neighborhood, I've noticed a few "under-cover" cops, often Korean, who walk around with their hands under their jackets, fingering their guns when they go into Niko's The Greek, for a cup of coffee.

So it was no surprise that when I arrived at Emily's Place there were three cop cars with flashing lights and enough crime-scene tape to surround a football field, blocking access to an entire block. Three arguments were in full flower as Jose could not deliver his newspapers, nor could Alec Le Grand collect his bets, nor could the straggly, homeless man who collects bottles and cans, get to his garbage cans. And this was before the hard-working proprietors of the shops on 101st street and Broadway attempted to reach their destinations.

As Murphy helped me over the tape, I remembered what SuperMama told me about the trouble she had renting the apartment of the guy who was murdered there—and I couldn't help wondering about the fate of Emily's Place.

"I know it's a lot to ask," I said to Murphy, "but would it be possible to keep some of the more sordid details out of the conversations your guys are having with the locals?"

"Sure, "he smiled at me. "We'll tell everyone Freddie's heart just stopped when he saw that red satin shoe in the window."

When I finally got inside, it was even worse than I could imagine. The cops had moved all my displays around and the shoes had fallen off in mismatched piles, which seem to have been swept to the corners of the store. My lovely, comfortable, deep blue customer seats had been pushed around and stood at odd angles, a couple of them up-side-down, while all the mirrors, so carefully angled along the bottom of the walls to reflect the shoes a customer was trying on, were scattered so that only someone's belly could be reflected.

On the other hand, the policemen had figured out how to operate my coffee machine and the backroom, where, after all, the murder had occurred, was pretty much intact as three of them sat around happily munching on the cookies Sammy had baked, and using up all my napkins.

The less said about the NYPD, the better.

I was in this contemplative mode of mind when one of the arguments outside got so loud it I could no longer ignore it, and when I looked out the window I saw Giancarlo having it out with one of the brawnier of the cops blocking the entrance to the shop.

Murphy and I got outside about the same time and Murphy waved the other cop off.

"Hey," he said to Giancarlo. "You're the guy from Big Bingo, right? The guy who did the magic tricks?"

Giancarlo scowled and waved his fist at the first cop. He was wearing the same black tee shirt with the skeleton head so that might have given Murphy a clue as to his identity— although I have to credit Murphy with having a good memory for faces.

"Easy now," he tried to calm him down. "This is a crime scene and no one is allowed through."

That was when Giancarlo saw me and yelled, "Emily! It's me, Giancarlo. I got to go in. I got to see Freddie. Him and me—we were friends. I got to see him!" And with that, this large, goon-like person with the skull on his tee shirt sat down on the sidewalk and cried.

Murphy and I looked at each other and then Murphy put his hand on his arm and gently helped him up.

"Isn't anything to see," Murphy told him. "Body went off to the morgue downtown last night. But you're welcome to come inside for a while. Maybe have a cup of coffee, settle down."

Murphy waved his hand and another cop actually detached a part of the tape—they didn't do squat for me!—and let him through. Once inside, Giancarlo brushed off one of the seats in the showroom and sat down.

"Where did it happen?" he asked Murphy. 'I want to see the spot."

Murphy and I exchanged glances again.

"Not exactly sure," Murphy squatted down next to him. "Still dusting for evidence. How do you take your coffee?"

Giancarlo shook his head. "Can't think of nothin. Just want to see where Freddie was."

He looked up at me.

"Ms. Emily! He trusted you. He tells me over and over, "Ms. Emily. She's my friend. She helped me when I was down. Don't know what he was doin' here. Must have been hiding out."

He jumped up from the seat. “Must have hid out here from the guy who was lookin’ for who stole the shoes!”

That was when Murphy arrived with a cup of coffee. He nudged Giancarlo back into his seat and put the cup in his hand. Giancarlo kind of stared at it as though it were some stone from Mars. He looked for some place to put it down and finally choose the floor. Then he looked around and said, “I guess I’ll be going along now. Thanks for the Java.”

I suppose at that point he realized that he was sitting on a chair at the scene of a murder, surrounded by cops and that probably wasn’t the coolest place for someone like him to be. At any rate, when he tried to get up from the chair, Murphy gently held him back.

“So—You and Freddie were best friends. He told you he had stolen the shoes he sold to Ms. Emily here?”

Giancarlo shook his head. “I didn’t mean …Freddie didn’t steal nothin’. Some people might think so, ‘cause these shoes went missing, but Freddie didn’t do nothin’ wrong. Freddie—he would sometimes just find an opportunity to make a deal. Like any business person.”

He turned and stared at me.

“He was just trying to make a living.” I said to Murphy. “Like most of us here on Upper Broadway.”

Murphy raised one of his eyebrows. “Sure.” He said. “I grew up poor myself. Would you know anyone special who might have thought Freddie stole from him? Someone who might have been angry enough to shoot him in the head—Mafia style?”

At the word “Mafia” Giancarlo twisted in his seat. But he just shook his head. “Don’t know anyone would want to kill Freddie-the-Fox. Everyone I know liked him. Specially me.” And he bent over in the seat and covered his face with his hands.

Murphy put his hand on Giancarlo’s shoulder. “If you think of anything you want to tell us, give me a call.” He put one of his cards in Giancarlo’s hand.

I couldn’t help noticing, once again, the contrast between their hands. Both men being about the same size, it was interesting how Giancarlo's fingers, long and slender closed gracefully around the card, while Murphy's short, blunt fingers opened and closed like a vise.

"Thank you," Giancarlo said to both of us when he finally rose to leave, "for letting me see where Freddie was." And I believed he meant it. I walked Giancarlo to the door, and the cops made way for him.

When I came back inside, Murphy had picked up the coffee cup with his handkerchief.

"Finally got a set of his prints," Murphy said, and he walked into the back room.

It was clear to both of us that however strong the friendship was between Giancarlo and Freddie-the-Fox, Giancarlo had come because he was scared of meeting the same fate—from the same person—and that he had an important role in the shoe caper.

I sat down on the chair newly vacated by Giancarlo and waited for Murphy to return. "He's guilty of something." I told him.

Murphy nodded. "That statement is probably true of everyone in this neighborhood."

"Could be true of everyone on the planet," I said to him. "Don't Catholics believe in original sin?"

Murphy smiled. "I've lapsed in a lot of ways, but that's one idea I can still go with."

Together we surveyed the mess his guys had made of Emily's Place. "When can I open for business?"

He shrugged. "I'll do the best I can. We'll take down the tape in a couple of days. Then, it's up to you. At least now we have a murder. No more pussy-footing around. No more Mr. Nice Guy, hoping someone will return the evidence. Now I can get a warrant."

He stared rather deliberately at me. As usual, he was trying to blame something on me. He was still after the diamonds found in Sophia's Shoe.

"Does this make Sophia Sarfatti's death officially a homicide too?" I asked him.

Murphy averted my glance. "I got to look at the new evidence—find something specific linking the two deaths. Check-out these fingerprints from Giancarlo. Maybe get a match for some we found at the old lady's place. Check into the Mafia connection. This kid was executed Mafia-style, one shot to the head. 'Course it could be someone wants us to think that way…." His voice trailed off.

I still wasn't buying the Mafia connection. There was still Bellini to consider—and he didn't smell like Mafia to me. "What about the whole WWII war crime thing that might have sent Sophia over the edge?"

Murphy shrugged. "Could be a red herring. Old lady has visions of her past. Thinks she sees a ghost from the past. Could be she was getting a little ga-ga and it wouldn't take much to send her to the next world."

I shook my head. "There was something in that room. There was a smell of camphor—a fluttering of wings…." I shuddered.

Murphy wasn't buying it. " Most probably some rat who lived under the sofa. Old lady had about twenty years of dust under there. I'm not closing the door on anything yet. Just saying WWII's a long shot."

He gave me one more searching look. "Try to keep out of trouble. Don't buy any more shoes that fell off a truck."

"Wait a second!" I ran after him. Now that Murphy was sure Freddie was trafficking in stolen goods, was he trying to pin a felony on me? "Freddie never told me that the shoes I bought fell off a truck. He just said they were 'seconds.'"

For a moment, Murphy stopped in his tracks and looked me up and down.

"SuperMama never told me she was African-American but somehow I figured it out." He walked towards the door. "Patty says 'Hello'" he called over his shoulder, and he walked out into the street.

“So what do I do with my two ladies?” Harold Shapiro asked me the next afternoon.

We were sitting in our “garden.” Some, like my estranged husband Larry, might say “a cruddy cement courtyard”—but that just shows a lack of imagination.

Whatever. It might be a small space, but it was partly green and, although shaded by the apartment building next door, came rent-free with my apartment. I had to share it with the six other people who lived in the old brownstone but since most of them didn’t get up until about 4:00 in the afternoon, it was mostly just Harold and me, hanging out.

We had cleared away the old newspapers, beer cans, and other debris and had broken up a few more slabs of cement until we had enough room for a bench. Then we put in a few flats of impatiens a couple of pots of geraniums—and voila! An oasis of beauty in the cement jungle.

Harold bent over a small tomato plant he had put in the earth a week ago and sighed. “I’m beginning to feel more and more like Willie Loman in Death of a Salesman, pathetically trying to plant something in his little sunless backyard.”

I leaned back on the bench and yawned. It was a lazy day for me—a day without a destination since Emily’s Place was off limits—a rare opportunity to relax. “I’ve lived my entire life in this city and the only piece of green I could ever lay claim to is right here. “

I bent down and plucked out a weed.

“Ah!” Harold replied. “You are a woman of simple tastes. And it is a good thing because unless you can open the shop and sell some shoes, neither you, nor your good friends, Mary and Sadie, the most celebrated mannequins in the entire City, are going to have a place to live.”

I figured I could last a couple of months at least before things got desperate—and the police would surely be gone in a day or two. How my customers would respond to a murder in their favorite shoe store only time would tell. Anyway, I wasn’t too worried about Mary and Sadie. They were already notorious in the neighborhood—"The Upper West Side Improvement Society" had sent me a scathing letter denouncing the mini-skirt and breast-revealing tiger-skin Sadie sported a couple of weeks ago, so I was sure some enterprising store owner would pay a good price for them. And Harold had lots of jobs, plus a wealthy lawyer who was his devoted (if somewhat boring) life partner.

"I love Mary and Sadie dearly but they do take up a lot of room. Right now they are stashed in my bedroom. They look so realistic that they have already freaked out several of my friends, who have accused me of going straight. I mean, I do have a reputation to preserve."

My apartment was even smaller than Harold's and it was already bursting at the seams. I had left my old Central Park West apartment with little more than a toothbrush and all of my shoes, but I had managed to fill it up all the same. Shoes can take up a lot of room. Especially when you only have two closets in the entire apartment. I was already stashing them in the oven of my stove. So I wasn't looking forward to sharing my space with Sadie and Mary.

"Let's try to bring them back tomorrow. Even if the store isn't open, I may be able to get Murphy to give us a dispensation."

"Murphy!" Harold exclaimed and sat down next to me on the bench. "The last time I saw him he tried to arrest me for stealing."

"That wasn't Murphy." I reminded him. "That was one of his policewomen. And you were stealing."

It was about a year ago, during my investigation of Goodie One Shoes—but it still loomed large in our memories.

Harold smirked. "It was for a good cause. Anyway, I fail to see why Murphy should favor Giancarlo over me. If he thought I was a thief, for sure he'll believe Giancarlo is a murderer."

Hello! This was a strange thing to say. How did Harold know anything about Giancarlo? Sure, Giancarlo lived in the neighborhood but he was light years away from Harold in everything from education to social class. Besides, Giancarlo was homely—not the kind of guy Harold would even want to speak to.

And how would he know Giancarlo came to the store and was questioned by Murphy?

"Giancarlo? Sammy's boyfriend? How do you know Giancarlo?"

Harold laughed. "Sammy's boyfriend? Right! Like I'm Sadie's boyfriend!"

I must admit none of this made an ounce of sense to me.

"He's not Sammy's boyfriend? I always see them together. They had a booth together at Big Bingo!"

Harold fidgeted on the bench. "So? I had a booth with Sadie and Mary."

This was beginning to give me a headache. I got up from the bench and approached a patch of impatiens. Tearing off a few yellow leaves seemed to be about all I could manage at the moment.

"I wonder what Giancarlo will do now." Harold mumbled.

I returned to the bench. "Ok. I give up. I don't understand a word of what you are saying. What do you know about Giancarlo that I don't?"

Harold squinted at me. "Come on! You're kidding me!"

I shook my head.

"He's gay, of course." Harold finally blurted out. "I was sure you knew."

I shook my head again. I had never even given it a thought.

"How did....How come....?"

Harold scratched his head. "Now I did it. I thought you knew or I never would have said a word."

He turned towards me. "You know everyone knows everything in this neighborhood but even though people here can be tough, they can also be kind. Giancarlo grew up here. So did Freddie-the-Fox. Everyone liked them, even though they surely had their troubles. SuperMama, she used to take care of Giancarlo when his mother was in jail. Freddie-the-Fox? Beverly Bernstein gave him free lunches that were left over from the school. Freddie and Giancarlo hung out together. They became friends. Really good friends. "

"So Freddie-the-Fox was gay too?"

This all seemed so far-fetched to me. I found it all very hard to believe. On the other hand, I was sure Harold wouldn't be making it up.

Harold nodded. "Freddie was as queer as they come—but most people ignored it. To be a gay gangster is not a good thing. Both Freddie and Giancarlo were born into some of low-level connection with the Mafia. I think Freddie's Father did time for one of the guys so they used him to run some errands. Same with Giancarlo. There was an unspoken agreement in the neighborhood not to mention their sexual orientation to outsiders."

It's not often that I am speechless but I have to admit I couldn't think of anything to say.

I could believe Freddie-the-Fox might be AC/DC or something like that. I had seen him around the neighborhood with a number of younger men and there was something about his interest in shoes that went beyond the selling of them that once in a while struck me as a little odd. But Giancarlo? The skin-headed goon with the snarling bear tattoo on his thick neck?

I suppose there is no accounting for taste, or love whether you are straight or gay but try as I would, it was hard for me to see Giancarlo the Goon and Freddie-the-Fox as a couple. Besides, my feelings were hurt. Me—an outsider in my own neighborhood? Freddie had even told Giancarlo that I was a friend, and yet he never came out to me. How long does a person have to live here before you become an insider?

"So does everyone know all this except me?" I asked Harold.

He put his arm around me. "There are lots of others." He paused. "Jose, the newspaper delivery guy, for example."

That was not very comforting, as it was well-known in the neighborhood that Jose thought of himself as a very macho guy with no tolerance for any other kind.

"And Murphy, of course." I'd have to let Murphy know. It suddenly put Giancarlo's emotional visit to Emily's Place yesterday in a different light. He was telling the truth—at least about his feelings for Freddie-the-Fox.

And, for the first time, I could make some sense out of the relationship between Sammy and Giancarlo. Sammy was a cover for him—and perhaps he served as a cover for Sammy. I wondered what Murphy would make of it all.

I made an appointment with Harold to move Sadie and Mary back to Emily's Place the next morning, and I went back to my apartment to give Murphy a call.

"Murphy here," he answered on the first ring.

"Guess what? Giancarlo and Freddie were lovers."

There was a couple of minutes of silence on the other end of the line as Murphy digested this information. Like me, it seemed to leave him speechless.

"Maybe Freddie was killed by a jealous lover instead of whoever was sending diamonds in the heels of shoes," Murphy said at last, "but whoever did it, used a 1940's Italian Policeman's pistol."

"Bellini!" I blurted out.

"Or anyone else who could purchase a gun of that vintage," Murphy reported matter-of-factly. I'm not getting much from Immigration. Seems Bellini came to America about ten years ago. Applied for citizenship seven years ago. Had an old mother who died when he was a kid in Italy. No information about his father. Came here alone, with no family. Not sure where that leaves us."

"It seems to me he's a better suspect that anyone else we have."

"Problem is we can't find any link between Bellini and Freddie-the-Fox or Giancarlo. I still think this WWII connection is a red herring. Maybe the Mafia is deliberately trying to make their involvement look like something else. Anyway, my boys are just about done here. You can clean up and open for business tomorrow."

I sat down on my kitchen chair and stared at the ceiling. I knew it would take me hours and hours to clean up the store. And then. Would anyone come? Or would the unquiet spirit of Freddie-the-Fox keep all the customers away.

I opened my bedroom closet and pulled my black pants from the hanger.

The small round diamond I had pocketed still rested there. Was it my imagination or did the entire pocket seem to glow with some strange, pulsating rays of light? Had I captured a pebble from Hell that cast its hideous power over everything related to me and Emily's Place?

I shoved the pants to the back of my closet, and hid them under a couple of pair of shoes where I hoped the Angel of Death would never find it. Nonsense, I said to myself, as I slammed the door shut. There is no such thing as hell or The Angel of Death. And if there was, no closet door would deter them.

SEVEN

Shoe laces were first used in 1790 in England. Before that, shoes were fastened with buckles. Shoes gradually become less structured with less heel—more slipper-like and comfortable—without the squashing of toes.

"How's your Italian?" I asked my neighbor Angelina.

She waved her hands in the air, "Buongiorno! Arrivaderci!, Mama Mia! Santo Cristo! Amore! Figaro! Rigoletto,! Pucci! Gucci! Pasta! Basta! Bella! Bene! Caro! Linguini! Tortellini! Baci! Cannoli!"

She bowed. Henry flew overhead squawking "Ca… Ca… cannoli!"

"Wait a minute. Half those words are food. "

Angelina shrugged. "You asked me how much Italian I know. That's about it. I grew up in the Bronx—on Jerome Avenue, with all the Jews. Maybe if I had lived on Arthur Avenue, in the middle of "Little Italy" I might have learned a few more things."

"It was Arthur Avenue that I had in mind," I told her. "Think you are up for an outing to encounter your heritage?"

Angelina motioned to Henry who settled on her shoulder. She looked to the right and then to the left.

"What kind of day is it Dolly?" she asked me. "You know I don't like to go out in the sun. Not good for my complexion."

I went to the small window in her kitchen and peeked through the blinds.

"So so…kind of over-cast. You'll be fine." I reassured her.

In fact, Angelina was a bit of a recluse who often slept till noon and rarely left the apartment before dark. I knew if she said "yes" it would take a real effort.

"Think of poor Freddie-the-Fox, who never had a chance. Think of his Mother, waiting for him to come home."

Of course it was all over the neighborhood within hours that Freddie-the Fox had been murdered at Emily's Place and donations for his funeral and his mom were already being collected. Angelina was one of the neighbors who always fed Freddie in return for his fixing her sink or taking out her garbage, and I knew she would want to help capture his killer if she could.

Angelina took a deep breath. "What do you think Henry?"

Henry chewed pensively on a strand of her hair.

"How far away is Arthur Avenue? I don't think I've been there since I was six."

"We'll go by taxi. My treat. You'll love it. You can dress in black. Like a Sicilian widow."

She pulled herself to her feet. "I'll do it! I've got just the outfit! I may not speak Italian Dolly, but I can play an Italian any day! Give me one hour and we'll go."

I hugged her—surprised at how slender and frail she really was under all that red hair and flowing kimono. Angelina was true blue.

I went back to my own apartment to wait for her. I had gone back to Emily's Place yesterday with Harold and our two mannequins, Sadie and Mary. The place was a mess, and the police were still poking around, opening all the shoe boxes and moving every display case. They seemed to take great joy in all their destruction. Kind of like when the firemen come in swinging their axes and breaking all the windows, even though the fire has been out for two hours. It's as if putting on a uniform unleashes all these fierce male hormones.

For a moment I pictured the tarnished brass button with the blue threads still attached. Fascist police. Another uniform that loosed a deadly fury. Was the wearer of that uniform or one of his descendants roaming the Upper West Side.Was he living on Arthur Avenue, the city's most authentic Little Italy, hoping to blend in?

I was getting impatient with Murphy's opinions and the pace of his investigation. He was stuck on this Mafia idea and was only going through the motions of searching for a WWII connection because I kept annoying him.

I was ready to do some research of my own on the origins and character of Massimo Bellini. And I was sure Angelina and me, even without knowing any Italian, could learn a lot more than Murphy and his boys in Blue. Since Emily's Place wouldn't really be ready for business for another day or two, it was the perfect time to visit Arthur Avenue. At the least, we would come back with some fresh pasta and some lovely olive bread—and at the most, stake out a killer.

I met Angelina in the hallway between our apartments one hour later. Bent-over and clinging to the doorknob, was a little old lady, gray hair pinned back in a bun, wearing a long, baggy black dress that reached down to her ankles. Around her neck was a heavy gilt cross. On her feet were rolled down stockings and a pair of worn-out ballet slippers.

She would have passed for a widow even in Sicily.

She leaned heavily on my arm and shuffled toward the door of the building.

"Where'd you get the get-up?" I asked her

She smiled. "Once played a nun in a skit for the Jolly Be Nightclub on 42nd St. They kicked us out after two performances. The black material was too good to throw away."

I nodded to the two teenagers smoking pot on the top step, who parted politely for the elderly widow.

"Have a good one, granny," one of them said, "Be careful crossing the street."

I hailed a cab and we set out for Arthur Avenue.

I had the cab stop a block from the address Murphy had given me where Massimo Bellini supposedly lived. It wouldn't do to pull up in a cab and immediately announce you were from somewhere else. Trust was important in these neighborhoods. Besides, I wanted to try out Angela's Italian personality before we reached a critical point in our investigation.

I had worn a tee shirt with a St. Antony's medal pinned to it that someone had lost in the shop, a pair of faded jeans and my sneakers in case I had to make a quick getaway.

Angelina straightened up a little when we got to the curb and loosened her grip on my arm. She looked around her with pleasure. The low buildings, many with the windows open, framing white haired ladies in black looking much like Angelina; women in tee shirts and jeans pushing strollers and calling out to Gianni, Tino and Sophia, fresh fruit stands brimming over with tomatoes in different sizes and shapes, broccoli rabe, the biggest and the smallest artichokes I've ever seen, a giant meat store with rabbits hanging upside down from hooks in the window; an appetizing store with barrels of olives out front.

"I smell formaggio," she said happily. "Buongiorno!" She nodded to a couple of men playing cards on a small table set out on the street, and gripped her cross in her other hand.

One guy stood up and nodded his head as if he actually knew her.

"Prosciutto di Parma!" she uttered in a sprightly tone.

The man pointed down the block.

"Bene! Bene!" Angelina intoned with gratitude. She lifted her cross and muttered a few syllables, of which only "Santo" was intelligible to me.

Both men smiled and then went back to their cards.

"How much money did you bring?" Angelina whispered to me,

I reached into my pocketbook and extracted my wallet. "About $60.00" I told her.

"Good. After this we should go shopping. I'm getting hungry."

I tightened my grip on her arm. "Let's not get distracted. We're here on business. If all goes well, I'll buy you dinner."

We continued down the block until we came to Bellini's apartment building.

Like most of the others on the block, it was a three-story walk-up with a couple of food stores in the front. Fiarucci's Bakery, and Leonardo's Olives were doing a bang-up business with people waiting on line out into the street.

"I need an olive," Angelina told me, "for courage."

"Later," I promised her, and pulled her round the corner where the stairway to the apartments was located.

The door to the building was locked and there were several buzzers. I found Bellini's button and pressed it. There was no answer. We were about to give up when a voice behind us called out, "Can I help you? Who did you want to see?" And a young girl in her twenties holding a baby in her arms, fit her key in the door and ushered us in.

The hallway was dimly lit but very clean and smelled from the fresh bread being baked just outside.

'Signor Bellini," Angelina mumbled, "Amigo Mio!"

Even I could tell this wasn't Italian but luckily the kid spoke English like she was born in America and probably couldn't tell.

"Oh Massimo!" She said, "Sometimes he plays opera and doesn't hear the bell. I'll go up with you."

She led the way to a door on the first landing and rang the bell. We followed more slowly. I could see Angelina wasn't acting. The stairs were a challenge. She clung to my arm. The young woman knocked and called out "Massimo! Visitors!" a few times and then turned towards us.

"Sorry. Guess he isn't home. "

She looked at Angelina who was breathing hard.

"Maybe your mother would like to sit down for a few minutes."

Angelina bent over and kicked me. "Bene! Bene!" She muttered.

The woman moved over to the next apartment and fit her key in the door. She opened the door and ushered us into the living room. "Just a minute," she called out, and she disappeared with the baby into another room. The room was clean and neat. Lace dollies covered the large credenza against the wall. Across from the sofa in a gilt frame, was a color portrait of The Pope.

"Can I get you a glass of tea?" she asked us

"Bene! Bene!" Angelina answered, nodding.

I shook my head. I felt a little guilty coming here under false pretenses. I wanted to do our business and leave as quickly as possible. The woman disappeared into the kitchen and returned with a glass of tea. She handed it to Angelina.

Angelina grasped her hand, "Grazie, Grazie!" she intoned, and pulled the hand up to her lips.

The young woman smiled and withdrew her hand. I saw her wipe it nonchalantly on the lower part of her shirt.

"So," she turned to me, "how do you know Massimo? Do you live around here?"

"Not far," I told her. "Further downtown. It's my Mother who knew him—in the old country."

Angelina pinched me, and mumbled a flow of words ending in vowels. The only words I recognized sounded like "Puccini, Figaro, and tortellini."

The young woman shook her head. "I don't understand. I guess she's speaking a dialect. My own mom doesn't speak real Italian at all. Just a few words. What town is she from?"

"Riggoletto!" Angelina answered happily.

I gulped. "Yes, We're from Riggoletto—or rather my mother is from Riggoletto. It's on the south end of Sicily. I grew up in Brooklyn myself."

"Sounds familiar. Too bad my mom's not around right now. She went to the doctor. Should be back any minute now. Bet she'd enjoy meeting your mom."

I glanced at Angelina, who, I could see was eyeing a bottle of wine on the coffee table. If I wanted to find out anything, I'd have to work quickly. It was time to get to the bottom of this "Fotinni Fatale" connection. The photo on the internet was a dead-ringer for Massimo. He had to be his son. There was no record in

Immigration of an old father coming with him to America, but that didn't mean it didn't happen. If the old guy was a war criminal, he would have had to sneak into the country some other way.

There was only one way to find out. I took a chance and plunged in.

"Well," I said, "Mom knew Massimo's dad too, from the old days. Is he still alive?"

"Oh no," the woman answered, "He died a couple of years ago. A really nice man too. Like Massimo. He always gives Tino…that's my baby…a toy…something from Italy…whenever he sees him. Gave him a real Baci ball last week…even though he can't even walk yet."

I was right! Massimo's father had come to America! I was so excited I could hardly think of the next question to ask. I took a deep breath.

"So—I suppose Massimo has a lot of friends in the neighborhood—lots of people from his home town. Milan. Momma told me he was from Milan."

Angelina nodded in agreement. She waved her arms. "Milano! Milano!"

"Yes. He told us he was from Milan. Don't think he really has that many friends in the neighborhood though. He kind of stays alone a lot. Specially after his father died."

We were really on a roll now.

"His father—He was in the war, no?"

The young woman clapped her hands. "Was he ever! Was a policeman. Even saw Mussolini once. Saved a lot of people too. Used to give the Jews phony papers so they could escape to Switzerland. He had so many stories!"

She sighed. "Massimo really changed when he died. Looks sad all the time. Doesn't get many visitors. Think he'll be sorry he missed you. Want to leave a note?"

"Si! Si!" Angelina threw out before I could protest.

All I could think of was to get out of there before this woman's mother came home and started speaking in dialect to Angelina. The young woman disappeared into what I figured was the kitchen and came out with a piece of paper and a pencil. I lunged for it before Angelina could get it and scribbled my name on it with my telephone number.

"Tell him it was the lady from the shoe store," I told the woman. "I found two more pair of the shoes he liked. I think he'll remember me."

"And your Mom—she knew him in the old country?"

"Amore! Baci!" Angelina yelled out, and then suddenly sank back into the pillows on the sofa, and moaned. Her moans contained words that sounded like" Santo Cristi, Santo Prosciuto."

Fortunately, the baby started howling in the next room. I hoped the woman couldn't hear Angelina too clearly. She glanced over her shoulder at the room the baby was in and then looked back at Angelina who was breathing heavily and feverishly kissing her gilded cross. The woman looked at her with concern.

"Perhaps your mom would like a little vino…sometimes that can perk a person up."

"Bene! Bene!" called out Angelina.

But this time I was ahead of her.

"I don't think so" I winked to the young woman. "I think it is time we were headed back home. Thanks so much for being so kind."

And I lifted Angelina to her feet and literally swept her out the door and down the steps.

"Rigoletto! Give me a break!" I admonished her when we got outside.

"It worked, didn't it Dolly?" She answered. "Between Opera and food, we have all the Italian we need."

"We were lucky." I told her. "What if her mother had come home? She'd see through you in an instant."

Angelina gripped my arm tighter. "Slow down a little Dolly. I'm not used to wearing such flat shoes. When can we eat?"

I smiled at her. Skinny though she was, she had the ability to eat like a person twice her size. We deserved a nice Italian meal. We had gotten what we came for. Bellini's father must have been the infamous Fotinni Fatale, who had somehow made his way to America illegally. And Bellini Jr. was getting extortion money from WWII sent to him here through shoes manufactured in Italy.

We walked slowly down the Avenue. Here was Pucci's Parmigano ; Dante's Appetizer Pavilion; Enrico's Fresh Fish Market; Figaro's Vegetable Garden. Here the important names of the past were alive and well. And the aromas of newly baked bread, spicy olives, and tangy Parmesan cheese had probably not changed since the 1800's when many of the Italians in this neighborhood arrived. Right now, all of this together was certainly making our mouths water.

I was just about to cross the street over to the Colombo Restaurant whose outdoor tables were still filled with customers—and it was already three in the afternoon—when we passed a shoe store. Now, as the self-appointed Mistress of Shoes in the Western World—at least on the Upper West Side of Manhattan—any shoe store anywhere will capture my attention.

But Italian shoe stores were still Class A for me; the workmanship, the design, the smell and feel of the leather,the whole Italian aesthetic embodied in that one small item, was something that always turned me on.

So, naturally I had to make a short detour before we settled down to our well-deserved lunch.

"Take a look at this," I pulled Angelina over to the window.

"Those are nice," she said, pointing to a pair of yellow sandals with a three inch platform.

"I'm not sure they'd go with your current outfit," I told her, "but you picked a good one."

Even through the window I could tell they were good Italian leather.

I moved closer to the window. There were only three pair of shoes on display in the window. The yellow sandals; a pair of black silk pumps with skinny, stiletto heels; and a pair of red satin slides, with rhinestone bows. Very high style for Arthur Avenue. And no prices. Very odd for a window display, meant to attract customers. Besides, the shoes all looked to me like size 9—for sure not the average shoe size for Italian women who, in my experience, since most of them were short, wore size 6 or 7. The window itself was smudged and dirty—not at all in keeping with the type of shoe they were trying to sell.

I didn't need to be the Shoe Maven of the Western World to know that something was wrong.

I looked up and around, trying to find a name and number for the store. Being a woman of a certain age, I am a little near sighted, and I finally had to take out my glasses in order to make out the small sign over the door which read PERIGGI & SON.

Oh boy, I thought to myself. Paydirt!

The manufacturer of the very shoe whose heels were filled with diamonds.

"We're going in," I told Angelina. "You can take a rest before lunch."

"Dolly, the only thing I like better than good Italian food are good Italian shoes."

I took her arm and pushed on the door. Nothing. I peered inside and saw a couple of people moving about. The lights were on. The store was open. I searched around until I found a small buzzer and pushed the button. A young, heavy set girl of about eighteen or nineteen opened the door.

"Yes?" She looked us up and down. Not the most pleasant welcome for potential customers.

"I'd like to see a pair of shoes," I said, "Are you open?"

"Sure," she answered without enthusiasm, and led us inside.

The inside of the shop was an dingy and dusty as the display window. The carpet was a mixture of gray and black tweed, with assorted stains here and there. There were only four seats for customers, rickety folding chairs that were probably borrowed from one of the card game tables down the block.

"Marcella!" the girl called out, and another young girl, tall and slender, wearing a tee shirt with a Mickey Mouse picture on the front, strolled out wearing four inch red pumps with matching red sequin bows on the front. The other girl retreated to a desk on the side of the store where she quickly lost herself in what looked like a movie magazine.

"Can I help you?" she asked me.

Before I could answer, Angelina rose to her feet and started gesticulating madly at the window.

"Yellow! Gucci! Puccini! Santo Cristi!" She grabbed on to Marcella's arm, and pulled her towards the yellow sandals in the window.

"Momma!" I tried to hold her back but Angelina had her eye on those yellow sandals and there was no stopping her now.

I shrugged. "Size six." I told Marcella. "Her grandson is getting married next month and she wants something new to wear."

Marcella shook her head. "I don't know," she said. "I'll have to check the back."

"While you're up," I called out, "I'm looking for a different kind of shoe. Something I could wear every day. Maybe in a patent-leather with a two-inch heel."

Marcella brightened up. "Oh," she said, "That style I know we have. What size do you wear?"

"7" I told her, and pulling Angelina back down beside me, I crossed my legs in triumph.

A couple of minutes later she returned with one shoe box which she put on the floor next to me.

"Sorry," she told Angelina. "We only have a couple of sizes in the yellow sandal—8 and 9."

Angelina slumped in her chair at this news. "Santo Cristi." She said, in a resigned manner, and fingered her cross.

I opened the box of shoes and, sure enough—there they were! The very pair.

I slipped them onto my feet. They felt soft, lovely. I got to my feet and walked around.

"Do you have a mirror?" I asked Marcella?

She shook her head. "Sorry," she said. "We've only had the store a couple of weeks. Things aren't set up yet."

I walked a few more steps. I didn't feel any extra weight or discomfort in either shoe. I sat back on my seat and took off the shoes. I waited until Marcella walked away and I shook each heel close to my ear. If there were any stones in these shoes, they were stuffed in so tight that nothing rattled.

"I'll take them," I called out to Marcella, "How much are they?"

Marcella hesitated. "I've got to look it up." She retreated to the desk on the side of the room where her friend was still deeply engrossed in the latest romantic turmoil of Brad Pitt.

"$250!" she proclaimed at last.

"$250! That's ridiculous!" I was selling these shoes for $54!

Marcella waved her hands. 'That's the price. They are hand-made in Italy."

I took the shoes off and held each one up to the light. I had seen my customers do this very exercise many times.

"Ah ha!" I exclaimed. "Look at this!" I pointed out a slight scuff mark.

"These shoes are damaged!"

Marcella looked confused. "Damaged? They are brand new shoes. I don't what you are talking about!"

I held the shoe up to the light again and pointed to the scuff mark.

"I'm not paying $250 for shoes marked up like this. There should be some discount!" I folded my arms in front of my body and scowled at her.

I must admit I was beginning to enjoy being the customer. It had been more than four years since I was on this side of the sale.

Angelina now started mumbling "Caro! Caro!" getting gradually louder with each utterance.

Marcella shook her head

"I'd like to speak to the manager," I said.

"Nicola!" Marcella called back to the desk and the young woman put down her magazine with an annoyed look on her face and walked over to our side of the showroom.

"Lady here says this shoe is damaged. She wants a discount."

I held up the shoe to the light and pointed out the scuff mark.

Nicola grabbed the shoe and made a face.

"Listen lady. There's no discount. You either buy the shoe or you don't. I don't have time for this stuff."

"I insist on speaking with the manager," I protested.

"I am the manager!" Nicola stated, hands on her hips.

This took me a little by surprise. I was hoping to get a look at the person who was importing the shoes.

"You're the manager? You look much too young!"

Nicola stared at me. "And you look much too old to be wearing any of our shoes." She picked up the shoes and started putting them back in the box.

I'll show her who's "too old," I thought to myself. I was just about to kick her in the shins when she turned to me and said, "What are you some kind of sexist? You don't think a lady can run a shoe store?"

I could feel my face getting very red. "Well, no…I mean yes…I can understand a woman running a shoe store. I just wanted to speak to the person who actually imported the shoes. Maybe he…or…she would understand how I feel."

Nicola shook her head. "That's my Uncle Antonio…and trust me, he wouldn't give you no discount either! Anyway, he's in Italy right now, at the factory. "

I could see this Nicola person had no experience whatsoever in dealing with customers and I was trying very hard not to slap her.

I pulled the box of shoes from her hands. "It's like this. I'd really like to buy these shoes. As a matter of fact, I'd like to buy two pair of these shoes…but they are just too expensive. I need some break on the price."

Nicola sat down on my newly vacated chair and stared at me with disbelief. "I don't get this. First you tell me the shoes are too expensive to buy at all. Then you tell me you want two pair. Why would you want to buy two pair of the same shoes?"

It was a good question but I was ready: "It's for my sister. She saw these shoes in a store in Manhattan and they didn't have her size. And she always wants to wear the same shoes as me."

Nicola tapped her fingers on the side of the chair. "Wait a minute. Your sister could not have seen these shoes. We are the only distributor of Periggi & Son in the country."

I shrugged. "Maybe she made a mistake. Anyway, I'd like to buy two pair…if the price is right."

Nicola thought about this for a minute and then she disappeared into the back storeroom.

Marcella straightened the chair. "I don't think we have any more. They only sent us a few styles in a few sizes."

Nicola returned without another box of shoes. "We're sold out" she said. "No discount."

I scowled. "All right. I'll take the shoes. Maybe I'll give you a call in a couple of weeks…in case you get some more in. Can I have your card?"

Nicola threw up her hands. "Card? What kind of card? Do you think we are Duane Reed and every time you buy a pair of shoes you get a stamp…until you get something for free?

She shook her head. "People come to this neighborhood…they think we're stupid or something. I'm really tired of it."

At that point I really did lunge for her throat but Angelina grabbed my arm and started yelling "Pasta! Tortellini! Canolli! Formagio!" and tugged on my arm, pulling me towards the door.

I took a deep breath and tried to get control of myself.

"My mother is very hungry." I explained, patting Angelina on the arm. "This will just take another couple of minutes Mama," I told her.

"A business card." I explained to Nicola. "Do you have a business card with your name, address and phone? Perhaps your uncle Antonio left you some cards with his name, address and phone number?"

She looked at me as if I had two heads. "Why would I need a business card? Anyone who comes into the shop and really wants to buy a pair of shoes knows where to find me. And Uncle Antonio doesn't come around very often."

So no business card. No contact number. I could only hope Murphy could look up the necessary documents and find out who was behind this whole ridiculous scheme.

I opened my pocketbook and took out my American Express Card.

"Don't take American Express," Nicola said, folding her arms and glaring at me. "We're a cash-only business."

I glared back at her. "You know, a person could get in trouble with the law running a business like that."

She smiled at me. "Laws like that don't bother people on Arthur Avenue."

Not yet, I thought. But soon. I took another deep breath. I don't like to lose an argument. On the other hand, I reminded myself, better to lose a battle but win the war.

"I really want those shoes." I told her. "The shoes here are really special. I have a lot of friends, would like to know about this place. Rich ladies, who wouldn't ask for a discount. How about a personal check?"

Nicola looked from me to Angelina and then back again.

Angelina smiled. "Bella! Bella!" She said, and she grabbed Nicola's hand and kissed it.

Nicola tried to pull back her hand but Angelina held it tight. Nicola scrunched up her face. "Come sta?" she finally asked her .

"Bene! Bene!" Angelina bobbed her head up and down. Then she let go of Nicola's hand and rubbed her stomach. "Mange! Mange!."

Nicola pulled back her hand and wiped it on her jeans. Maybe she just wanted to get rid of us at that point so she finally relented.

"Ok." Nicola said. She handed me the shoes. "Make it out to cash and put down your telephone number. If it comes back marked "insufficient funds" you'll have to answer to my uncle."

I held the shoe box close to my breasts. I put it down just long enough to write her a check.

"Don't worry about it." I told her. I grabbed the shoe box in one hand and Angelina's arm with the other and we walked quickly out of the store.

EIGHT

After Elias Howes, inventor of the sewing machine in 1846, adapted it to sew soles of shoes to uppers in his new shoe factory, heated arguments broke out between shoe-makers skilled in hand-work and the new breed of unskilled factory workers, as to who could make a better shoe.

"You look pleased as Punch," I said to my sister Shana. "Like the cat that just swallowed the canary."

Shana settled herself on the seat and fluttered her eyelashes at me. We were seated next to each other on the sea-blue chairs in Emily's Place.

"You know, I think your entire personality would improve if you slept with that cop you are always talking about."

The things that come out of my sister's mouth never cease to amaze me. As if she, the Goddess of Bad Choices, had anything reasonable to say about anything—especially men. I ignored her attempt at prying into my private affairs—partly because I actually agreed with her in this case—and partly because she was the younger sister and therefore required advice, whereas I....I was currently floundering in many different areas and would rather not discuss any of them with her.

When I got home from my Arthur Avenue investigation, I felt so good. Excited. Part of it was the fresh pasta and vino happily swishing around my gut after one of the best Italian meals I'd had in years—but most of it was because I knew that Angelina and I had gotten information about Bellini and the phony shoe store that Murphy would never have found out. Information that brought us all closer to finding out who had killed my friend

Sophia Sarfatti and poor Freddie-the Fox, whose entrepreneurial ways had fatally backfired.

But when I pried off the heels of my very expensive Periggi & Sons new shoes, there was not even a rhinestone stuffed inside. And to make things worse, Murphy was underwhelmed by my detective work.

"So good, you found an unsuccessful shoe store in the Bronx and learned this Bellini guy's father might have sneaked into the U.S. illegally. Unsuccessful shoe stores in the Bronx are not necessarily connected to homicides. And as for illegal immigrants, do you have any idea of how many immigrants from all over the world have sneaked into our country ? Don't get me started on that one. And yeah, some of them are criminals. We still have no way of proving this particular man was that Fotinni Fatale you keep talking about. And what if he was? He's dead. We can't deport him and we can't put him on trial for war crimes. What we need is something real to link Bellini with the shoe laundering operation, and so far, we haven't got it."

I gave Murphy the street address of the shoe store on Arthur Avenue and he said he'd see what he could dig up about who owns the lease to the store. In the meantime, he would go visit the Russian girl and take back the shoes she bought as evidence.

The only good thing about this whole mess was that the police finally cleared out of my store and, guess what? My customers all came back. Instead of staying away because of evil spirits prowling the territory, they flocked to Emily's Place to see the site of the execution—and they even brought their friends.

"Hello there Emily! Sandra Minkoff told me someone famous was murdered in your shop!" Cindy Rosenblum, my ex-next-door neighbor on Central Park West called out to me, waving from across the showroom. "Good to see you Shana! Love that shade of blond! "

Shana smiled and waved back. "If there is one thing I don't miss about your old apartment on Central Park West, it is Cindy

Rosenblum." Shana muttered under her breath. "Was this, what's his name, 'Freddie-the-Fox' a famous person?"

"Only in this neighborhood." I patted her hand. "He was not a rock-star if that was what you were thinking."

I hadn't told Shana anything about the jewels hidden in the heels of the shoe, or even that poor Sophia Sarfatti had probably been murdered as well. I knew my sister well enough to know if she knew there was anything valuable in the heels of the shoes she had, she'd never give them back to me. She only knew what she had read in the papers—and that hinted at some Mafia-related murder, execution-style, that just happened to take place in my shop, but not much else.

"How come he was hiding out at Emily's Place?" She asked me now.

I hesitated. The best way to answer questions I really didn't want to answer, I've found, is to tell as much of the truth as I could, even if it was only a half truth. That way, I didn't have the trouble of trying to remember the lie I told.

"He was a kid with a drug habit, trying to go straight. I had given him a hand-out from time to time so he counted me as a friend. I guess he thought no one would look for him in a woman's shoe-store—and I certainly wouldn't squeal on him."

"Vitamin D." Shana said. "You should have sent him to me for Vitamin D. tablets and our special Russian Bath massage therapy. Would have cleared out all his yearnings for drugs. He'd be alive today."

"Our Russian Bath Therapy?" The "our" linked with "Russian" made me nervous. It meant her newest boyfriend Vladimir was probably taking advantage of her like all the others.

"Is this Russian Bath therapy something new?"

"No. It's actually very old.Vladimir tells me the Russian Czars used it in the 17th Century."

"Vladimir. Does this therapy take place in his gypsy cab?" I asked her.

"He's given up the gypsy cab. We're partners. My patients adore him!" Her face clouded for a minute. "My patients! That

Tanya Solowitz called me again. She said she'd take $5000 to settle her law suit against me."

"Is that what her life is worth? I don't get it. If she is really dying, what will she do with $5000? Tell her you'll pay her funeral costs instead. If she doesn't like that, she can take you to court!"

Shana shook her head. "I can't afford to go to court. I'll lose all my patients. Just when everything is going so well with Vladimir!"

She brightened. The sun coming out from behind a cloud. "Why don't you bring that Murphy guy down to Brooklyn and we'll give him a freebie. As a matter-of-fact we'll give both of you a freebie." She giggled. "A Russian Bath and some cacao tea from Peru and I guarantee you'll fall in love."

I was not very happy with the direction this conversation was going. Besides, I had a store full of customers clamoring for details about the latest crime in our neighborhood, and they all wanted discounts on the season's newest shoes.

I handed Shana a pair of black patent-leather Ferragamo shoes with a low, two inch heel.

She slipped one on and stretched out her leg. She turned her head from side to side.

"I'm kind of tired of this style," she said. "They look just like those shoes I've been wearing. Do you have anything else in my size?"

"Hundreds." I threw up my hands.

I did not have time for this. Shana had already conveniently forgotten that the shoes I just gave her were supposed to look like the ones she was returning. They were substitutes.

"Just give me the shoes that I need back for the factory recall, and you can pick something else when I'm not so busy."

She reached into her backpack and pulled out the shoes. A little scuffed and worn down, it was true, but the shoes I wanted.

I grabbed them out of her hands before she could change her mind and cradled the shoes in my arms. Then I helped her up from the seat and kissed Shana goodbye. Out of the corner of my eye I could see Cindy Rosenblum, bearing down fast from the other side of the showroom.

"Emily, Shana, sweetheart," she cooed. "It's been such a long time since I saw you both. You should come to visit. "

"Sure." I told her. "I know Larry longs to see us."

Shana straightened up and adjusted her back-pack.

Cindy grabbed her arm. "You doll you! Every time I see you, you look younger and prettier. Are you married yet?" Cindy asked

"Three times," Shana told her, and slipping out from under her hand, she walked towards the door.

When the last customer finally left, I locked the door, put up the CLOSED sign rushed into the back room. I had been anticipating this moment all afternoon. What treasure would I uncover in Shana's shoes? Was I hoping to help myself to another if I found what I hoped to find in Shana's shoes?

Certainly not! I still didn't know what I was going to do with the diamond I had taken from Sophia's shoe. No. I had learned my lesson on that score. These jewels were bad news, bad luck, bad Karma as my sister Shana would say.

Especially since, as I was believing more and more strongly, they belonged to dead Jews sent to concentration camps during WWII.

I took a deep breath and grabbed a pair of pliers. I tugged. I twisted. The heel stubbornly refused to separate from the sole.

Finally! I closed my eyes for a minute and shook out the heel.

Nothing! Damn! I pulled apart the heel of the other shoe. It came off much more easily.

Nothing there either! I stared down at the mutilated shoes on the table in front of me. What did it mean? Had Shana or, more probably Vladimir, helped themselves to the diamonds hidden inside the heels?

I had always thought it was a little strange that this Vladimir, driver of some run-down gypsy-cab, would be so eager to track down and return a worthless back-back filled with junky pseudo-medicines and strange food-additives, plus, probably a bunch of useless face creams and other beauty aids that Shana usually carted about. Unless, of course, he had been keeping tabs on Shana, who, since the break-in, he would know owned a pair of the shoes containing the diamonds he was desperate to retrieve. If he were part of the money-laundering scheme—if Russian Mafia were the culprits—and the Italian connection was really a red herring, perhaps planted by the Russians to throw everyone off the track—then Vladimir might want to befriend Shana because she was my sister and perhaps would have access to other pairs.

And who was this Slavic Slut, Tanya Solowitz? Was it just coincidence that she and Vladimir both became such a presence in Shana's life at the same time?

I threw the shoes into a shopping bag. Murphy might want them for some reason or other. I had had enough of his yelling about my tampering with evidence.

I stared at the ceiling. There was another possibility of course. That Vladimir really was an honest guy. That he remembered Shana because she is pretty—and memorable in her own nutsy way. He returned her knapsack without ever opening it. And he really wanted to hang out with her because he liked her. In that scenario, it would be Shana who would have discovered the diamonds in the heel.

I took the shoes out of the shopping bag and looked at them more closely.

Shana would have tried to wear them. She had told me they weren't very comfortable.

She might well have taken some tool—a simple screw-driver would do—and pried off the heel, hoping to readjust it in some way.

I stared into space. I could picture the expression on Shana's face when she took off the heel and dozens of diamonds spilled out from the heel.

I could picture it because I could still remember how I felt when I made the same, surprising discovery. And I could picture it, because she was my sister. However I liked to think of us as different—she the eternal child, optimistic, naive; me the careful, fearful, cynical older sister—we were tired together by genetics and blood.

And if I could not resist putting one diamond into my pocket, I knew that Shana, bless her greedy little heart, would have pocketed the whole lot. Like the child she once was who ate an entire bag of chocolate chip cookies and gave herself a stomachache.

So vivid was that picture in my mind that the sound of the telephone made me jump up from the chair.

"Murphy here!" The less-than dulcet tones of Murphy's voice brought me quickly back to the present.

"How's business?" he asked. "Any more customers looking for our favorite shoe?"

"Not yet. Did you find out anything about that store on Arthur Avenue?"

"Looks like a blind alley to me. Lease is in the name of Antonio Gerrini. Italian-American, born in the Bronx. His grandparents immigrated—legally—from Sicily in 1910. Has some cousins in Milan. One of them, named Periggi. Owns a shoe factory. Gerrini is the exclusive representative in the U.S. Used to sell a few pair here and there to Saks and Neiman Marcus. Just opened the store a few weeks ago. Looks like he was trying to increase business. All the paperwork is in order; corporate financial statements, taxes, customs receipts—not like some people I know."

"I guess some of us are better Americans than others." I threw back at him.

"You said that, not, I, me lovely." Murphy responded." Did you manage to get the shoes back from your sister?"

I was afraid he was going to ask me that. "Actually yes," I told him. "but the heels were empty."

For a moment all I could hear was heavy breathing.

"And how do you account for that?" he asked at last.

He didn't say a word while I ran through my Russian Mafia theory. I decided not to share my suspicions about my sister Shana—he'd never really understand.

When I was done he said, "Could be Vladimir took the loot. Could be your sister discovered it by accident and decided to keep her mouth shut. But it could also be that there was nothing in the shoes, that in fact, there were only two or three pair, marked in some special way we haven't yet found out, that contained the jewels. "

He paused. "Even if we don't find the jewels, we need to collect the shoes so we can figure out what kind of mark sets them apart. Then maybe we can take them off the truck on the next shipment. Besides, any mark we find might give us some clue as to who marked the shoes, which in turn will lead us to who put the jewels in the shoes in the first place."

"We'll, I've got the shoes," I said, glancing down on the mutilated pair in front of me. "All I can see is a bunch of scruffs and looks like some dog dew clinging to the bottom."

"Try not to mess them up any further," he cautioned. "Tell your 'friend'—whoever is holding the old lady's shoes, that now they are evidence—big time and they should be delivered Tout Suite, as your friend Merissa would say—to me personally immediately. You know the address."

Larry and Murphy the Cop? Give me a break! That was surely a scene to be avoided. "I'll take care of it," I told him. "What about the pair the Russian girl had bought?"

"Another immigrant group I could do without. She looked at me with these big brown eyes, kept trying to give me a glass of vodka, and insisted she couldn't understand a thing I said. I have to come back with an interpreter."

"Funny—she had no trouble making herself understood when she came to buy the shoes at Emily's Place. Why don't you leave her to me—and your friend Merissa."

Merissa's beauty and her feminine charm, I had learned from experience, were only skin-deep. That was an aspect of Merissa that I very much admired. She had the manners, when she cared to turn them on, of an African Queen—elegant, aristocratic, above the hardscrabble road that most of our customers on upper Broadway had to tread. But what you saw was only a polished surface. People who knew her well knew that Merissa also had a tough, street-wise side that no one with half a brain would want to mess with. And, even though I was a woman of a certain age, I was no shrinking violet myself. Besides, I had my own reasons, wrapped up in the person of a Russian sweetheart who had plunged a knife into my twenty year-old marriage, to want revenge on that sorry group of fortune hunters. If the Russian Mafia was involved, and that slinky, fish-eyed Galina had anything to do with the murder of Sophia Sarfatti and Freddie-the-Fox, she would have to answer to Merissa and me.

"Ok with me," Murphy replied. "At least she won't be able to claim Police brutality."

By the time I had hung up the phone, I found my own hands flexing and un-flexing in the same manner I had so often observed with Murphy—my own fingers inching to squeeze the life out of somebody.

"Mon Dieu!" Merssia exclaimed as she stared up at yet another staircase. "Russian Mafia must be really cheap to stash a lady in a place like this."

She grabbed on to the dirty railing and removed her four inch Jimmy Choo yellow-patent-leather pump.

"How you walk anywhere in those things is beyond me," I chided her. "You knew we were going by subway."

Even if the rest of the trip ended up being on ground level, she still had to negotiate those stairs. I took the opportunity to rest myself, even though I was wearing ballet slippers—the current fashion statement, yet quiet and comfortable. We had already walked up three flights and the fourth loomed ahead of us.

We were deep in Brooklyn in an area near Prospect Park, not far from where I myself had grown up. Eastern Parkway, the Champs Elyse of Brooklyn, as my friends jokingly called it, was where the rich people of the neighborhood lived. The large apartment buildings, some within walking distance of The Brooklyn Museum and Grand Army Plaza—a great arch across the Avenue—as well as the majestic building housing the main branch of the Brooklyn Public Library, seemed like they dated back to the 20's and 30's—not too different from their grand cousins on Central Park West. But now they were battered and neglected by generations who stopped here only briefly on their way to Manhattan. Some, it was true, still retained their air of elegance, with handsome, sandblasted exteriors and heavy, gilded lobby doors—discovered by some ambitious developers who hoped to attract a new generation of young professionals and their families—people who appreciated the easy access to the Park, the Museum and the main branch of the Public Library. And clearly the neighborhood was reinventing itself again. Some of the side streets were flush with new money showing off their newly renovated brownstones with lovely front gardens, and stained glass windows. But other streets were unrepentantly shabby—graffiti scribbled walls and cracked steps leading up to scuffed doors and dank hallways.

Gallina Kaplanoskya actually lived above a McDonalds, located on Bedford Avenue, that seemed caught between these two worlds, one irretrievably shabby and the other newly gentrified. While the face of the building housed the usual McDonald's facade, the entrance to the apartments upstairs was around the corner and through an alleyway. Bigger than a brownstone, without its old-world shabby dignity, it had a kind of hang-dog appearance in its yellow-brick exterior that broadcast an aura of resignation.

It reminded me of those shoes made of dull black plastic called "leatherette," in the 70's. It had given up all pretense and just offered a cheap covering between the foot and the sidewalk.

Why someone who lived in Brooklyn would come all the way to Emily's Place to buy her shoes was a question that needed answering. Of course I would like to believe it was the fame of my enterprise that had spread all the way to the boroughs—and it was true that occasionally someone wandered in from Staten Island or The Bronx but usually they were visiting a friend or making some business call and catching sight of my fabulous window display featuring Sadie and Mary in all their glitzy finery, came inside to look around.

And Gallina had visited Emily's Place before. Did she work nearby? She told me she was a model—but cynic that I am, especially in the case of Russian women, I thought it more likely that she was a call girl. Her breasts were too large, her behind too round for the runway. On the other hand with her long, slender legs, pretty face with those Slavic cheekbones and long, straight, blond hair, it was always possible she was telling the truth.

In the end I had to admit to myself that aside from the question of Gallina's profession, her motivation for visiting Emily's Place was probably more complicated than just looking for the best discount in town. No. It was a particular pair of shoes that attracted Gallina Kaplanoskya. Or more precisely—a particular pair of heels.

"Not even an African-American would be dumb enough to live in a place like this," Merissa moaned."Walkin' up and down would kill a person straight-off—specially if they was built like SuperMama."

I bristled. "There are lots of white people live worse than "African-Americans, so you can quit singing that song. One of you managed to live in The White House."

"It still called The White House." Merissa grumbled.

I was not interested in arguing with Merissa, especially about race. As Merissa was fond of telling me, she had as many white people in her family as I did in mine. She was just getting grouchy because her feet hurt.

I was not in such a hotsy-totsy mood myself.

"I bet Murphy never got beyond the first landing. He made up that whole story about having to come back with a translator."

"Why I come with you, anyhow? Is this not my day off? Are you not taking advantage of my good nature? Just 'cause

Fredie-the-Fox couldn't do an honest day's work his whole life—have to steal a little from everybody, have to get killed in the only store dumb enough to do business with him—why do I care? Now, half the people come to Emily's Place, only want to see some blood. Ask a lot of questions but don't buy nothing. Why you can't let that dumb cop solve the case his own self?"

I was beginning to wonder the same thing myself. But the truth was the situation was more complicated than Merissa knew. I hadn't told her about finding diamonds in the heels of Sophia's shoes—or rubies and emeralds in the heels of Beverly Bernstein's shoes. I figured the fewer people who knew the whole story the better.

I told Merissa that there was "something going on" with the shoes that Freddie-the-Fox had sold me, because that guy Bellini was after them, and whoever killed Sophia was searching for them too. And whoever broke into Emily's Place and hacked into my computer wanted the names of who had purchased them.

Were they marked in some way—like clues to a stash of hidden treasure? Or possibly used to transport something illegal? I threw out these ideas and let Merissa come to her own conclusions. The shoes were essential to solving the puzzle, whatever it was, and essential to finding who murdered Sophia and Freddie-the Fox. She was perfectly happy to come with me when I asked her yesterday.

"I come with you, Madame Emily—someone put that stuff in the tea I give to that old lady—good thing I hate tea, or I be dead now myself and you be talkin' to the Angel of Death."

But that was before we found ourselves climbing up a staircase to the sky.

Complaining only made the situation worse and after a couple of minutes we resumed our climb. I had called Gallina and told her there was a recall on her shoes. I was bringing her a much more expensive pair. Unlike Beverly, she didn't seem to think it was unusual for a store-owner to come all the way to Brooklyn to give her a present. Who can explain the mind of a Russian?

"Hello! I am happy to see you," Gallina said in good English with just the trace of an accent.

Murphy was a dope—and a dupe. The inside of her apartment glowed with light.

"You come in now. I give you some good tea—you come up all those stairs."

"No Thanks." I said immediately. "Merissa and me, we only drink coffee."

Gallina frowned. "I don't have any coffee." She brightened. "How about a little vodka?"

I admit I was sorely tempted but I felt a sense of responsibility to my mission. We both shook our heads. "A little cold water would be fine."

As soon as Gallina left the room, Merissa grabbed my arm, her eyes wide.

Although the room was small, a crystal chandelier hung from the ceiling with dozens of candle-shaped light bulbs. On the floor was a dark blue and burgundy oriental rug. The sofa was covered in pink silk. No plastic covers here. The furniture arranged carefully along the walls was a kind of French Baroque—white with gold accents and lots of curves. And on top of the credenza was an ornate silver samovar.

"Where a gal like Cette Femme get stuff like that. No way!" She shook her head. "I work for twenty years can't get no rug look like this," Merissa said, taking off her shoe and digging her toes into the thick pile.

I had no time for a reply.

"So..what do you bring me?" Gallina asked, handing us each a heavy cut-glass full of cool water.

I ignored her question and took a long swallow of water.

"You surely have a beautiful home, here" I told her. "I love your carpet."

Gallina smiled. "Yes. It was a present from a friend. A rich friend!"

"Does he have a friend for me?" Merissa asked, "That tea pot ain't bad neither."

"I'm glad you like my things," Gallina said. "What is the trouble with the shoes?"

I put my glass down on her gilt and white coffee table, and opened the box I was carrying.

"Oh, the factory said there was a problem with the heel. It wasn't attached properly and could fall off. Then the woman could fall down, get hurt, make a lawsuit. So they are asking everyone to return the shoes. Instead, the manufacturer will give you these Ferragamo shoes. They sell for $300 in Saks. It's a great deal."

I took out the Ferragamo shoe and showed it to her.

"Size 7 right?"

Gallina took the shoe and ran her hand over the soft leather.

"So soft!" she said. She reached for the other one. Then she cradled them both in her arms.

"I love these!" she said. "I can have them. Yes?"

"Yes!" I said. "I just need the pair you bought from me to return."

Gallina scowled and sat down on the sofa. "There is problem."

Merissa glanced at me and bit her lip.

"I don't have those shoes any more. I don't like them. They don't feel good. Like you say. Something wrong with the heel. I give them away."

Merissa snorted. "You give away new shoes like that? Mon Dieu! Why you didn't try to bring them back to Madame Emily? She give you back your money!"

Gallina shrugged. "I don't know American stores. I don't know they return money like that. These were discount no?"

"So who did you give them to?" I asked her. "I can't give you these unless I get back those."

Gallina looked crestfallen. "I like them so much!" She said. "Maybe I give you something you like and we trade!"

"I'll take the teapot over there" Merissa said.

I glared at her. "We need the shoes." I told her. "I've got to return the shoes."

Gallina hesitated a minute. “Wait. I trade you something beautiful.”

She disappeared into the other room.

“No!” I called out. “I need the shoes!”

Merissa put her finger to her lips and whispered, “Let’s see what she has.”

Gallina returned wearing a fox stole. The thick, silky reddish fur draped elegantly around her shoulders. She strolled slowly across the living room, hips and shoulders twisted towards us, like the model she claimed to be, on the runway.

“Mon dieu!” Merissa leaped up from the sofa. “Que Belle Chose!. Por Moi?”

She pulled it right off from Gallina’s shoulders and draped it around her own.

“For you.” She looked from one of us to the other. “You share. Real fur. From Siberia.”

I must admit I was tempted. Me, who protested animal testing in the 80’s and 90’s. Me, who refused to wear the mink coat Larry bought me for my fortieth birthday.

“Wait!” I cried out. “I need the shoes. They are dangerous—a lawsuit—lawyers, judges, people asking questions. Nobody wants that.”

I knew enough about Russians to push the right buttons.

Gallina literally began wringing her hands, right in front of me. “But they are gone.”

“Gone where?” I asked her. “I’ve got to get them back. Who did you give them to?”

Gallina threw up her hands. “I give them to—I give them to—my friend Sergio. He has flea market on Sundays. He said he would sell them for me. “

She smiled. “I ask $100 for them. I only pay $50.00.”

“$54.00 with tax.” I corrected her. “Give me the name and address of your friend. Also the location of this flea market. “

I looked at Merissa who was happily parading around the living room in the fox stole.

Gallina followed my gaze.

"I have even better!" She said happily. "I have whole jacket!

You would like to see?

Merissa and I exchanged glances.

"Not really…."

"Biensur!" Merissa called out and pinched me on the arm. I nodded.

In less than a minute, Gallina was back, wearing a stunning white fox cropped jacket with a high collar that framed her face. I had to physically restrain Merissa from grabbing it off her body. I decided to reserve the right to fight with Merissa later. For now, I'd chalk all this up to "research."

"You have more beautiful furs?" I asked her. "I am looking for a coat?"

Gallina hesitated. "You tell me. I can get what you want. Right now. I have only two or three things. No coats. But I give you special price. This jacket only $500. Only in Siberia they have furs like this. Thick. Long hair. I get special straight from Russia!"

Merissa clapped her hands. "You can get me mink? Sable?"

Gallina nodded. "I must talk to my friend. Then we see. You give me the shoes? You take the stole?"

"Yes," I told her. "I just need the name and address of your friend."

Gallina disappeared again into the other room and came back with a scribbled name and address on a piece of paper."

I handed her the Ferragamo shoes.

"I wrap up the fur?" Gallina offered

Merissa shook her head. "I think I'll wear it home."

Considering it was May and about sixty degrees, this was not the most practical decision. Nevertheless, I could understand the strength of passion even when I was not in the throes of it myself. On the stairs on the way down, Merissa said. "Poor little Darkie that I am, I thank you Madame Emily for this fur."

"Oh give it a break," I said to her.

Merissa held on to the railing with one hand and stroked the fox jacket with the other.

"You think these furs fell off the truck coming from Siberia?"

I laughed, "They fell off a plane, a boat, and a truck. Russia is a lot further away than Italy."

I suddenly thought of the mink coat I had left hanging in the closet on Central Park West. When I left Larry, I took little more than the clothes on my back. That was all I wanted at the time. But now I wondered what had happened to that coat. Had Larry given it to his Russian Babka? Just the thought of that almost made me trip on the stairs.

Right there and then I made up my mind to get that coat when I went to collect the shoes Larry was keeping for me. I might even decide to sell it to Gallina.

NINE

In the 1880's people began calling shoes with rubber soles and canvas tops sneakers because people wearing them could "sneak up" on others. .

"So, what do you think?"

Nancy held the diamond I had given him between his thumb and first finger. He held it up to the light on his desk. Then he took out a jeweler's loop and peered through it at the stone.

"I'd say you had a good-lookin' stone here. "

He put down the loop and took out a pair of calipers. He fit them carefully around the stone.

"2 /1/2 Karat, Very clean—tiny spec on the side, otherwise perfect—Color, very good. Very white. The best. How much you pay for this baby?"

I laughed and sent the question back to him. "How much do you think it's worth?"

Nancy sat back on his chair and looked me up and down, as if he had never noticed me before. In truth, although we met often in the neighborhood, at the Korean grocery store on the corner, and just recently at Big Bingo, we had never had a real conversation before. And I could see my response had won some respect.

"That depends on whose asking," he shot back. He leaned over the desk towards me. "For you? I know you in the neighborhood. I could give you a deal you shouldn't refuse. Right now—I call my friend—I give you $20,000 cash."

Wow. I sat back on my chair. $20,000 for such a little thing!

I shook my head. "It's not mine," I told him. "I'm selling it for a friend. I've got to give it some thought."

Nancy got up from his chair and sat on the edge of the desk. He composed his features into what he thought was a professional businessman's look, indifferent, cool. He focused his eyes on some point over my head. In less than a minute, however, his gaze sought mine and his demeanor changed to that of a secret agent, exchanging important information. His shoulders rounded and he bent over towards me, lowering his voice.

"I'm going to level with you. Nothin' is worth anything, less you have a buyer. You want to work with me, we can maybe get more. Here's the thing: Retail value…put it on a black velvet cushion…fancy neighborhood…a customer looking for an engagement ring to knock someone down…$35,000…as is. You put it in a platinum setting, maybe add a couple of diamond chips, cost you maybe three hundred bucks…the right customer you could get $40,000. Me? I don't have a fancy customer. I got to sell it to someone else. Then he, my friend, he got to sell it to someone who has the customer. We come up with the right price and everyone makes money." He smiled and went back to the seat behind his desk.

One of the things I liked better about business than teaching English in college was the creativity of the people I met. You think Chaucer had talent? Nancy, Nancy Nino, sitting opposite me in a torn undershirt with half a day's beard on his not very clean face, who probably had dropped out of high school when he was sixteen had just made himself my partner in a deal worth $40,000!

I shook my head. "I might just buy it from my friend and wear it myself."

Nancy bit his lip. A clear disappointment. But he recovered quickly

"Why not? A pretty lady like you. What were you thinking? Maybe a simple pendant in a platinum setting—just a couple of prongs. Nothing fancy."

I reached for the stone. For a minute I thought I'd have to wrestle him for it, but Nancy opened his hand and dropped it quickly into mine.

After meeting with Galina, the possibility that the Russian Mafia was involved was very much alive. She wasn't buying those furs in Saks. Whoever she was involved with though, didn't seem to have a special interest in shoes. Of course it was possible that she was some kind of "pony"— a carrier of hot stuff—a messenger of sorts—and didn't realize what was inside the shoes she had bought and then delivered elsewhere. Her specialty was hot furs, not hot shoes. On the other hand, there were thousands of independent 'entrepreneurs' in New York City and the fur business might belong to one of them.

My gut feeling was that Gallina was too stupid to be Russian Mafia. Besides, I couldn't get over the idea that whoever had imported those shoes had some knowledge of shoes—the way Bellini smelled the leather still stuck in my mind. And so I was following up the Italian connection—with a favorite Italian fence in the neighborhood—Nancy. If anyone would know who had hot diamonds to sell, it would be Nancy. And now that I had established my bargaining credentials with him, we were ready to get personal.

"Do you ever do any business with a guy named Massimo Bellini?" I asked him.

Nancy looked up at the ceiling. "Never heard of him" he told me.

"Think carefully. I think you play Poker with him every Thursday night."

"Oh," Nancy answered. "Fancy-dressed guy, talks Italian? Could be. I'm not too good with names."

There are some people, it seems, who can't tell the truth no matter what. I was hoping to learn something about who might be trafficking these diamonds, but now I was wondering if I could believe anything Nancy said, even if I could get him to say anything worthwhile.

"Listen," I bent over the desk closer to him and lowered my voice. "I don't expect you to tell any stranger who comes in here the secrets of your friends. But this is Emily, you are talking to. Emily from Emily's Place. I do business in the neighborhood, just like you do. One of our friends…yours and mine…Freddie-the-Fox…has been murdered and I don't want to let them to get away with it. We owe it to Freddie."

Nancy stared at me for a minute and then he leaned back in his chair. "I don't owe nobody enough to get myself knocked off for them. Sometimes it's better to let sleeping dogs lie if you catch my drift."

"I agree," I said to him, "But one of those dogs jumped up and bit me by murdering Freddie in my store. And I want to make them pay for it."

Nancy stared down at his hands for a minute. Then he raised his head.

"Yeah. Maybe you could do that. You have what I call "reinforcements." That cop you hang out with…the one whose kid got lost at Big Bingo. Tried to give me a tip!" Nancy threw his head back and laughed in a distinctly unfunny manner. Clearly it was not neighborhood practice to tip someone for finding their kid.

"How about I make you a nice pendant out of that rock you have in your hand—two, three sapphires on each side, platinum prongs—cost you $500."

"I'll consider it," I promised him, "This diamond. There are more where that came from."

Nancy shook his head, " I don't like to do work for nobody I don't know where the stuff comes from. Could be I'm stepping on someone's toes I don't want to step."

"It's ok," I told him. "I got the stuff from an old lady. She's dead. You might say I inherited it."

Nancy considered this for a minute. "Ok. I can live with that. Who told you to come to me?"

I smiled. "Everyone on the Upper West Side knows you're the go-to man for some kinds of services. A man who doesn't ask too many questions. A man who knows how to keep his mouth shut." I waited a minute to let the compliments sink in and then I added the clincher. "I got a personal recommendation from Alec Le Grand."

This was a stretch of the truth but so what? It had an immediate effect.

Nancy smiled. "Why didn't you say so in the first place. Now it's coming back to me—that black gal, hangs around with Alec—she works for you right? "

I nodded. "Bellini—he doesn't live in the neighborhood. Lives up in Arthur Avenue in that Little Italy. What's he doing down here? Came into my store, snooping around, a few days before Freddie was killed. What's his story? How come he plays Poker with you guys every week? "

Nancy shrugged. 'Bellini—he's a good guy. Paisano. Came from Milano—same as my grandpa. His papa and mine—used to play cards. Then both the papas died and we just kept playing cards with each other. Alec le Grand, Jose, the other guys, they all said, sure, why not—we all play together. "

I wondered if every Italian family in New York claimed to have originated in Milan—the home of sophisticated gentlemen. I held up my hand.

"Fine," I said, "But what does he do? Is he Mafia? He came into my store looking for some shoes that Freddie-the-Fox sold me. Is this guy a shoe-maker?"

Nancy made a face. "Bellini? No. That guy has class. His papa worked for Mussolini—an ambassador or something. Don't have anything to do with shoes. Owns an apartment building on Arthur Avenue."

"He never said anything to you about any diamonds? You never maybe helped him sell or reset any stones?"

Nancy shook his head. "Bellini? Nothing. Freddie the Fox and his friend Giancarlo—that's a different story."

This was getting interesting. "Freddie? Giancarlo? I didn't think they had a dime, let alone diamonds."

Nancy shook his head. "Not diamonds. An old gold brooch; a string of pearls, a pair of earrings—stuff they picked up from here and there if you get my drift. Nothing big. Those guys were always losers."

I threw up my hands. "So tell me, if someone, say, the Italian Mafia, had something big—diamonds, emeralds, rubies—where would they take it?"

Nancy laughed and pointed at himself. "Me. I'm the go-to guy. You said so yourself. There isn't anyone on 47th street will give you a better deal than me—and everyone knows it. If it didn't come to me, it didn't come to anyone."

That was interesting as far as it went. That was the kind of information I had been seeking. But I needed more. There were other suspects." But what if wasn't an Italian job. What if the Russian Mafia got hold of something. Where would they go with it?"

Nancy turned and spit on the floor. "Turds! Russian Mafia I wouldn't even let in the door. They go somewhere in Brooklyn. Brighton Beach maybe. I don't have no truck with Russian Mafia!"

I rubbed my fingers once more around the smooth curves of the diamond I had taken from Sophia's shoe and slipped it back into my pocket.

"$20,000" I said. "I've got to give it some thought."

Nancy got up and walked me to the door.

"I have one more question," I turned to him. "How come they call you Nancy?"

He laughed. "Ever hear a song 'a Boy Named Sue'?" One of them country Western guys sings it. Man names his son Sue 'cause any boy with a girl's name would need to be strong enough to beat up anyone who teased him. He'd for sure grow up tougher than anyone else. So my pa names me Nelson Nino—and this neighborhood kid, calls me Nancy and I bust his jaw and I'm only ten. After that, everyone call me Nancy as a sign of respect."

Did I get it? Sort of. I would have to think about it. One thing I did get though, was that Bellini was not laundering money by selling stolen jewels. I took what Nancy said about the Italian Mafia with a grain of salt. I didn't think he was shrewd enough to handle really big jobs. For the number of diamonds I had found in the heel of Sophia's shoe you needed fancy connections—legitimate stores with rich customers. That he did the occasional favor for some low-level Italian Mafia, was probably true. But that was as far as it went. So I couldn't count out the Italian Mafia and that still left the Russian Mafia and a lot of unanswered questions about Bellini and the shoes he was so eager to buy.

I put my hand in my pocket and rubbed the diamond for good luck. It looked like I would need it.

I had just gotten home, thrown off my ballet slippers, and opened the refrigerator to see what odds and ends of food might be lurking there, when I heard the buzzer ring.

"Merissa and Alec," Merissa announced.

I buzzed them in.

Although Merissa and I were friends and colleagues, our friendship only went so far. I could never quite trust her after finding out how she was willing to abandon me to the clutches of Goodie One Shoes, and for lying to me about her own origins. After concocting an elaborate story about her Haitian/ French background, she turned out to have started life as a poor black kid in Washington D.C. who left at an early age to shift for herself. The truth was I admired the survivor more than the French Princess but a lie is still a lie and I was still smarting from it.

Then there was the undeniable fact that I was "The Boss Lady" or, in Merissa's pseudo-French, "Madame Emily" who paid her salary and expected her to show up on time.

And so, there was a certain distance in our friendship—questions we didn't ask each other—personal facts we didn't share with one another. One of these was Merissa's relationship with the men in her life. They came in different shades and sizes. They came and they went. Merissa painted herself as too savvy to trust a man. They were okay in their way, for sex and money, but after that, it was each one for themselves. All this aside, she had been hanging out with Alec le Grand for longer than most. I knew that under that hardened exterior, Merissa had a softer side. And who knew what was under that? Like an onion, one could continue to peel the layers off Merissa's center, and I hadn't gotten very far as yet.

"What you goin' round barefoot like poor white trash, Madame Emily. Company here!." Merissa greeted me.

Alec Le Grand bowed politely. This evening he was wearing a white straw hat and his signature red bow-tie. Merissa was decked out in a red satin turban, flowing blue silk dress baring one shoulder and three inch red Manolo Blahnik sandals. The fact that Merissa was at least three inches taller than Alec in her bare feet never interfered with her dress code.

Now she sat down on my sofa and rubbed her feet.

"I haven't been here, so long, I forget those stairs up the stoop—then down the stairs to your place. Mon Dieu!"

"That's why I like to walk around barefoot," I told her. "I may be the Goddess of Shoes at Emily's Place but between you and me, there's nothing more comfortable than walking around barefoot."

Alec grinned. "That's what I tells my little honey-pot but she don't pay me no mind."

"Can I get you something to drink?" I asked them. "Seltzer, Vodka, Gin, Coffee. That's about all I've got on hand."

Merissa and Alec exchanged glances and both shook their heads.

"Madame Emily—we got business to discuss and when we got business we got to keep our heads clear."

I nodded.

"This is real important, Missy Emily." Alec began. " We knows you are a brave, strong woman. Everyone in the neighborhood, they say, Missy Emily—she a good woman. Want to help everyone. Maybe it's true she's rich—maybe it's not. But it don't matter. Missy Emily treat everyone good."

First time I ever heard people in the neighborhood thought I was rich. Wonder where that came from. That I used to live on Central Park West? Or was it the sentiment that Giancarlo had expressed to Sammy 'those Jews always have money?' This was going to be interesting.

"What Alec means," Merissa interrupted, "is that we are your friends. Only friends can talk to one another like we talk to you."

I nodded again.

Merissa took a deep breath. "What you doin', lookin' all over for them shoes—shoes that fall off a truck—ain't doin any good for the neighborhood. Freddie-the-Fox—he dead now. Nobody do him any good any more on this earth. Why you keep lookin', here, lookin' there? Creepin' all the way to Brooklyn for God's Sake! Find some dumb Russian girl selling furs! How that be our business?"

I glared at her. "It's our business. It is sure my business. Freddie-The-Fox was murdered in my store—in our store. In case you didn't notice, murder is against the law."

"Ha! The law!" Alec le Grand called out.

"What we care about the law?" Merissa picked up her argument. "What the law ever do for me? What the law ever do for you? It's that cop. That's the only thing, count with you these days. That cop! And what that cop ever do for you?"

I was both embarrassed and annoyed at this joint attack. I stood up and stared from Alec to Merissa and back again.

"That cop saved the life of your niece Fifi. He put that killer Goodie One Shoes in jail for life, so he couldn't kill me or kill you." I scowled at both of them. 'This person, killed Freddie-the Fox. How do you know he won't try to kill you, or Alec or me or Shana or Beverly or, yes, Gallina? How do we know what he wants or why, or what will stop him?"

Merissa stood up from the couch, hobbling over to me with one shoe.

"We know that killer want them shoes. Maybe somethin' in those shoes. Ganga. Coke. Maybe there be names in that shoe of people do them wrong. We find them shoes we all in trouble. Game over for this black girl. Don't need trouble with gangsters don't even live in this country. Don't need no more trouble with the law neither. Why you keep helping that cop? This world you got to help your own self."

Alec le Grand nodded. His small frame bobbed up and down. "We don't want no cops coming round to this neighborhood lookin' into everyone's business. People here got to make a living. They come here with nothing—they don't have education, parents, money. They got to live the way they got to live. You know that Missy Emily. Why you want to bring the law down here?"

Before I could even formulate an answer, Merissa came up closer to me. Even with one shoe on and one shoe off she was six inches taller than me. She bent over and looked me in the eyes.

"It's that cop. That's all it is. That cop don't do nothing for you. That cop don't even get into your pants."

How dare she talk to me that way! How dare she even think that way! What right does she have to picture what Murphy and I do or don't do in bed? I was so outraged I couldn't think of anything at all to say.

I walked over to the couch and sat down. I grabbed a pillow and smacked it. "How dare you!" I managed at last.

Merissa turned round and walked towards me. She hit herself in her chest.

"Me. I your friend. That's why I can say this. No one else in this whole world tell you how it is. That cop nothing but trouble. Trouble for you. Trouble for the whole neighborhood." She plopped down beside me on the couch. "Who that cop help ? All that cop want to do is hurt someone. I watch his eyes. I watch his hands. All he want to do is punish somebody. You say he save Fifi. No. I save Fifi. And I save you. I give that Goodie One Shoes killer to that cop. I give him a gift. He give you, me, Fifi, nothing."

Alec Le Grand put up his hand. "She right. No cop care for you like Merissa. This neighborhood. We take care of our own. Now you one of us. We don't need no cops, come to Upper Broadway, ask who have what piece of paper, who pay money to some government wouldn't even give food to people flooded out of their house—living on the street like dogs. We take care of you now."

I covered my eyes with my hands. Much as I hated to hear it, there was some truth in what Merissa and Alec Le Grand had to say. Still, they didn't know the whole story—that a fortune in diamonds and jewelry were hidden in those heels and whoever murdered Freddie and probably Sophia wasn't going to stop until they got everything back—and that was beginning to seem more and more impossible. I uncovered my eyes and rose from the couch with as much dignity as I could muster.

"You didn't take very good care of Freddie-the-Fox. You didn't take very good care of Sophia Sarfatti either. I think this is bigger than our little neighborhood. I think there are many people at risk of getting killed here, and I don't think any of us sitting here can go it alone." I walked over to Merissa and glared at her. "And as for Murphy the cop and my pants, that's none of your business."

Merissa adjusted her turban and said nothing.

"I think you should both leave now." I told them, and I pointed towards the door.

Alec Le Grand bowed and taking Merissa's arm, walked slowly towards the door. When they were gone, I went to the refrigerator and took out a bottle of vodka from the freezer. There was only a smidgeon of pomegranate juice left and I poured it into a glass, followed by a double shot of vodka. I decided I'd skip dinner tonight. There was nothing worth eating in the refrigerator and all I really wanted to do was go to sleep.

"Sorry, I'm late. I had a little problem."

Larry bent over to kiss my cheek. I ducked.

He sat down heavily across the table from me and motioned for the waitress.

"I'll have a scotch, Johnny Walker Blue Label and she'll have a Mojito, rum on the side."

Larry looked more rumpled than usual. His shirt was open at the neck and one shirt tail was hanging out of his pants. It looked like he had even lost a few more hairs from his balding head. It did my heart good to see him in such a state. It showed me how much he needed me. He unfolded the napkin and placed in on his lap. It slid off. For a minute or two he tried to retrieve it from under the table, but bending down seemed to be a difficulty. I was beginning to feel sorry for him, but this was a trap I know he engineered deliberately for me.

When the drinks arrived, I poured in the rum, sipped the Mojito before me and tried to look unconcerned. I had suggested we meet here, at the local Turkish place around the corner from my ex-apartment. It was neutral territory—neither too plebian for my fancy estranged husband, nor expensive enough for him to think he was doing me a favor. The only problem with it was they cheated you on the mixed drinks. I had learned the only way to get an honest serving of rum in my Mojito was to order it on the side. At least he remembered that about me.

I was annoyed that Larry didn't seem to want to meet me at my former apartment on Central Park West where he still lived. I had come to get Sophia's shoes back from him to give to Murphy—but I also had decided to retrieve my mink. I wasn't exactly sure what I would do with it. I really had no interest in wearing it. I just wanted to make sure he didn't give it to his Russian Babka.

I smiled to myself. I thought it might be kind of fun to sell it to Gallina. There seemed to me to be some kind of poetic justice in that. Larry would go nuts when he found out—and of course I'd make sure he did.

When Larry finally retrieved his napkin, his face red, and the napkin filthy, he motioned to the waitress again and demanded a new napkin.

I ignored this little drama, played, I was sure, for my benefit, and asked him, "How come you didn't want me coming upstairs to the apartment? Is she living with you?"

"Who living with me? What are you talking about?"

"You know who I mean—your Russian borsch-berry.

"You know—you are really crazy. That was four years ago. She bothers me enough at the office. Believe me, I have no interest in anyone living with me except you."

I scowled. "So why wouldn't you let me come upstairs?"

Larry readjusted his new napkin and made room on the table for our drinks which finally arrived. He held up his glass and reached across the table for mine. "Good to see you," he said.

I nodded. I couldn't bring myself to say the same, although I had to admit that it was getting harder for me to nurse my resentment against him. Four years ago I had caught him in bed with his Russian secretary and I pulled the plug on my marriage.

It was, of course, much more than that. I hadn't gotten tenure at the University; I was tired of living the boring life of a rich, spoiled lady, I was tired of trying to satisfy another person's demands and whims. I was tired of picking up Larry's dirty socks and changing the water in his disgusting fish-tank.

I guess, looking back, you could say I had a mid-life crisis. I used Larry's affair as an excuse to do something entirely different. And now I was happier than I had been in years, running Emily's Place. Doing whatever I felt like when I felt like it. My own boss. In some sense, I suppose, my discovery of Larry's infidelity was a good thing for me. Whatever my feelings were for Larry, I knew I didn't want to live with him. And Sasha, Masha, Babka, whatever her name was, was a good excuse. Besides, all I had to do was think about her and my thoughts turned to violence.

"The apartment doesn't look so good." Larry took another drink of his scotch. "Not that you were much of a housekeeper," he added dryly. "But now I can see it's a mess. You'd only get mad."

I chewed on a leaf from my drink. "Why would I care? It's your apartment. You can live the way you want." I settled back in my seat. It did my heart good to hear how completely hopeless he was at home without me.

"I got a dog. I think I made a mistake."

I almost choked on my leaf. "A dog! You got a dog! You're scared of dogs!"

"Yeah. Well. He's a little dog. A puppy. He chewed up my Ralph Lauren pants.

"Ralph Lauren pants! Since when do you wear Ralph Lauren pants?"

Larry fidgeted in the chair. "I'm been trying to change my image. My clients. They're rich now. Not like before when I was a prosecutor. I got to look good."

I rolled my eyes.

"I saw him staring at my fish tank."

The disgusting fish-tank. The one I had wrecked vengeance upon before I left the marriage. Larry had replaced all the fish I had so happily flushed down the toilet-bowl.

Of all the things he loved, his antique watch collection, his chess pieces, his cactus plants, the stinking, disgusting fish-tank with dead things periodically floating in it, was his favorite..

Despite my best intentions, I was beginning to feel a little sorry for Larry again. "Maybe you should think of getting rid of the dog."

He finished his scotch and motioned to the waitress for another. "Let's forget about the dog," Larry said. He reached down into his briefcase and took out the shoes.

"Where are you going to keep these? There's a fortune in hot rocks in here—and two people are already dead because of them. When are you going to hand them over to that cop?"

"As soon as possible. Probably tomorrow."

Larry scowled. "Did you bring a bag? Something to carry them in? How will you get them home?"

I reached across the table for shoes. Then it was my turn to fumble underneath the table.

I kicked off my ballet-slippers and slid my feet into the shoes. I stretched out my leg for Larry to see.

"I wear size 7. Remember?"

Larry shook his head. "How would I know that? I never bought you a pair of shoes. I did buy you a mink coat once though."

"Yes, You did. As a matter of fact, I wanted to talk to you about that. I decided I want it."

Larry picked up the menu. "How come? I thought you hated fur and you hated me."

I shrugged. "A person can change their mind."

“I’ll bring it to you.” Larry said. “We’ll have dinner together. You name the day. I’ll bring it with me.”

There he goes again. You never get anything for nothing from Larry. But I didn’t have much choice. “Ok. I said. “Next Wednesday night. You’ll bring the coat?”

Larry said nothing. “I don’t like the idea of your wearing my coat with that cop. What’s his name? Murphy? Maybe I’ll keep the coat. You told me everything in the apartment was mine.”

This was clearly going to be painful. Why did I have anything whatsoever to do with this man? I took a deep breath. “I promise you I won’t wear the coat with Murphy. OK?”

“Deal.” Larry reached across the table and we clasped hands.

He held on to mine. “I still care about you. You know that. I even care about your ditzy sister Shana. She called me you know. Something about practicing medicine without a license. She’s a menace. She should really be prosecuted.”

We gave the waitress our orders. In a way I agreed with Larry, but Shana was my sister—and, according to the promise I made our dying mother—my responsibility. Of all the things she had tried in the past, physical trainer (she had dislocated somebody’s arm); hair-dresser (she had burned somebody’s hair); life-coach (she had told somebody to leave her job and she ended up on welfare); this seemed the least dangerous and the only one to earn her enough money to live on.

“Shana is Shana. She’s too ineffectual to really do anyone any harm. She reads auras for God’s sake. It’s some Russian character, trying to hold her up.”

Larry nodded. He was with me on that one. “Yeah. She gave me the name of some low-life. Tanya Solowitz. Runs some errands now and then for the Russian mob. Tell your sister all she has to do is get her friend Vladimir to lean on Solowitz. Let her know that he knows she is working for Ivan Ivanoff—“The Big I.” If she ever bothers Shana again, she’ll be arrested. That should be enough to scare her off.”

I squeezed Larry’s hand. “Thanks. I appreciate it.”

Larry took a bite of his Shish-kabob and chewed thoughtfully. “And another thing. I don’t think the Russian Mafia has a hand in this shoe thing. They don’t do shoes. And they don’t do diamonds. Furs—since we are talking about it—furs and drugs are their thing. I think this Bellini guy—he’s the one to watch. It’s like I said, anyone who is named for a drink at Harry’s Bar in Venice is not to be trusted.”

I smiled and extracted my hand. “Just for the record,” I told him, “Bellini was a painter in Venice before he became a drink.”

“I knew that.” Larry replied.

That was one of the things I could never stand about Larry. He always had to have the last word.

TEN

Nancy Sinatra's single album, "These Boots Are Made for Walking" declaring the independence of women in no uncertain terms, sold more than four million copies.

"How do you know your 'friend' didn't help herself or himself to the booty—pardon the pun—inside the heel of this shoe?"

Murphy shook poor Sophia's left shoe close to his ear to hear the diamonds inside rattle around.

"How does Jim know he can trust Huck?" I countered. "Let's just call it experience." The truth was, while I knew Larry could bend the truth into a pretzel when he wanted to, he was scrupulously honest when it came to other people's property.

Murphy bent over the coffee table, twisted off the heel, and poured the diamonds onto a small plate on my coffee table. He had come to my apartment to collect all the shoes I had been able to recover so far—Shana's, the pair I had just bought at the shoe store on Arthur Avenue, and Sophia's. Of the three, only Sophia's contained a treasure.

I had dressed in a form-fitting black tee and straight-leg jeans, with a pair of long dangling silver earrings I had bought on a trip to Mexico. I thought I looked inviting but not deliberately dressed up. It was a look that took me hours to think up. I had invited him at 5:00 after I left the shop, in the hope that I might encourage him to stay a while.

But Murphy didn't seem much interested in me. It was the diamonds that had captured his attention.

The stones sparkled and glowed on the porcelain plate. Hell Fire to me now. To Murphy maybe that pot of gold at the end of the rainbow those leprechauns never did give him.

Murphy picked up a couple of stones and squeezed his hand shut around them.

"So, me darling'," he said to me, "is it Brazil you'd like to live? Or perhaps the Cayman Islands?"

I sat down beside him and picked up a few stones and let them dribble through my fingers back onto the plate. Magical. Awesome. Dangerous. Tiny prisms sending rainbows of light onto the ceiling of my living room. I could understand how they could drive a person wild.

"No one would know," I promised him. "If three or four were missing."

"I would know." he said. Me and the Angel of Death. And I'm not planning on wrestling with that one."

"Is it fear of Hell, then," I asked him, "that keeps you honest?"

He stared at me for a minute without answering. "It'll do." He said at last. "That and the fact that I don't have much use for crooks. And I suppose, I really don't have much taste for fancy living either."

"I guess we'll have to settle for Coney Island," I quipped. "Or rather, Brighton Beach. I don't really buy Galina's story about selling the shoes. Thought me and Shana would take a trip to that flea market tomorrow and check it out."

Murphy opened his fingers and allowed the stones he had been holding to slip back on the pile before him. Then he carefully filled the heel one by one, and twisted it shut. Then he picked up one of Shana's empty shoes. "Could be your little sister may be planning a trip soon. What do you think?"

I shook my head. "Let me put it this way. My sister Shana is not much of a planner. She has a tendency to consult fields of energy invisible to you and I and then floats off in whatever direction the wind is blowing. If she were going to Brazil, she'd be there already. Now Vladimir. He might be creating enough of an energy field to pull her along. Have you been able to find out anything about him?"

One of the interesting things about being with a cop is that he had access to secret information. Some of which, he occasionally decided to share with me. He sat back against the cushions. "Haven't been able to come up with much. He seems to have entered the country legally—although it's always possible that he is traveling under the name of someone who died years ago.

"Dead Souls." I said to him. "Gogol."

He looked at me. "Right," he said.

I bit my lip. Why did I have such a need to show I knew more than him? "And Galina? Could you find out anything about her?"

Murphy snorted. "Other than she lied to the police…me nothing. She works in the garment center for some Russian furrier. Models the furs. She has some papers—visitor's permit. Who knows where she got them. Those Russians. They are all desperados. Survivors. They had to lie and cheat to get by in Russia. They had to lie and cheat to get out of Russia. And they lie and cheat to get by here."

"People once said all those things about the Irish. And the Jews."

Murphy's eyes twinkled. "Ah! But the Irish had St. Francis to look after them and the Jews had Moses to lead them out of the desert. The Russians are lost in transit."

I had my own reasons for disliking the Russians—not something I wished to share with Murphy. Still—it seemed to me that it was okay for me to feel that way—but the law—the law should be above prejudice. I should know better by now.

"Russian Mafia? If it were them you'd probably be lying next to Sophia. They don't worry about collateral damage Now the Italian Mafia—they have some rules of conduct. But the truth is, with all this Mafia talk, there doesn't seem to be much that connects either of them to this shoe thing."

Murphy reached down and took a couple of white cloth bags out of his briefcase. He wrapped each shoe carefully in a bag. He took a magic marker out of his briefcase and carefully labeled each shoe, Right, Left, Sophia, Shana. Then he tucked them into his briefcase and locked it closed.

"Yeah—Giancarlo and his friend Freddie-the-Fox ran a few errands for some Mafia guys. This Galina has a boyfriend who carries messages now and then back and forth for the Russian Mob. None of this is high level enough to account for those diamonds. And the diamonds might be just the tip of the iceberg. There is something bigger going on here. And I think it has to do with that Bellini guy who came into your shop."

I didn't want to point out to Murphy that I had said that from the beginning. It's like dealing with a child. You've got to let men think they have discovered it for themselves. I crossed my arms. "Oh," I said. "Good thinking."

Murphy ignored me and continued." I want to deal with him without calling in the Feds. The Feds are worse than the Russians."

I knew he had a turf war with the Feds but I didn't know how deep it ran.

Murphy's hands began that "Executioner's Dance" I had seen before. The fingers opening and closing, as if aching to wring somebody's neck. "Someone left me a message on my cell. Told me to 'ditch my investigation of certain parties having an Italian connection if I knew what was good for me and my family."

I tried to stifle a gasp, but it slipped out. I knew this kind of thing came with the territory if you were a cop and Murphy was not a man who would scare easily. Still, it was hard for me to swallow. Murphy might not be scared—but I could see immediately that he was angry. Or, shall we say, angrier. The threat had just upped the ante for Murphy. This was personal. A clear slap in the face. What my estranged husband would call "a tort,"—an attack and provocation. What Alec Le Grand would call "Disrespect." If duels were still fought in the United States, Murphy would be cleaning his weapon.

I edged closer to Murphy on the couch. I could smell the metal of the gun he kept hidden somewhere on his body. It mixed with the scent of his after shave lotion and something else—something woodsy and musty. The scent of excitement? Fear? Hatred? I wondered if he could ever put away his gun long enough to make love to me. If he would ever make love to me. He thought of himself as Super Cop. But he was really just a man. And a man who now was in danger.

"I'm sorry." I said to him. "What will you do now?"

"Now I've got to find them before they get to me. It's what I do for a living."

He put his hand over mine. "Don't worry about it. I'll get them first. I always have."

'But if Bellini is a war criminal—if there is an international ring of murderers who have escaped for so many years—they will do anything to keep their secret."

Murphy released my hand and picked up his briefcase. "I think their time is running out." He looked at his watch. "And so is mine. I got to pick up Patty at the after-school center today."

I tried to keep the tone of disappointment out of my voice. "How about a cup of coffee before you go?"

"Next time." He said.

When he got to the door I called out, "Give Patty my love."

"I will," he answered, "We'll be in touch."

"I wouldn't give a rat's ass for anything in this whole fair." I held on to Shana's arm as we wove between the aisles of tables set out in a grassy field.

"You always have such a picturesque way of putting things" Shana commented. "These are not your antique dealers who bring out Victorian watch chains in the school yard on Columbus Avenue in Manhattan. "

"I can't believe you are still angry that I sold Mom's watch chain. You told me you didn't want it."

Shana pursed her lips. "That was then. I was only fifteen. Why would I want a Victorian watch chain?"

“I gave you the money I got for it.” I told her.

“That was in 1980 dollars.” Shana pinched my arm. “Look at that doll!”

Shana pulled me over to one of the tables overflowing with junk. Rusty tools, dusty glass bottles, a couple of broken picture frames, a few dirty-looking dolls, one with a missing eye and matted straw-colored hair.

“You’ve got to be kidding,” I told her, as she picked up the doll and cuddled it.

“Don’t you ever watch The Antiques Road Show?” she asked me. “This is just the kind of doll you buy for $2.00 and it turns out to be worth $20,000.”

I pulled the doll out of her hands. “Don’t you read the newspapers? About the bed-bug epidemic? That’s a hell of a lot more likely than an undiscovered treasure.”

Shana moved over to the bottle collection. Blue, green, yellow with strange labels in Cyrillic lettering. I picked one up and peered in. There was a thick black liquid congealed on the bottom. It smelled like old cough medicine. “Why on earth would you want such a thing” I asked her.

“It’s for my new beauty creams—make them look really authentic.”

“Right. Authentic Soviet issue shit—like that Tanya Solowitz creature who’s been bothering you. Did you finally get rid of her?”

Shana scowled. “I told her The Big L was going to get her but she just laughed.”

“The Big L? What are you talking about?”

“I just did what your “Estranged husband” Larry-the-lawyer told me to do. He sent me an email—something about threatening her with the Big L.”

“It’s the big I! For Ivan The Terrible! I think you need glasses. It’s time you began acting your age!”

She scowled. “You were just born under the wrong sign; Venus was in decline. That’s why you always have such a negative attitude.”

I had to admit she was right about Venus being in decline—although I doubt that was responsible for my attitude this morning. The day was gray and overcast and the field was muddy. I didn't even know there were fields like this in Brooklyn. I had already stepped into what I was sure was bull dung. It was way out in the low-lands somewhere—some swamp one of those Russians rented for nothing. My Stuart Weitzman $300 ballet slippers were caked with who-knows-what and all around me were heaps of junk being recycled from one Russian to another. Shana had already bought a shopping bag full of dusty old bottles which, she informed me, she would soon fill with a wonderful new skin cream she and Vladimir were mixing up—a cream that not only softened your skin but had wonderful healing qualities as well.

Over-weight women with dyed red hair and tight low-cut tee shirts pushed past us carrying shopping bags. A group of little kids sat under one of the tables eating oranges and throwing the peels on the ground. A couple of men with big bellies stood smoking under the only tree in sight. A peroxide blond lady wearing an apron was selling some kind of sticky buns. A couple of teenage boys roamed the aisles selling CD's. Somewhere a radio blared Russian music.

I stopped at a table filled with old bed and table linens. They had a damp, musty smell as if they had been in someone's basement for years. I picked up a blue flowered table cloth that looked just like the one my mother had when I was growing up. It had a wide yellow stain in the center.

"A vase of flowers. That's what they kept there. That's why the stain. $12.00. You put it in a little Clorox and you got something, good as new." The heavy-set lady minding the stand started wrapping it up.

"Bed-bugs!" Shana whispered to me and pulled me away.

"I wasn't even thinking of buying it. She has some nerve!"

Shana glared at me. "Give it a break. She's just trying to make a sale…hey…look! The shoe table!"

Across the aisle was a table filled with shoes. I don't know if it was "The Shoe-Table" or "A Shoe-Table" but nevertheless it looked promising. There were more people at that table than anywhere else.

We pushed through the crowd and dove into the pile of shoes before us. There didn't seem to be any rhyme or reason to the assortment. Men's shoes were mixed up with ladies and children's shoes. Right shoes were separated from left shoes. Some seemed like new shoes—others had clearly been worn. And there were no prices.

What a mess! Emily's Place was Fifth Avenue in comparison.

Nevertheless, the crowd seemed to love it. People dove into the piles of shoes, extracting one or another, holding it up and yelling. If they liked one shoe, they shouted to their friend to try to find the mate. Shoes were thrown from one end of the table to the other, in a constant game of "find the shoe."

Presiding over all this chaos was one of the tallest men I had ever seen outside of a basketball court. In his hand he held a wad of bills to which he was constantly adding and subtracting. From his mouth dangled a cigarette, that he managed to keep on smoking no matter how much talking and yelling he did.

He had wild gray hair and a soiled gray sweatshirt with the words Harvard College printed on it. Every time someone held up a shoe, he would shout out a price.

"$16.50!"

"$19.95!"

"$7.00!"

"$79.00!"

This last price was greeted with laughter.

"I'll give you $50.00!" Someone shouted.

"$35!" shouted another.

Where were these prices coming from? It seemed to me that Big Guy was just making them up! The crowd either agreed with it or challenged it.

Talk about free markets!

This was half circus, half auction, half super-sale. And the crowd loved it!

I picked up a blue woman's shoe, size 9. Big clunky heel. Heavy, cracked leather. It looked like Soviet issue, 1978. Who would want such a thing at any price?

Even though I have been called by The Amsterdam Avenue News the Shoe Queen of The Upper West Side I have to admit I had a hard time identifying most of the shoes sold here. I imagined them coming by boat steerage about thirty years ago. The leather on most was dull and cracked. The shoe laces were knotted. The heels were worn down.

On the other hand, I did manage to catch sight of something that looked very like last year's Chanel pump—and another that could have been Prada from a couple of years ago.

"Anyone need a size 8 ½ ?" Big Guy shouted out.

A couple of hands went up and he tossed over a pair of ladies black shoes in the direction of one of them.

Shana pulled away from me and dived right in as if she were born to it.

"Take a look at this one!" she tossed me a gold-colored shoe with a plastic bow.

"I saw the mate on the other side of the table." She called out and ran to the other side.

Before I had a chance to follow her, I caught sight of a black sequin heel sticking up from the corner of the table that I would swear was a Jimmy Choo, but before I could grab it, a hand shot out with long, red fingernail polish and plucked it out.

"Size 6!" She called out in disgust. "Too small!" She tossed it back on the pile where it was scooped up by my baby sister on the other side of the table.

"Mismarked!" she announced as she slid her size 7 foot into it easily.

"Where's the mate?" She yelled out to the crowd. Then she held the shoe up in the air and scurried to the front of the table.

"How much?"

"$36.95!" Big Guy called over.

This sent Baby Sister into high gear and her enthusiasm seemed to have caught the attention of a couple of teenage girls who tossed the shoes this way and that around the table until one of them triumphantly held up the mate.

"How much for the mate lady?"

This stopped Shana in her tracks.

"$1.00!" she offered, opening her bag.

"No deal," the dark-haired one said. "$10.00. Finder's Fee! Ten bucks or I keep it myself."

Apparently there was another aspect to this show I hadn't noticed. The hunt for the mate to the shoe someone wanted to buy was a real treasure hunt.

I walked over to the kid. "Excuse me," I said to her. "Can I see that for a minute?"

"Sure thing," the girl handed it over.

"Now you'll take $5.00 or you'll get nothing at all." I took out a five dollar bill and waved it in front of her.

"Hey!" she yelled.

"Finder's Fee today is $5.00."

For a minute I thought she was going to push me and make a grab for the shoe but something made her think twice about that. It could have been the glint in my eye or the large scissors I had extracted from my purse—but whatever it was, she mumbled something in Russian I didn't understand and grabbed the bill.

I handed Shana the shoe.

As if Shana needed another pair of shoes. "Emily's Place isn't good enough for you?" I asked her.

She ignored me and slipped her feet into her new shoes.

Yup. Jimmy Choo. Last year's model. Almost new. Shana had caught the feeding frenzy attitude of the place. She ran right back to the table and started rummaging through the shoes.

Big Guy smiled at us and threw a few more pair of shoes on to the pile.

"Anyone looking for a size 7?" he shouted.

Low and behold! The shoes he held up were Galina's Shoes! The very shoes we had come to find.

I held up my hand, the same time as another woman on the other side of the table.

Big Guy threw one shoe to me and the other to her. "$80.00 Imported Italian leather!"

he shouted out.

I grabbed the shoe and pushed my way to the other side of the table. A skinny blond-haired lady about Shana's age had slipped it on her foot. Her friend, a sloppy-looking red-head with a double pierced ear supported her as she stood on one foot.

Shana came up alongside of me.

"Do you want that shoe?" I asked the lady.

Her friend translated for her. She nodded and held out her hand for the shoe I was holding.

"I'll give her $10.00 for the mate." I told her friend.

She duly translated. The lady shook her head and came out with a long stream of Russian words.

Her friend nodded. "She needs these shoes. She is going to a wedding next week and she needs a low-heeled, comfortable shoe. She has a bad back."

"Tell her I'll bring her another pair. Better. Brand New! "

The two women spoke in Russian for a couple of minutes. Then the lady with the shoe shook her head.

Her friend said, "No deal. She needs the shoe. She'll give you $3.00 for your half of the pair."

That wasn't even enough for a finder's fee! For a minute I contemplated pushing her over, grabbing the shoe and making a run for it—but I figured that wouldn't work. She would have too many friends in a place like this where I knew no one but Shana.

And then I had an inspiration.

"Bed-bugs!" I yelled out in a loud voice.

I pointed to the shoe I was holding and began to shake it.

"Bed-bugs! If they get in your house, you have to throw everything away! It was in all the newspapers! An epidemic!"

The other people at the shoe table stopped and stared at me.

"Look!" I called Shana over who cried out in a loud voice "Bed-bugs!"

The crowd around the shoe table immediately began to disperse. Big Guy looked completely confused.

The skinny lady's friend babbled excitedly to her in Russian. Then she dropped the shoe, grabbed her own and, shaking it out, moved quickly away from the shoe table.

I picked up the shoe quickly and put it in my bag.

"What you doing!" Big Guy put his huge paw on my shoulder. "Why you say Bed-Bugs? My shoes have no bed-bugs! You give me $90.00 now!"

"You said the shoes were $80.00!"

Big Guy squeezed my shoulder till it hurt. "You make my customers run away. Bed-Bugs!"

"Ok. "I said. "I took out $90.00 and handed it to him. While he counted it, I ducked out from under his hand, grabbed hold of Shana and made a B-line for the exit. Shana hobbled after me on her sequined high-heeled shoes.

"I can't believe you bought those shoes!" I admonished her. "it was like you had never owned a pair of shoes before."

Shana smiled. "That was fun!" she said. "I'm going to come back next week. I didn't even make it to the jewelry counter."

It just goes to show. Women love a bargain better than something for nothing.

"I still don't understand why you were so hot to get those shoes back," Shana complained as we relaxed back in her apartment. "It's a lot of trouble to go to for some factory recall."

I still didn't feel it necessary to tell Shana about the jewels hidden in the heels of the shoes. I was quite sure, that like Beverly, if she knew, she would demand a share. It was also, quite possible that she already knew, and had helped herself to whatever she found inside her own shoes. I didn't want to know too much about that myself. There was no telling what I might blurt out to Murphy in a weak moment. As for her being in danger—if she didn't have the shoes, and she really didn't have any information, she would probably be ok. In this situation, innocence was probably the best defense.

But I do admit it was hard to come up with a good enough excuse for my hot pursuit of Galina's shoes. "This company," I began, "is trying to establish a reputation in the U.S. They gave me an exclusive on their shoes. So when something went wrong, they were worried that their whole brand would look bad, unless they made everything right. So…they told me it was very important for me to get back all the shoes with the weak heels before someone fell and sued them and ruined the future of their business."

"Oh," Shana said. She looked down at her new shoes.

I didn't have to worry much about explaining my motivations to Shana. Her attention span was limited.

"I bet Vladimir will love these shoes!" She walked slowly around the living room.

I picked up Galina's shoes and put them in my oversized pocketbook. Then I told Shana I had to go to the bathroom. I could hardly wait to pry off the heels and see what was inside. I sat on the seat of Shana's toilet and took out the sharp scissors I had brought with me.

I picked up the right shoe and held it up to my ear. I shook the shoe.

Nothing.

Probably packed so tight there is no room for jiggle. I twisted the heel, inserted the point of the scissors, and pulled hard. I couldn't budge it. This heel seemed to be glued on as well as nailed like the others. It was hot in the bathroom and I was beginning to sweat.

I could hear Shana talking on the phone in the other room. Was she describing our afternoon to Vladimir? How much did she really know about that flea market and the merchandise they offered? Did Vladimir get some kick-back from stuff he located? Or was it even worse? Was he involved in the scheme to launder money in the heels of the shoes? And had he now somehow enlisted my sister Shana in his scheme?

I tugged once more on the heel. It came loose. I shook it out into my other hand. Nothing! I threw both parts of the shoe into my purse and took out the other shoe. The heel came off more easily. But the result was the same. Nothing!

Shana knocked on the door of the bathroom. "Is everything ok?" she asked me. "you've been in there a long time."

"Yes! I'm fine! Just a little upset stomach," I called out. I threw the other two parts of the second shoe into my bag and flushed the toilet. Then I turned on the water in the sink and washed my hands. Was all this just a game being played by Galina and Vladimir? Was my sister Shana in on it?

Was there a ring of Russian criminals using Emily's Place as a haven for laundering money? Or were Galina and Shana innocent victims in a scheme run by Italian war criminals? I looked at my reflection in the mirror. If my hair hadn't been gray before all this started, it would surely have turned gray now. I wondered how I would look as a red-head, like so many of those Russians I'd seen at the flea market. I wondered what Murphy would say when I told him the results of my wild goose chase.

I even wondered if I would get bed-bugs.

ELEVEN

Suffragettes wore heels to demonstrate their femininity, but it was in the 20's when the flappers wore high heels and short skirts, that shoes in American became sexy.

"The bastards took her! My baby girl is gone!"

I held on to the phone by the side of my bed. "What? Who?" My mind was still half asleep, although my mouth seemed to be moving.

"Patty! She's gone! The murdering bastards grabbed my baby girl!"

Now I was fully alert. Murphy! "Patty! When….tell me what happened!" For a minute all I heard were strange snorts and noises as if someone was moving heavy furniture around.

"Murphy! Where are you? What is going on? Are you all right?"

"I'm not all right! Never again all right while those Bastards live!" I heard a door slam and mumbled curses. Patty! Kidnapped! It was beginning to sink in.

"Murphy! Tell me where you are. I'll come. Tell me!" Patty! Gone! His little girl! I remembered how upset he was at Big bingo when she had slipped out of sight for a few minutes.

Heavy breathing into the phone. "No. I'll be ok. I got to figure out what to do. Those cops out there won't find her! I got to get to the Superintendent, the Mayor!"

I shook the phone. "Listen. You called me. Forget the Mayor. Give me your address."

Silence. "It's the middle of the night. It's not safe. No one is safe anymore in this city!"

"Just give me your address. I'll take a cab. I've lived in this city my whole life. I'll be fine!"

I grabbed a pen and scribbled his address on the back of an unopened Con Ed bill.

I slipped on my jeans and a pair of sneakers. Then I opened my closet and reached far into the back where I kept my dress-up shoes. I grabbed my trusty Tango shoe that had served me so well in capturing Goodie One Shoes and lifted it over my head. It was heavy enough to take down an attacker across the room—but for hand-to-hand combat I needed something else. I reached back a little further into the closet and pulled out a four inch stiletto heel, red Prada.

For a minute I held it in my arms. I had bought it in Paris fourteen years ago on a trip with Larry for our tenth anniversary.

I bit my lip. This was no time for nostalgia. I would probably never wear the thing again for a number of reasons—not least of which was they hurt my feet something terrible.

I threw it into my oversize purse, grabbed my keys and headed downstairs for a cab.

Some people carry pepper-spray for self-defense when they travel alone to unknown parts of the city. I carry a shoe.

This being the city that never sleeps, I had a cab within five minutes even though it was 4:00 A.M. The argument he gave me when I said I needed to go to Queens, and the amount of money I had to pay him to take me, is a story I'd rather not tell.

"Sorry. It took the cabbie a little while to find the street. He's not used to Queens."

Murphy was waiting for me in front of his door—a small brick-faced little house on a street filled with others that looked just like it. There was a front porch with a couple of plastic chairs set out and a little patch of grass going down to the sidewalk. A cat rubbed up against my leg when I entered.

Murphy led me into the living room. He swept the newspapers covering most of the sofa onto the floor with one motion, and made room for both of us. On the floor near the sofa was an ash-tray overflowing with cigarette butts. The room had a sour smell.

Across from the sofa was a broken coffee table, upended with a couple of legs reaching towards the ceiling. Murphy's shirt, usually so clean and starched was limp and grungy.

I didn't know what to expect when I offered to come to him. What kind of state he was in. I didn't have a clue what I could do for him to make anything better. I just knew I had to come.

I never had a child. My former assistant Kim was the closest I had come to the deep feelings between a parent and child. Her death has left a hole in my heart—and she was an adult—only part of my life for a short time. I had only met Patty a few times. I liked to think we bonded. I was a friend, not her mother, not interested in discipline or judgment—a grown-up playmate who enjoyed being with her and her father. And yet, I could already feel that empty feeling in my chest. I could only imagine what Murphy must be feeling. He looked pretty wasted.

He jumped up from the sofa almost as soon as he sat down.

"Get you a beer?" he asked me, moving towards the kitchen.

"Sure," I said. I picked up the overflowing ash-tray and followed him in.

The door to the kitchen hung on one hinge and Murphy held it up for me to pass. There were several empty beer bottles around the garbage can—as if Murphy had thrown them like a basketball from some distance away and only a few found their mark. I emptied the ash-tray into the garbage can.

"Looks like your kitchen door had an accident." I commented as we passed through again into the living room.

Murphy glared at me. "No accident. I kicked the thing off its hinges. And I don't want no lip from you."

I took a drink from the bottle and held it in my hands since the coffee table seemed to have had the same kind of accident as the kitchen door.

"What happened?" I asked when Murphy had settled down next to me and taken a gulp from his own bottle. The least I could do was to get him talking instead of destroying the furniture.

"I go to pick Patty up yesterday. My wife has her signed up for these activities, after-school. Dance on Monday, soccer on Wed, Art on Thursday, cause we both work…no one is home. So I go to pick her up and the teacher says, oh, your baby-sitter picked her up already, so I say, 'baby-sitter we don't have a baby-sitter.' She says, 'oh yes, your wife called. Left a message. Maybe she forgot to tell you.'"

Murphy put the bottle of beer on the floor and put his head in his hands. I put my bottle on the floor and put my arms around him. The cat jumped up and rubbed against us. A Siamese—sleek and gray with blue eyes. Murphy lifted his head and reached for the cat.

"Patty's cat." Murphy said. He cuddled her for a minute and then put her down on the floor.

"So I call my wife but I know already it's all bullshit. There's no babysitter. And my wife starts screaming on the phone. 'I knew one day this would happen' she says to me. 'I knew one day this would happen.'"

Murphy covered his face with his hands again.

"It's not your fault." I told him.

"I'm a cop!" Murphy said. "That's my fault! Holly Mary, Mother of God. It's all my fault!"

I pulled him closer to me. "It's all right," I mumbled. "It will be all right. You're a good man Murphy. We'll find Patty. I know it. We'll find her." It was as painful for me to see Murphy all broken up like this as I'm sure it was for him to expose himself like this to me.

"A man who can't protect his own family isn't much of a man." Murphy pronounced.

He got up from the couch so quickly he knocked over his bottle of beer. I went into the kitchen and fumbled around until I found a roll of paper towels. I came back into the living room and mopped up the beer.

"I'll get those fuckers!" Murphy yelled out. His moment of weakness had clearly passed. I saw his big hands open and close around the leg of the coffee table. He lifted it up and banged it once hard on the floor.

"What happens now? Is there a plan? Who's looking for her?"

Even though I had worked with Murphy to catch a criminal before, I really had very little idea of police procedure. I imagined there was some standard operating system for a kidnapping.

"Yeah. We've got it covered. Squad cars out combing the neighborhood. They threw me out of the car. Said I had to stay home in case the kidnappers called. What do they know?" Murphy sat down again on the couch. "It's not their kid. Yeah. They'll do their job. But me—I'll get those fuckers and they'll never even get to a courtroom! You think my kitchen door had an accident? Whoever did this to Patty is going to have an accident every creep in the city will remember!"

I offered Murphy the rest of my beer. Never did like beer. Vodka was my drink. I wished I could have one now but I thought better of asking for one. Didn't want to get Murphy started on the hard stuff. He was juiced up enough on beer.

"So how come you waited until four in the morning to call me? Did something else happen?"

Murphy finished off the bottle and put it down on the floor. "Smart thing, aren't you? Got a call from the bastards about 2:00 AM. Told me they would exchange Patty for the diamonds in the heel of the shoes bought by Sophia Sarfatti. How would anyone know I had those shoes?"

It only took me a couple of seconds to come up with a reasonable scenario.

"Whoever killed Sophia—and now we are pretty sure she was murdered—looked in her closet for her shoes. When they didn't find them, they must have assumed that I had them—remember that Bellini guy was in the store when Sophia returned them. Also, whoever hacked into my computer knew Sophia had bought the shoes from me. And anyone in my neighborhood knows you and I are friends and you were working on the case. Ipso Facto, you would have the shoes and the diamonds."

Murphy nodded. "Your neighborhood! Your 'vendors' who sell things that fall off trucks!"

"So now it's my fault?" I challenged him. "Why did you call me anyhow?"

He grunted. "Thought you were tough enough not to get hysterical like my wife—and shrewd enough to understand how your neighborhood operates." Murphy shook his head. "It's nobody's fault—except maybe that God damn Angel of Death who got stuck on the Upper West Side because of all the heathens who live there."

I could see Murphy was desperate to blame someone or something. There was no point in arguing. None of this would get Patty back for us. But maybe…just maybe…he was right in figuring that I might have some influence in the neighborhood.

"These Heathens can help get Patty back. Trust me on this one Murphy. The Neighborhood will hang together on this one." Could I really depend on people like Alec Le Grand, and Jose the newspaper man to help trap a kidnapper? Would Nancy the fence and Giancarlo help out anyone? I had to believe some of them would. I did believe it. And I would make Murphy believe it. I stood up to him and rested my head against his chest. Then I stepped back and looked up into his somewhat bloodshot blue eyes. "We'll get her back. Murphy. I promise you."

Murphy pushed me away. He began to pace up and down in front of me. "I'm supposed to make a drop—exchange the diamonds for my kid—two days from now—12:00 noon—somewhere in the Bronx. They said they'd kill her if I showed up with anyone else. Someone with an Italian accent. They put her on the phone. My girl! She said "Daddy! Come soon. Daddy, Come now!" Then they cut the connection."

He went into the kitchen to fetch another beer. I glanced at my watch. It was almost 6:00 A.M. When he came back from the kitchen I put my arms around him again.

I could feel the pounding of his heart and smell the sweat on his shirt. I moved back and looked up at him.

"We'll get them. Patty's a brave little kid. She'll be fine. I feel sorry for the kidnappers. They will want to give her back. I have a lot of friends in the neighborhood. We'll find her."

Murphy handed me his beer. I took a long drink and finished it off. "Maybe you should try to get some sleep" I suggested

Murphy shook his head. "Macbeth has murdered sleep. Sleep is finished."

"Maybe not." I took his arm and led him towards the stairway that I figured must lead to his bedroom.

The stairs creaked. Murphy held on tight to my arm and grabbed the railing with the other. He breathed heavily. "To the right," he directed me, when we came to the landing on top of the stairs.

Inside the small bedroom, all was neat and clean. The covers, army style were stretched tight across the bed. It had not been slept in. Murphy sat down on the edge of the bed and took off his shoes. He pulled me down next to him. His breath was sour. I stroked his face. I could feel the stubble of his beard.

"You'll be fine," I said to him. "Can you call me a cab?"

Murphy put his arms around me. "You don't have to get a cab." he said. "Why don't you stay with me for a while? I'll drive you back home…afterwards."

I looked at him. Wasn't this the moment I had been waiting for? Thinking about all those nights when I lay alone in my bed? Of course I did picture it rather differently, but that's the trouble with fantasies. Making love now might make us both feel a lot better. Better than beer and better than vodka.

I shook my head. "I don't want to take advantage of a man in a weak moment," I said.

I got up from the bed. Murphy mumbled something and lay down, his eyes already closing. I walked towards the door. I figured it was light enough to find a roving cab—even in Queens. "I'll be in touch," I told him and I shut the door behind me.

"Lordy! Lordy!" SuperMama shook her huge head slowly back and forth. "That little gal? They done took that little gal?"

I sat next to SuperMama and her daughter Sammy on the stoop. The "Senator" leaned against the door frame. "I need your help. I need everybody's help. We got to get Patty back!"

I had promised Murphy I would rally the neighborhood and I was going to do it. Yes, we had our share of heathen and hoodlums from all over the planet, but some of these same people had learned the value of loyalty the hard way. You take care of me and I'll take care of you. It was the way it had always been in neighborhoods like this. I remember stories my mother used to tell of her parents on the Lower East Side. You watch my kids; I'll watch your kids. It was the Italians and the Irish and the Jews back then. Now it was the South Americans, the Asians, and the African-Americans. No nannies there. No nannies here. Just a diabetic, nearly blind SuperMama, who took care of her people and didn't miss a trick.

The Senator bobbed his head up and down. " Che brutta! Brutta! La ragazza bella! The pretty little girl.

"Don't know nobody here, take a chile away like that. Even low-life Mafia don't do nothin' like that!"

SuperMama reached over and took Sammy's hand. "What you think, girl? Who do somethin' like this?"

Sammy looked down at the cracked step she sat on. She shook her head.

"Could be some stranger. Come from some other place. Maybe China."

SuperMama grunted. "What you talkin' about girl? What kind of Chinese person need a girl like that? I hears in China they try to get rid of girls. Let's them die right there in the fields."

It was a strange thing to say. Sammy was a lot smarter than that. I moved a little closer to Sammy on the step. She looked off into space. I put my hand under her chin and turned her face to mine. She met my eyes briefly and then lowered her own. Was Sammy acting strange—or was it my imagination? Murphy had indicated there was some woman, or women involved. A woman claiming to be his wife had called the school. A so-called baby-sitter had picked Patty up. I didn't think the school would have released Patty to someone who looked like Giancarlo. But Sammy? She was capable of taking both roles.

And Patty. Patty was a smart little thing. Would she have gone with a stranger? Even if the school told her, her mother had sent her?

Maybe. But it was more likely she would have gone along happily with someone she knew.

Sammy!

She had met her at Big Bingo. She and Giancarlo had done magic tricks for her that day. Patty would have followed her willingly.

"Where were you yesterday evening? Maybe you overheard something? Someone planning something they shouldn't be planning?

Sammy shook her head. "I was in class all day yesterday. Had a biology lab. Didn't get home till late."

SuperMama repositioned her huge thighs. She straightened her housecoat. "That's right. She don't come home till maybe 9, 10 o'clock. My girl work so hard in school. She goin' to be a nurse someday."

The Senator put his hand on her shoulder.

"Sammy help everyone in the neighborhood. She know how to make people feel better with just a few healthy herbs, a cup of tea. She always make Signorina Sarfatti smile."

Sammy got up from the stoop. "I got to go now. I have a class. English lit," she said to me.

I stood up and put my hand on her shoulder. I noticed she had no book bag with her. "If you remember anything suspicious," I told her, "You know where to find me."

Sammy nodded.

"If Murphy doesn't get his kid back safe and sound this whole neighborhood is going to have to pay a price."

SuperMama turned her big head in my direction. "What this neighborhood have to do with anything? This little gal, you tell me, she taken in Queens. Queens like another country. What that have to do with anyone here?"

"Sure. Patty was kidnapped in Queens, but the kidnappers want something that was hidden in poor Sophia Sarfatti's shoes. And she lived—and died—right here in your house. They want a pair of shoes that I sold her—a pair of shoes that Freddie-the-Fox sold me. And Freddie-the-Fox was murdered right down the block in my store."

"Poverina!" The Senator shuffled his feet back and forth. "Shoes! Someone want Sophia's shoes!" He shook his head. "She don't have fancy shoes. Why someone want to kill her for her shoes?"

I stopped short. How did the Senator know Sophia was murdered? So far as I knew, the word had been given out that the death was "suspicious" and still under investigation.

I looked carefully at The Senator. Did he know something the police didn't? Or was I just beginning to suspect everyone in the neighborhood? And then my breath caught in my throat. I had forgotten the biggest neighborhood connection of all. The people in this neighborhood knew that Patty was Murphy the cop's little daughter. He had come with her to Big Bingo. In fact—Patty had gotten "lost" for a while at the fair, and Murphy had made a public announcement—describing his daughter and making an emotional appeal for her return. It was Nancy the Fence who brought her back to the Manager's Booth.

Was all that a deliberate prelude to an actual kidnapping? Had Big Bingo provided the killer with the information he needed to target Patty.?

I sat down again on the stoop. If that were so, I was surely partly responsible for Patty's kidnapping. I pictured Murphy's haggard face. He had said something about the kidnapping being his fault because he was a cop. Then he said something nasty about "my neighborhood" and "shoes that fell off a truck." But he hadn't made the final, devastating connection. It was because of me that he and Patty had come to Big Bingo.

"Big Bingo. Murphy came with Patty. That's how the kidnapper knew she was the cop's daughter. If you ask me, the neighborhood connection is pretty damn strong. "

Sammy looked down at her own shoes—a pretty pair of Chanel pumps. And she didn't buy them from me.

"I got to go now," Sammy said, and she walked quickly down the stairs.

SuperMama and I watched her as she disappeared around the corner.

"She didn't take her books," I said.

SuperMama sighed. "My Sammy is a good girl. She all I got, Miss Emily. These young people. Sometimes they go their own way, no matter what you do or say. She have some friends—I don't know why she hang out with some of them people—but she do. My Sammy. She likes nice things. Things this old blind Mama can't get for her. But I tell you this. My Sammy never hurt nobody. Never have anything to do with anyone, would hurt a child. Don't need no cop comin' round trying to blame something on someone in my house."

The Senator sat down in the seat vacated by Sammy and looked up at me.

"The people here don't want any trouble. They have trouble all their lives. We look for la ragazza. We find her!"

SuperMama grabbed hold of the wrought-iron railing and pulled herself slowly to a standing position.

"If I hears anything, I come running," she said to me.

And the funny thing is, I believed she would.

"Tsk, Tsk!" Alec Le Grand sat on the bench on the island on Upper Broadway and straightened his bow-tie. "I tell you Missy Emily, you leave that cop alone. I tell you 'fore his little gal be taken. No good can come from being friends with a cop."

Merissa nodded. "Madame Emily. She don't listen to anyone her whole life. She have a fine husband, want to buy her furs and all things else but she don't "trust" him. So he find a woman once or twice. It's his nature. Can't no one go against their nature. But that cop. How you goin' trust that cop? What he ever do for you? Now the whole neighborhood in trouble cause someone snatch his gal."

I crossed and uncrossed my legs a couple of times while a big garbage truck went roaring by. When the traffic stopped for a red light, I lit into Merissa and Alec.

"We are not talking about my friendship with a cop. We are talking about the kidnapping of a little girl. A little girl who followed you around at Big Bingo like a puppy. Don't you care that her life might be in danger? It doesn't matter whose kid she is. We got to get her back!"

Merissa waved her hand. "Maybe she just get lost by herself, like at Big Bingo. Maybe that cop just want an excuse come nosing round the neighborhood making trouble."

I could see that human kindness alone was not going to get me very far with these two. I had to appeal to their more selfish instincts. "It doesn't matter if she ran away or someone snatched her. It's what Murphy believes that matters. And Murphy believes someone in our neighborhood is responsible for her disappearance. He's going to get my ass if he doesn't get someone else's—and if he closes Emily's Place you, my friend, Merissa, are out of a job."

Merissa smiled. "Mon Dieu! Merissa be out of a job many times in her young life. But your ass going to be in trouble."

Alec le Grand chuckled. We all going to be like asses if Murphy want to make trouble." He pulled on his little mustache. "I don't need to tell you Missy Emily that our neighborhood famous far and wide for its independent business men. 'Entrepreneurs.' Everyone on Upper Broadway know who owes Alec le Grand money and who Alec le Grand owe to. Everyone know who wins and who loses in my poker game. Everyone fine with that. Everyone fine with Jose who run some numbers now and then and Nancy, he set stones for his friends. Freddie-the-Fox, may he rest in peace, not the only personage here who sell merchandise that fell off a truck. Everyone know Beverly Bernstein sell some ganga now and then. We all right with all this."

Even Beverly Bernstein, the Kindergarten teacher had a racket!

Merissa clapped her hands. "Biensur! What the priest say? He who without sin cast the first stone? We all sinners here. We all ok with that. 'Cept that cop. He think he better than the rest of us. Like he never tell no lies. Like he never take some money under the table. I bet I ask around I find out plenty about Murphy the Cop."

"It's not about Murphy!" I yelled at her. I wanted to shake her. Why couldn't I make them understand?

"It's about Patty! We got to find Patty! And if we don't, there will be Hell to pay—and the entire neighborhood will have to pay it!" And then I stopped short. What if Merissa and Alec Le Grand already understood? What if Merissa and Alec le Grand were somehow involved in the kidnapping?

Patty would have gone with Merissa just as she would have gone home from school with Sammy—willingly and happily. Merissa and Alec had already warned me to get Murphy out of their hair—and out of the neighborhood. Alec had a number of illegal businesses all over the Upper West Side. He was a gambler—and maybe he lost more often than he won. It was possible that he and Merissa found out about the shoe filled with diamonds from Bellini—or Giancarlo, or Freddie-the Fox himself before he was killed. They decided to kidnap Patty to scare Murphy off the trail. Then they could keep the diamonds for themselves, and get rid of Murphy at the same time.

I scratched my head. Was everyone a suspect? What kind of person was I to suspect one of my best friends? Was I so eager to blame someone else so that I could get off the hook? I kept going over that Sunday of Big Bingo. Murphy had come because of me. And now his child was in danger. I didn't need Murphy to punish me. I felt guilty enough without his help.I would never forgive myself—or the neighborhood—if anything happened to Patty.

I turned towards Alec Le Grand. "You have a poker game every Thursday Night. There is a guy who plays, name of Bellini.

I think he's mixed up in the kidnapping. Maybe also the murder of Freddie-the-Fox. "

Alec Le Grand stared at me for a minute. "Don't know anyone, name of Bellini. "Cept it is a drink, I hear tell, somewhere in Italy."

"Come off it, Alec. I saw him at Big Bingo. I saw him go into your tent where the game was going on. Francis the Fence told me he's a regular."

Merissa and Alec exchanged glances.

"Oh. That Bellini! Massimo."

I nodded. "I want you to put the word out on the street that Patty must be returned unharmed immediately. And I want in on your next poker game—Tonight!"

Alec shook his head. "I tell my friends we don't stand for no kidnapping, innocent kids on The Upper West Side. No way. But you can't play no poker game. Even my honey-pot here don't come, Poker night. It's Men Only."

"Your rules just changed." I said to him, over the roar of a large furniture delivery truck and the tinkle of Mr. Softie bells. "I play or I tell Murphy you got an illegal game going every Thursday night."

Merissa actually hissed at me. I threw her a dirty look.

Alec le Grand reached into his pocket and took out a silver dollar. "I'm a gambling man. Been a gambling man my whole life."

He flipped the coin up into the air. "Call it—heads you play, tails you don't !"

"Heads!" I yelled out.

The coin hit the ground and Alec covered it with his shoe.

He bent over and picked it up. "Heads it is!" he shouted above the screech of a fire truck rounding the corner. "I'll see you later tonight. Merissa knows the address!" He got up and kissed Merissa on the cheek. When the light changed, he walked quickly across the street

"Luck favors the bold," I said to Merissa.

She laughed and scribbled an address on a small piece of paper she found on the ground.

"My man. He don't take no chances with luck. He have himself a two-headed silver dollar for chumps like you."

Sometimes I wondered about the thin line between friends and enemies.

TWELVE

Manolo Blahnik's metal spike heeled stiletto had to be taken off the market because it was regarded as a lethal weapon.

"Wait a minute! All my cards are red! Doesn't that beat a full house?"

Alec le Grand straightened his bow tie. "That depend, Miss Emily. Do they all look the same? You need to look at the shape. What shape do they be?"

Harold rolled his eyes and took a sip from the glass of scotch next to him. "In other words, are they all hearts or all diamonds? They have to be the same suit as well as the same color."

Jose chuckled. "Don't think Miss Emily need any suit. She lookin' real good in that tee shirt."

He took a swallow from the bottle of beer in front of him and passed it to me.

I shook my head. It looked to me as if everyone brought their own refreshments. It would have been nice if someone had told me. I surely could have used a straight vodka.

Nancy the Fence chimed in, "She lookin' good to me too. You know what she has in common with a pack of cards? They both can be staked!" He took a drink from a silver cask he carried with him.

Giancarlo smiled and reached over towards me. "The lady has a flush." He made some shuffling movement with the cards and seemed to extract an Ace of Diamonds from my ear.

"Hey—where'd you get that Ace of Diamonds?" Nancy called out "Talk'in about diamonds—what did you do with the one you showed me? Still want to sell it?"

The room seemed to grow quiet.

I stared at Nancy. I wasn't prepared to talk about this. Whatever happened to honor amongst thieves? "I've got to think about it." I said. And then I added, There's more where that came from."

Bellini made some sudden move and knocked over his glass of Compari. Giancarlo literally dropped his cards on the floor. For sure these two knew something about the diamonds hidden in those shoes. Jose and Alec hardly twitched.

Bellini poured himself another glass from a bottle he had on the floor. Giancarlo picked up his cards and rearranged them in his hand.

"What's this about diamonds?" Harold inquired. "Have you been holding out on Sadie and Mary? Can I now afford to dress them in designer clothes instead of Salvation Army rejects?"

I stared at my cards. "You guys are just trying to distract me. I got a flush and I win." I leaned over to the center of the table and swept a pile of 10's and 20's in front of me. Considering I hadn't played poker since I was about twelve, I thought I was doing ok. The problem was, I was a little rusty. And besides, I was sure they were all cheating in one way or another, and laughing at me. Even Harold, my window-dresser and neighbor seemed to enjoy making fun of me. It was making me mad.

I had been instructed to come up the back stairs of this ancient apartment building where apartment 4B had been rented just for the evening. That meant climbing up four floors of broken-down stairs and enduring the smells—mostly of urine—that this building had absorbed over the years. It seemed silly to me to have a floating poker game with a secret address when everyone in the neighborhood knew the game was taking place.

But I suppose the secrecy, such as it was, and the dimly lit, smelly hallways added to the excitement of the experience. In truth, I couldn't really figure out how anyone could be arrested for having a friendly poker game. But I suppose if the police wanted to harass people, they would find a reason. At this point I wasn't worried about the police. I was annoyed at the guys I was sitting with.

They were a motley crew. Jose the newspaper delivery guy (boy was no longer applicable in his case) wearing a shabby pair of jeans and a stained blue tee shirt that said "Superman" on it; Harold Shapiro, my window-dresser and neighbor wearing one of those wrinkle proof white shirts from Brooks Brothers; Nancy The Fence, his grungy white tee shirt full of holes; Alec le Grand, in his signature little red bow tie ; Giancarlo, his tight black tee shirt cut sleeveless to show his muscles and tattoos and Massimo Bellini, in a black turtleneck with a tweed sports jacket over his shoulders.

The room reeked of cigarette smoke and booze.

I'm not sure what Alec le Grand told them was the reason for allowing a woman to trespass onto their sacred space but whatever it was, it didn't make them happy. Nancy the Fence actually groaned when he saw me and pulled Alec into a corner for a quick "conference."

What was there about a group of guys together that made them all regress to adolescence? Even the gay guy had a sense of solidarity with the others.

Between Jose making jokes about my breasts, Giancarlo peering at my cards, Harold's eye-rolling, and Alec Le Grand, analyzing each hand as if he were talking to a five-year-old, I had begun to wonder if it was worth coming at all. But things were beginning to get interesting.

The dapper Bellini managed to concentrate once more on his game—whatever that really was. He played smoothly, ignoring the silly banter around him, smiling occasionally out of politeness and smoking a string of cigarettes. But his reaction to the mention of a diamond was unmistakable. Bellini was the clear winner tonight. Alec was losing steadily. I wondered how much they cared, about who won and who lost. Was this really a friendly little neighborhood game or were the players dependent on the outcome of these games to pay their rent? I wondered how many hundreds were really exchanged in these weekly games. Did Jose depend on winning a certain amount to make ends meet? He certainly wasn't making much delivering newspapers. And how much did Alec le Grand depend on winnings for his own needs? This game was one of several "businesses" Alec ran in the neighborhood. The players had to put up some money in order to get into the game. Merissa had indicated that he got a percentage of everything, but if he gambled himself that would clearly eat into any profit. And what if he participated in the horse-bets and numbers game as well? And I wondered how much of what was going on here was being staged for my benefit.

Giancarlo took the deck and shuffled it. He handled the deck like a magician. I wondered how many cards he had up his sleeves and how the others handled his handling of the cards. Was he dealing a few cards now and then from the bottom of the deck? And if so, did Alec le Grand know it?

I was coming up with more and more questions, and no answers. I glanced at my cards. Two aces. Black ones this time. I asked for three new cards. Giancarlo's hands were quicker than my eye so I couldn't tell where they came from. All I know is I had two kings, red ones. I opened with a $20. Bellini glanced at me and then threw two $20's on the pile. I added a $20. Everyone else folded.

"So, I said, "I never realized that Italians liked to play cards so much. My poor old friend Sophia Sarfatti used to love to play cards with another elderly Italian, lives round here. We all call him the Senator."

Alec le Grand looked across the table at me and shook his head. "Now who tell you that? That all wrong! Miss Sophia? She don't never play cards. She like the ponies—that one really like the ponies. Used to tell me she rode when she was a girl, back there in Italy." Alec looked up at the ceiling and pulled on one end of his mustache. "When the Angel of Death done come for Miss Sophia, I waitin' there to get her last bet." He nodded to me. 'I don't never tell anyone but I make a bet for her that day—I knows she likes the fillies, so I put a $10 on Pride of Sue, prettiest little filly I ever did see, run out at Belmont that day. Damn if that little filly didn't run home. She be a long-shot at 10-1. I make $1000 I donate it to her funeral casket, may she rest in peace!"

Jose clapped his hands. "You did a good deed, my man!" he said. "Miss Sophia, she always good to me. She like some people, and she don't like other people. Now, "The Senator? You tell me he say he play cards with Miss Sophia? That not even funny! Miss Sophia, she never even speak to that man. She much too high-class for his kind. I see he come trying to visit when I come to the door with her paper and she quick shut the door. Almost caught my hand that time."

Hello! Here's an interesting piece of news. So The Senator wasn't in the building to play cards with Sophia? What was he doing there and why did he lie about it? "So what do you think," I asked Bellini. "Do Italians like to play cards? Did you ever meet The Senator?"

Bellini puffed on his cigarette and stared down at his newly dealt hand.

"Ah, Signora, This "Senator" you mention, I don't know. And cards? Do Italians like to play cards?"

He hunched up his shoulders. "Do Americans like to dance? Perhaps some do and some don't."

I couldn't much argue with that answer. I suppose it was a silly question. I just wanted to try to keep the conversation going.

"Sophia Sarfatti. Do you remember her? She was in my store when you came in to buy some shoes."

Jose whistled. Nancy laughed. "Hey," He poked Bellini. "What were you doin' in a ladies shoe store?

Is there something you're not telling us?"

Giancarlo and Harold exchanged glances. Bellini seemed embarrassed and confused.

"I have a girlfriend," he admitted. "Bellisima! The shoes were for her."

"Yeah! Yeah! That's what they all say. Bet it was a size 11!" Jose quipped

Everyone laughed at that one, except Bellini.

"It was a size 7." I said. "It was one of the pairs of shoes that I had bought from poor Freddie-The-Fox."

Bellini said nothing. He rearranged his hand and tossed another $20 dollar bill onto the pile.

"Poor Freddie," Harold said. "He never had much of a chance."

I put my cards on the table. Two aces and two kings.

"He was shot in the head with a World War II Italian police revolver." I said nonchalantly.

There were groans all around the table. This piece of information had been carefully withheld.

"Bastards!" Giancarlo banged his fist down hard on the table. The mound of bills in the center of the table flew about.

Bellini downed his new glass of Compari. He set his cards carefully face-down on to the table.

"You win." He said.

"Show me your cards," I said to him.

He ignored me and got up from his chair. He put on his jacket and nodded to the group.

"Troppo tardi," he said. "I have a distance to go. "Arrivederci."

Alec le Grand put his hand on his shoulder: "Massimo, my friend. You can't leave when you're winning."

"But I just lost," Bellini said, nodding in my direction. He picked up half of his winnings, sitting in a pile in front of him and pushed the rest into the middle of the table.

"I have to go now," he said again. "You can play without me."

This seemed to mollify the group.

Harold kissed him on both cheeks; Nancy gave him a hug; Alec shook his hand; Jose patted him on the back; Giancarlo waved goodbye. Bellini bowed to me and nodded to the group, and then he was gone.

Alec le Grand stared at me. "What this business with a World War II revolver? Who have a W.W.II revolver, 'cept my great uncle down in New Orleans, got it off a dead Italian soldier he done shot through the heart in 1943."

"You tell me," I asked the group. "Could be Russian Mafia trying to blame it on the Italians."

"Fuckin faggots!" Jose spit out. "Only Russian I ever like is a dead Russian."

Harold got red in the face. "Remember, there's a lady present."

Jose mumbled something and sat back down at the table.

I picked up the cards Bellini had thrown down. He had three Jacks's and two queens. A Full House. Even I knew a full house beat two pair. I mixed the cards in with the others and handed them back to Giancarlo.

"Something bad is going on in our neighborhood," I said. "And I don't think Russian Mafia has anything to do with it. "I looked slowly around the table. "I think this is entirely a home-grown situation. There has been a kidnapping in our neighborhood," I announced.

For a minute everyone was very quiet.

"My friend Murphy the Cop's little girl Patty was snatched yesterday from her school in Queens.

The same people who murdered Sophia Sarfatti and Freddie-the-Fox have taken his girl. If she isn't returned immediately—tonight—unharmed—the whole neighborhood will have Hell to pay!"

Nancy got up from his chair. "Hey—lady! I ain't done nothing. What do you mean the whole neighborhood? The kid was snatched in Queens!"

Alec Le Grand got up from his chair. Giancarlo looked down at his hands. "Anyone takes a kid—got to answer to me!" Alec looked slowly around the table. "We don't steal kids. Even Mafia trash don't steal no kids. Sure isn't no one I knows in this neighborhood want to make trouble for us all. We make bets. We sell merchandise. We all here are "businessmen." Anyone take a kid—got to answer to me!"

I looked around the table. Most of the bottles and glasses of whiskey were done. A couple of ash-trays overflowed with cigarette butts. No one made a joke. No one made a sound. Then Alec le Grand swept the pile of bills that remained on the table into a little bag he carried and zipped it closed. There was a shuffling of chairs and the sound of clothing being moved about. Clearly the mood in the room had changed.

"I'll treat you to a ride home," Harold said. I held on to his arm and we walked down the back- stairs of the old apartment building. "What's all this about diamonds and a World War II Italian police revolver?"

"It's much too complicated to explain," I said to him. "But I think that Bellini guy knows the answers."

I stopped and held on to the banister for a minute.

"How well do you know that guy? What's he doing in this game anyway? He doesn't even live in the neighborhood."

Harold shrugged. "Alec Le Grand arranges the games. I think Bellini is a friend of Francis. He's been playing for about a year. Nice lookin' guy. Too bad he's straight as an arrow." Harold shook his head. "Can't see Bellini with diamonds or a WWII revolver. Certainly not snatching a kid. Grand Opera is more his style."

"There are some pretty terrible things that go on in Opera." I reminded him.

We continued down the staircase.

"I hope Murphy gets his kid back," Harold said. "For her sake, for Murphy's sake, for your sake, and for all the rest of us."

"Jesus, Mary and Joseph! Me girl Patty is back!"

I gripped the phone tightly and glanced at the clock near my bed. It was a little after 3:00 A.M.

"Oh Murphy! I'm so glad!" I shook my head to try to clear the cobwebs away. Was this a dream or had Patty really been found?

"Tell me! Tell me! Where is she now?"

"She's here, right here next to me. Fell asleep, she did almost as soon as I got her in my arms. I can't bear to take her upstairs. Want to keep her right here next to me all night."

"Is she ok? Is everything all right?"

"Right as rain. Perfect. Not even scared. The bastards gave her some piece of shit doll to play with. I got my baby girl back home."

I pictured them together on the couch in Murphy's living room. I hoped he had gotten rid of the beer bottles.

"How did she get free? Where did they find her? Tell me what happened!"

I wondered if my little speech at the poker game had really made a difference. Maybe all those things I had been telling Murphy about our neighborhood were really true. They would hang together to help one of their own—at least if it was sure to help them as well.

He laughed. "Can't hardly believe it. Patty, me baby girl, call on her cellphone. My phone rings—the private number. I hear her whisper—'Daddy Daddy—come get me.' Seems neither one of the creeps thought to search a little kid like that. Good thing she had it hid—from her mom—kept it in a special pocket. In a pair of socks I got her. Under her jeans. So I say where are you? 'I don't know' she says. 'I ran out the door when they weren't looking and I'm on the street.' So I tell her, 'run to the corner and look up at the sign on the corner. Spell the words. And, would you believe it, me sweet baby girl, she does it! She start spelling A-r-t-h-u-r….Holly Mary Mother of God—she's up there in that WOP neighborhood in the Bronx on Arthur Avenue! So I tell her to keep talkin' and I go call the guys on the other phone and I tell her wait there for a patrol car and don't talk to no one. And, and, then, maybe five minutes later—seems like forever—me friend Simmons get on the phone and he say 'I got her Murphy. She's OK!"

I was so excited I started jumping up and down on the bed. "Good for Patty! Good for you! Good for Simmons!"

What a lucky ending for us all, I thought. I trembled when I thought of what might have happened to her.

"Do you want me to come?" I asked Murphy. "Maybe give her a bath—get some breakfast ready?" I pictured Murphy's dirty living room and the sink full of dishes. A time like this a girl needs a woman's touch—someone to shampoo her hair and make her warm milk. And of course, Murphy could use some comforting too. Someone to share the celebration of Patty's return. Someone who will listen to his story and ask the right questions.

Murphy hesitated. "No. No. Her mom is coming over. She's kind of hysterical. She's been up all night. I'm sorry. I just wanted to let you know that my girl is OK. "

I stopped jumping on the bed. "I understand," I told him. And I did. But I really didn't want to. I put the phone back and lay back down on my bed, staring at the ceiling.

I pictured Murphy's ex-wife although I had never seen her. She would have the broad hips of that police woman Denise who worked with him, a soft belly and Angel blond hair. She would arrive at the apartment with home-made cookies—Patty's favorite doll. She and Murphy would hug each other and look down at the sleeping Patty between them. She would brush away a strand of Patty's hair and puff up the pillow. And then she and Murphy would give thanks to Mary, Jesus and The Holy Ghost.

It wasn't my family. And it never would be.

THIRTEEN

The elegant stiletto shoe with its four or five inch heel and pointed toe is never very comfortable. This is a sacrifice most women are willing to make.

"Get over it!" I told myself the next morning. I had a life of my own. Maybe it didn't include a husband and daughter but I had lots of friends—a whole community of creative, amazing, multi-talented friends. Besides, I had a purpose. People needed me. I gave them pleasure. I gave them advice. I was a power in the community.

Hadn't I helped to free Patti? I was sure my message at the poker game had resonated with someone, who told someone who told someone else, who actually did something. That was the way it was on the Upper West Side. Of course, I did have to give some credit to Alec le Grand. He had a long reach in the neighborhood.

And, of course Patti herself deserved a lot of credit. Gritty little creature, wasn't she? I couldn't help smiling when I thought of her running off and calling Murphy on her secret cell phone. Guess I still hadn't gotten over it.

So, here I was waiting on Mary Ellen Rimolovski, who needed a bigger size Prada brown leather pump because of her bunions, trying not to think about Patti and Murphy the Cop when who should arrive, shoes newly polished and shined, after-shave lotion cutting a broad swath through the layers of perfume and deodorant scented air of Emily's Place, but Himself—Murphy the Cop, cleaned up and glowing with energy.

Me, sweaty, worn-out feeling sorry for myself after a night of little sleep.

"I think we got him now," Murphy said, smiling brilliantly down on me where I squatted on the carpet next to Mary Ellen's bunions.

"The Bastard is finished!"

I pulled myself to a standing position with the help of Murphy's offered arm and led him to the back of the store.

I poured him a cup of coffee with two sugars and a little milk. I hoped he appreciated that I remembered things like that. I wondered how much he remembered of the almost-affair we had, the night Patti was snatched. Might things be different now between us if I had said "Yes, yes, yes!" like Molly Bloom, instead of "No, no, no," like a silly woman who couldn't make the leap between reality and her own romantic fantasies? There was surely no sign of intimacy now.

"Which Bastard are you going to get?" I asked him.

"All of them, eventually," he said, stirring his java."Me Baby Girl, God love her, told me it was someone from the Fair." He averted his eyes but the sneer on his face was unmistakable.

"The Fair? Big Bingo? Are you referring to Big Bingo?"

In a whole city full of criminals—more, a whole country full of criminals—he wants to pin everything on Big Bingo! And of course, by extension, on me. For sure he remembers enough about that night in Queens to know he was rejected. Even though I knew there was some truth for what he was saying, I wasn't going to take all the blame.

"So now it's all my fault?" I pulled the cup of coffee out of his hands. Some of it splashed onto his shoes. "Maybe you should arrest me too!"

I guess my reaction took him by surprise. Either that or he was trying to be friendly so I would return his cup of coffee, but when he looked up his eyes were kind. "Sure no one is blaming you for anything. Believe it or not Ripley, I came here to thank you."

That took the wind out of my sails. Thank me! That was surely a first for Murphy the Cop. The least I could do was to refill his cup and hand it back to him.

"Who did Patti say it was?"

"Remember what happened at the Fair, when she disappeared? I had told her never to talk to strangers and she told us the person wasn't a stranger she was talking to. She had met him at the Roulette Table."

I nodded. "I remember. That was Nancy, right? The Jewelry guy."

I was about to say the "jewelry fence" but I stopped myself in time. I still had that diamond in my pocket. There was some honor amongst thieves.

"Are you going to tell me it was Nancy?"

Murphy scowled. "No. Don't think so—although he could have been in on it. All of your lovely neighborhood "businessmen" might be in on it, for all we know now."

Here we go again. What was it Merissa had said about Murphy? He was always trying to punish somebody for something. "Most of those 'businessmen' you're referring to, didn't have your advantages."

"Right," Murphy took a napkin and wiped off his shoe. "I was born with a silver spoon in my mouth."

"Maybe not," I countered, "But at least you had a spoon in your mouth—and someone to feed you."

Murphy held up his hand. "They can all tell their stories to the judge—if they make it that far. It is entirely possible that they will have a fatal accident before they reach the precinct."

Murphy flexed the fingers of his right hand.

"Patti said the guy who took her wore a Santa Claus mask with a big beard but he was too skinny to be Santa. He wore red sneakers. Also, there were two of them. One was a woman. She was wearing a Pumpkin Mask."

"If the person was wearing a mask, how did Patti know she was a woman?"

Murphy's face lit up. "Her shoes. She was wearing ladies shoes." Murphy chuckled. "You women sure start young. First thing she noticed."

"It could have been a transsexual."

Murphy sat back on his chair. "Sure. Could have been one of them trained bears you see at the circus, but it wasn't. Give it a rest Emily. I didn't mean anything personal. Patti may be a little kid but she can tell a man from a woman. Said both of them were funny. Tried to make her laugh. Santa Claus even did some magic tricks."

"Oh boy." I said, I knew Giancarlo wasn't too smart but this is ridiculous."

Murphy reached into his pocket and withdrew a cigarette. He fingered it for a minute and put it back into his pocket.

"What'd you say the name of his girlfriend was? Some guy's name, right?"

"Sammy. SuperMama's daughter. You met her at the Fair."

"My men tell me that Giancarlo is connected to the Mafia. Low-level kind of guy. Runs errands now and then. No one seems to think he is smart enough for much else. But this girl, he hangs around with. This Sammy. She's a smart one. Could be she's the real Mafia connection. She just brought him along to do the heavy work."

"But why would they murder Freddie? If what you say was true, Freddie was in it with them."

Murphy snorted. "Freddie might have kept too many shoes for himself. Selling them to you. Keeping some for himself. Guy like that—what's a few more pair of shoes fell off the truck? His friends didn't like it. Anyway, it's not absolutely clear that the same person or persons who murdered the old lady and Freddie were the same who did the kidnapping. I 'll settle for getting them for the kidnapping first. Then we'll figure out the rest."

Murphy put his coffee cup down and flexed the fingers of his right hand until they made a tight fist. He was going to twist the life out of one of them for sure.

I walked Murphy to the door. "What's the next step?" I asked him.

"I got to get my girl Patti to do an ID on Giancarlo and Sammy. I'm going to take a ride over to their neck of the woods and do a drive-by. Don't want to traumatize my girl any more than necessary—make her peer at a bunch of low-lives through a window downtown. She'll sit next to me and point them out. I'll do the rest."

We stopped by the door. "I'll need your help to set them up. Get Sammy and Giancarlo together on the stoop of the brownstone where the old lady was killed. Maybe see if you can get that Nancy guy out too. And that teacher—the one who did the puppet show—it wouldn't be a bad idea to have her come over too."

"A whole neighborhood reunion," I said. "We can make it a street festival."

"Don't be so snide. This is murder and kidnapping we're talking about. Most of the people in your neighborhood are guilty of something. It wouldn't take much to push them over the line into homicide."

Murphy seemed to be one of those guys who believed listening to music could lead to dancing which could lead to sexual promiscuity so that anyone who liked music was a potential pervert. There were actually a lot of things about Murphy that I didn't like.

Murphy put his hand on my arm. "Patti says hello. "

"Hello. Tell her it was a good job she did—looking at the shoes. She'll either be a detective or a fashionista. "

Murphy grunted and mumbled something. These were clearly not the goals he had in mind for his baby girl.

"Let's try and set up something for this Sunday afternoon—aim for about 3:00. I don't want those bastards breathing free air longer than that."

He opened the door. " I'll be in touch." He said, and then he was gone.

"Who tellin' you stories, Missy Emily?" SuperMama asked, "Giancarlo can't hardly tie his shoelaces without someone helping him along. He sure ain't no kidnapper, murderer or nothing like that. 'Bout the only thing he do right is smoke ganga and play his music. That he do real good."

SuperMama tucked her dress under her large knees and stared out onto the street.

After Murphy left, I was so agitated I couldn't concentrate on selling shoes. Every time I decided he was just a waste of time, a sneaky cop like all those who ticket your car when you're five minutes late moving it on Alternate Side Parking day, or give you a fine for employing an illegal alien, he pulls out something like "Patti says hello" that makes me go all soft inside.

For the rest of the week until Sunday dawned, bright and lovely, I kept going over everything in my mind about the kidnapping and murders of Freddie the Fox and Sophia Sarfatti. I just couldn't go along with Murphy's hypothetical explanation of events. Giancarlo and Freddie-the-fox were lovers, for God's sake. There was no way he would have killed him. And, as for kidnapping Patti, it was possible but he was far too ineffectual to carry something like that out by himself. He would need an accomplice. More than an accomplice—a leader whose orders he would obey. Was that leader Sammy? They were friends but Sammy was only a kid herself—not likely the kind of character to engage in elaborate plots. Besides, as far as I was concerned, there was another, much better suspect—Bellini.

It was Bellini who threw down his cards when I talked about the WWII pistol. It was Bellini who had come into Emily's Place looking for the very same shoes Sophia Sarfatti had just bought and returned—the shoes with the diamonds in the heels. If anyone was giving Giancarlo orders, it was Bellini.

Another suspect in my book was Alec Le Grand. He had somehow turned up in Sophia's apartment right after she was killed—and also arrived at Emily's Place right after my computer had been hacked into. And it was Alec who said in no uncertain terms that Patti had to be released. Had he realized he had gone too far in antagonizing Murphy by ordering her kidnapping?

As for any woman involved, Bellini could have a girlfriend. Gallina was a possible accomplice. And, yes, Beverly the "saintly-socialist" kindergarten teacher who refused to give up her booty was a suspect as well. If Sammy was involved, she was taking orders from someone else.

At any rate, I couldn't find any real reason not to go along with Murphy's plan of an informal line-up on the stoop of Sophia Sarfatti's old brownstone, and so I called the "usual suspects" and asked them to assemble at 3:00 to discuss "some irregularities" in the treasury of the Big Bingo Festival. But I decided to go an hour early in the hopes of finding some time alone with SuperMama, who usually sat all day on the top step.

SuperMama is kind of like the blind seer of Greek mythology. She sits all day out on the top of the stoop staring into space but she sees and hears a lot more than she lets on. If anyone knew anything special about the kidnapping and murders, it would be her.

I told her Murphy the Cop had it in his head that Giancarlo was the one who kidnapped Patti and he was mad to blame it on somebody.

"Tisk, tisk," SuperMama shook her huge head back and forth. "That boy get himself in trouble his whole life, he so dumb. Hope that Cop look somewhere else. Somethin' go wrong in this neighborhood, someone blame Giancarlo, he don't even know enough to tell a lie. But he real kind. Mr. Adams, lives in 6 C, has himself a dog with only three legs. Run over by a motorcycle, they tells me. Giancarlo see that dog and he start to cry. I tell you true, Miss Emily, that man start to cry. Next thing I know he has made a leg for that dog. Made it out of plastic and tie it on some way, I don't know, but that dog go up and down those stairs now, like any dog in this world. Giancarlo—he don't have much goin' on in his head but he have magic in his fingers."

SuperMama put her hand over her heart. "Thanks to the Lord that little gal come out ok. That cop should light a candle over there in his church and leave the rest of us folk alone. We got plenty of troubles of our own, don't need any more from him."

I glanced at my watch. It was 2:45 and not a sign of anyone I had invited to the meeting. I know people in this neighborhood slept late on Sunday but this was ridiculous.

I stood up and looked up and down the block.

A cat jumped from one garbage can to another; A gypsy cab stopped to pick someone up; A Carvel Truck started it's tingly song.

And then the big outside door to the brownstone creaked and The Senator walked out onto the stoop. Was it my imagination or did he look older, frailer and more stooped than the last time we had met, just a couple of weeks ago at Big Bingo?

He took out a white handkerchief and wiped his brow. It was warm for the formal striped vest and suit jacket he wore. He extended his hand and I took it—his long fingers surprisingly cool.

I held on to his hand for a moment. The white cuffs of his shirt hung out from his jacket, exposing what looked like a gold cufflink. It was round and ornate, with some kind of crest. He was always decked out like some aristocrat—although according to Jose who delivered the papers and my own friend Angelina, he had been little more than a peasant from Southern Italy, and was just giving himself airs. Apparently his self-aggrandizement had worked pretty well. We did all call him "The Senator." As a matter of fact, it suddenly occurred to me, I never knew him by any other name.

"Nice to see you Signora Emily," he bowed slightly. "And How are you today SuperMama?"

SuperMama stared into space. "Thanks the Lord, I still here," she answered, "Who you been seeing this day?"

The Senator shook his head back and forth.

"Tsk, Tsk. Been visiting Mr. Clemento, 7B. Not doing well. Not doing well at all. Brought him some of my special herbal tea. He couldn't manage more than a mouthful."

He shook his head and stared up at the sky. "Don't think he is long for this world, I'm sad to say. "

He nodded to us both once more and then slowly made his way down the steps, clinging to the wrought iron railing. I watched him go step-by-step down the stairs. Hardly more than a skeleton himself.

"How old do you think The Senator is?" I asked SuperMama.

She sighed. "Lordy, Lordy." She moved her big head back and forth. "he old as them pyramids, they got there in Egypt."

I laughed. "Do all the people The Senator visits, do so badly?"

SuperMama sniffed. "Sure as I sits here, Miss Emily, I don't want no truck with that man." She leaned over closer to me. 'That man... That man… That man is The Angel of Death himself!"

The Angel of Death! I could still hear the whisper of wings in poor Sophia Sarfatti's bedroom. Could The Senator have had something to do with her death? They were about the same age. He claimed he knew her in Italy. Could she have known something about him that was so terrible he had to kill her?

"Tell me something, SuperMama. Do you know if that Clemento guy, The Senator just saw, takes Coumadin? It's a blood-thinner lots of elderly people take to prevent strokes."

"Sure do know what Coumadin is Miss Emily. Been takin it myself for three years. Half the people in this building takes Coumadin."

That was interesting. It wouldn't be difficult then for The Senator to take some Coumadin from one person and give it to another, now would it? He could have been saving it up for weeks to feed to Sophia in one lump dose.

I looked over at SuperMama. And what of SuperMama herself—and Sammy? They would both have had easy access to the drug, as well as access to Sophia's rooms. Since I was pretty sure they both believed "Them Jews all have money," they would have had a motive. And Sophia already had Sammy's trust.

There certainly were lots of suspects—but no way to prove anything—yet.

I glanced at my watch again. Still no one from the executive committee.

"I could sure use me one of them Carvel sundae's," SuperMama said to me, "but my diabetes acting up again lately. Got to let it go. I ate too many apple pies at Big Bingo. Now I got to pay the price. How much money you say was missing?"

I shrugged. "Didn't say. Was just looking at the account we have over there at Citi-Bank. I know Harold sold more tickets to dress up Sadie and Mary than was set down there. And I know Alec le Grand took in about $2000 at the Roulette Table. I'm not even counting the game he had going on in the back of his booth."

"Lordy, Lordy!" SuperMama, chuckled. "Alec le Grand always got a game going somewhere. That man wager his own grandma if he had one. But he don't cheat. Not that man. No one want to make a bet with a man who cheats. Bad for business."

I had to admit she was probably right. "Know anyone would hold out on the neighborhood kids, like that?" I asked her, Take in money from the games but put it in their own pocket?"

SuperMama stared out into space. She slowly began to shift her position on the stairs. First one leg, then the other. "The Lord giveth and the Lord taketh away. Don't know how I got this big and old." She pulled her skirt out from under her thighs and reached around until she found a pocket. Then she extracted a wad of something wrapped in a pink handkerchief. Without changing the position of her head, she handed me the handkerchief. It was torn and ragged, but clean. When I unwrapped it, I found a wad of five and one dollar bills.

"My girl Sammy and me, livin' hand to mouth. I don't say nothing to my girl. She want to go to nursing school, so I say sure, yes indeedy, Lord give me strength. She just a kid—don't know stuff like money it cost to go to school. Even over there, Brandeis High School, I got to give her money so she have a cell phone and them games they all got."

She turned her head and stared blankly into my face. "Miss Emily—where I goin' to get enough money, do those things? Sure, I bake and I cook and I sell some of my stuff, over there at the Korean grocery. I make cookies those chinks never see before. I get rent free here 'cause I Superintendent but can't live on that. I gets my disability for diabetes and stuff but where I goin' to get money send my girl to school?"

I bit my lip and slowly counted the money SuperMama had handed me. It came to $175.00.

"So Big Bingo come and I cooks and I bakes. Everyone here need something extra. Specially the kids over there at PS 96. So I works all day and all night for one whole week and I sell out every crumb. So I say to myself, "SuperMama, you got a kid too. You keep a little for your own."

She reached over and took the empty handkerchief out of my hand and blew her nose into it. Then she put it back into her pocket.

"Miss Emily, when you call, I feel ashamed. Ashamed! I take that money and I know the Lord see all that I do and maybe he punish my girl Sammy, use that money, and it bring bad luck down on my own sweet girl. So here it all be, truth be to God."

I folded up the bills and put them into my pocketbook. I took SuperMama's big hand in mine and gave it a squeeze.

"You're a good woman, SuperMama. " I told her.

"How much you got there?" she asked me.

"$175 bucks. Enough to buy some paints and crayons I would think."

SuperMama smiled. I wondered how much more she had put in her pocket. But who was I to judge SuperMama? I reached down deep in the pocket of my jeans where a two karat diamond that Nancy had appraised for more than $20,000 lay hidden. And as if my own thoughts had conjured him up, there was Nancy himself bounding up the stairs.

"Hey there Ms. Emily, SuperMama. Glad to see ya."

He nodded to me and pointed to an area on the steps, on the far side of SuperMama.

"Just need a private word with this lady," he said to SuperMama. "We got some private business. Be with you in a minute."

Nancy looked nervously out over the street and checked his watch. He turned his back on SuperMama and reached into the pocket of his jeans. He took out a wad of something wrapped in toilet tissue. He stood over me while I unwrapped it. It was filled with $10 and $20 dollar bills.

"There's $400 bucks there. Made a mistake when I counted up the cash I got from selling that junk Chink jewelry at Big Bingo. Put those bills in the pocket of a jacket I was wearing—forgot all about it till you called. "

He looked down at the cracked stairs below us, and stuffed the toilet paper back into the pocket of his pants. Obviously, junk jewelry was a better business than apple pies. I wondered how much more Nancy had made.

"Do you want a receipt?" I asked him, as I put the wad of bills into my pocketbook.

He shook his head. "Just between you and me," he said, "Don't need to tell SuperMama. She talks too much."

I nodded. For the first time it occurred to me that "the executive committee" who had so happily volunteered to help make Big Bingo a success had something besides charity on their mind. Did everyone in this neighborhood have an angle?

The next one to arrive was Harold, my genius window-dresser. "Hi there my darlings!" Harold gave me a kiss on both cheeks and threw a kiss to SuperMama. He nodded to Nancy. "A word—just a word—if you will excuse us. I need a consult. Tomorrow I change the windows at the elegant Emily's Place." He pulled me after him down the stairs. "Would you believe—when I was checking over the leopard-print blouse I had gotten ready to put on Sadie, what should I find, but a wad of bills in the pocket."

Harold put his hand in the pocket of his camel hair blazer and extracted a brown leather wallet with the Coach symbol embossed on the outside. He took out a handful of crisp bills and put them into my hand.

"I swear I forgot all about them. Never gave it a thought until I started to dress my girls. Must have stashed the bills there during Big Bingo. It was such a zoo! "

The first bill was a $20, the rest were $5's and $10's. All new and crisp. Harold had obviously discovered the money in time to take it to the bank and change the bills.

I wondered what he needed the money for. I thought his decorating business was very successful. But I suppose everyone feels they could use a little extra. I started to count the bills but Harold put his hand over mine." There's $200 there. "He looked nervously up and down the street and then up at SuperMama and Nancy sitting together on the top step.

"Put it away." He said, closing his hand over mine. He glanced at his watch. "Don't know if I can stay for the meeting."

"Et tu Brute?" I said to him, but he only shrugged his shoulders and mounted the stairs.

The next one to arrive was Giancarlo. This was really getting interesting. I could hardly wait to hear his excuse. He was wearing a black Spiderman tee shirt and red sneakers.

"Hello Miss. Emily. Hope I'm not late," Giancarlo called out.

I looked at my watch. Five minutes to 3:00.

"No—there's plenty of time," I told him.

He shook my hand and bounded up the stairs to join Super mama and the others on the top step. I followed him and pulled on his arm, just before he got to the top.

"So....Is there anything you want to tell me before we join the others?" I asked him.

Giancarlo scratched his head. "What about?" he asked me.

"You knew there was some money missing from the Big Bingo treasury?"

Giancarlo made a face. "Yeah. That's why you called us right? We got to find out what is what. God damn low-lives. Don't know anyone would steal from children. Maybe someone made a mistake."

I looked him in the eye. "Did you make a mistake?"

Giancarlo shrugged. "I put all the tickets the kids give me in the yellow envelope. Then I put all the money from the tickets in the green envelope. Just like you told me. Did I put the money in the wrong envelope? You said green was easy to remember because it was the color of money. That's where I put the money. "He wrinkled his brow and stared back at me. "Did I do it wrong?"

I shook my head and let go of his arm. "No," I assured him. "I think you did it all right."

He took the last two steps in one leap and sat down next to SuperMama at the top of the stoop.

Now it was my turn to scratch my head. When I turned around I saw Beverly and Sammy approaching quickly from the Broadway side of the street.

I walked back down the stairs to greet them. Beverly gave me a high five and started walking up the stairs.

"Thought you might want to know," she whispered to me as she passed by, "someone broke into my apartment and stole my shoes."

She paused for a moment, her eyes glittering. "Too bad they didn't find anything at all in the heels. I've got the stuff stashed in a much better place."

She chuckled, and continued up the stairs.

I held on to Sammy and pulled her back. "So…How are things Sammy? Haven't seen you for a while."

Sammy looked down at her shoes and kicked a pebble out of her boot. Expensive boots they were too. Looked like Cole Haan. $450.00. Last time I had seen her she was wearing sneakers. I pulled Sammy closer and lifted her chin so her eyes met mine.

"You know anything about any missing money from Big Bingo?"

Her mouth twisted. "Can't believe anyone would steal from school kids. No one I know. Maybe the money got lost. There were so many people. We all had to clean up—I lost my jacket. It was a real mess towards the end. There were all these napkins and papers. We put the money in those green envelops. Maybe someone threw them away by mistake. "

She looked longingly at the group of people on the top stoop. I loosened my grip on her arm and let her go.

Three O'clock sharp and here comes Alec Le Grand. I headed him off on the first step.

"Hi there Missy Emily. Glad to see you."

Alec shook my hand and glanced around. His small red bow-tie was tied neatly around his throat as usual and his small mustache carefully groomed.

He waved to the group on the top of the stoop and took a couple of steps closer to me.

"Shame! Shame! Some people have no shame. Put their needs ahead of anyone else. Bad times, Missy Emily. These are surely bad times for some." He pulled on the sides of his mustache. Then he put his hand in the pocket of his tweed jacket and extracted a wad of something, wrapped up in a racing form.

"Guess some of the money from Big Bingo got lost under your Racing Form and never made it to the bank. Could happen to anyone," I offered, holding out my hand.

Alec Le Grand squinted up his eyes and looked at me in a funny way. "What you sayin', Missy Emily? Alec Le Grand don't never lose anybody's money. They lose it their own selves on the ponies and poker. Now, Big Bingo? Roulette. Roulette is harder for a man to track but I real careful. A businessman like moi, always have to be real careful. "

He handed me the wrapped up bundle and extracted a small notebook from his breast pocket. Funny—it looked just like the one Murphy the Cop carried close to his heart.

"I got to keep track of my business. Write down everything. Got names, dates. Anyone want to know who put down what, when, I got it right here."

He moved closer and showed me the carefully ruled columns of numbers and names. On the bottom was an amount of money, circled in red.

"This here, now—this red circle. That the amount of green I put in the bank the day after we have Big Bingo."

I stared at the red circle. Inside the circle was the number $3041.

"I got me a receipt for it all, right here."

Damned if he didn't produce a yellow receipt out of another pocket as magically as Giancarlo could do it.

Now I was really confused. If Alec le Grand had deposited all the money he claims his booth made at Big Bingo, what was this bundle I was holding in my hand?

I started to unwrap it. Alec grabbed my hand. He tilted his head in the direction of the group on the top of the stairs.

"No need for everyone, know our business," he said. "Inside that Pony-sheet I give you is $2000. Yesterday my gray horse, everyone said can't run worth a dime, come in third and I hit the daily double big time. 'Tween you and me, some people round here need money so bad they steal from kids. I ain't pointin' no fingers at no one. But I think, hey, I'm a lucky dude. Don't got a family to support. Don't owe anyone anything. Hey—I give a little more to PS 96. That way, Missy Emily, you don't need be pointing fingers at our Executive Committee. Make some people look bad, feel bad. Some people just can't resist temptation. I figure, it's kind of like alcohol. You puts some bills in front of people, they can't help themselves. I thinks $2000 should cover any moneys happened to fall off the truck if you get my message."

Then he winked at me and walked quickly up the stairs. I opened my pocketbook and put the new bundle inside. Was he telling the truth? Maybe like Hawthorne, he wasn't telling the exact truth of how he got his hands on the money, but for sure he was telling the truth of the human heart. I could vouch for the pull of temptation. I patted my pocketbook and made sure the clasp was secure. I was feeling pretty good. I might not be able to finger the murderer or kidnapper but I had just recovered close to $3000 of charity money I didn't even know was missing.

I stood at the bottom of the stairs and stared upwards at the members of "The Executive Committee." A greedy-socialist Kindergarten teacher, an ambitious high school senior, a half-blind superintendent, a gentlemanly bookie, a Mafia errand-boy, a sneaky window-dresser and a jewelry-fence. My friends. Maybe Murphy and Larry had a point about the company I had been keeping, but the truth was I liked them all. Sure they had their failings—but so did I. And they had a strength I admired. A strength street-tested and iron-hard that made me believe they would stand by me when I needed them.

But what about me? Here I was, a turn-coat, doing a Cop's bidding, gathering a bunch of my friends into an informal line-up so that Murphy could send one or more of them to jail for a very long time. I have to admit I was on the verge of telling them all to go home. After all, the pretense for the meeting, to find out what had happened to some of the Big Bingo money had been already solved.

It was at that point that I heard the screech of a car behind me .Everyone on the top of the stairs became absolutely still. It was as if a film that had been running in real time had suddenly been frozen.And then a small, shrill voice called out," That's him, Daddy—the one in the Spider-Man tee shirt with the red sneakers!"

I turned around and saw the pale face of Patty, at the open window in the back of the squad car—her arm extended and her finger pointing at the group at the top of the stairs.

Then the two front doors opened simultaneously and Murphy and another cop burst out, guns drawn. Murphy bounded up the stairs much faster than I had ever imagined he could move—and he grabbed Giancarlo roughly by the shoulder. The others, as if in slow-motion moved a couple of steps away, surprise written clearly on all their faces.

And then Sammy ran over to his other side and yelled. "Leave him alone. Giancarlo hasn't done anything!"

Murphy pulled Giancarlo's arm out of her grip and fastened the handcuffs behind him. Then he grabbed Sammy by the arm and called down to Patty. "What about her? Was she the woman who held you?"

Patty hesitated.

At that moment, Beverly Bernstein moved over and grabbed Sammy's other arm. "What the hell do you think you are doing?" she yelled at Murphy. "This isn't a Police State. You can't just ride in here and arrest people!"

Murphy ignored her and yelled back down to Patty. "How about this one?" he pointed to Beverly. "Do you recognize her?"

Patty shook her head. "She was wearing a Pumpkin Head!" Patty yelled back.

My head was turning back and forth so fast I was getting dizzy. I felt I should be doing or saying something to someone. Whose side was I on, anyway? And then the group at the top of the stairs seemed to mobilize themselves. Harold stepped forward.

"Giancarlo. You have a right to a lawyer. He can't just drive by and arrest you. He hasn't even read you your rights!"

At that, Murphy began in a loud voice, "You have a right to remain Silent…."

Then Alec Le Grand approached him. "My man, we don't treat people like this here in my neighborhood. We got to sit down and talk man to man,' fore any one of my friends gets carted off to jail. What has he done? You ain't even mentioned what this man has done."

Murphy looked them over as if they were just turds in the street. I could feel his contempt all the way down to the bottom step. "I don't answer to you. I got a warrant in my pocket, says I can pick up this man. You don't like it, write a letter to City Hall. "

He glared at Beverly who stood with her hands on her hips blocking his way down the stairs. "As for you," he told her, "Mind your own business, or I'll take you downtown for obstructing an officer."

That was a mistake. Murphy had no idea who he was tangling with. Beverly was about to give the whole neighborhood a lesson in civil disobedience.

She folded her arms in front of her body. "Well isn't that just ducky! Maybe you have a police dog you want to set on me too—Giancarlo might not know his rights but I sure know mine!" She turned to her friends around her. "Anyone here see me obstructing an officer? I'm just asking for some information."

There were mumbles of approval from the group.

Alec Le Grand said, "Sure don't seem like anyone obstructing anything I can see."

Nancy grunted. 'Why don't you go home and watch the football game?"

And then Beverly noticed me, standing silently on the bottom step, trying to blend in with the cracked cement.

"And what have you got to say about all this?" Beverly challenged me.

I took a deep breath. It was time to choose sides. And I knew where I stood.

"Someone kidnapped Murphy's little girl. A little kid. Might have killed her if he had the chance. Maybe traumatized this little girl for life. Maybe now she'll be scared to go to sleep for the rest of her life. This Cop would not arrest Giancarlo if he didn't have enough evidence to hold him. This cop obeys the law."

Did I believe what I was saying? Only the first part, about Patty being traumatized, a word that most of the assembled group didn't understand. As for Murphy being a cop who obeyed the law—I thought it was a toss-up. I had never seen him do anything dishonest. Certainly he didn't seem very interested in money. On the other hand, those hands of his, always inching to squeeze the life out of someone. I believed he was capable of murder, in defense of his little girl. That Giancarlo might have an unfortunate accident on the way to the station was a possibility. I consoled myself with the knowledge that there was another cop in that car. And there were lots of witnesses to the fact that Giancarlo put up no resistance whatsoever. And the fact was, Patty did identify him. By his red sneakers. How dumb can you be?

I don't know how I became the spokesperson for the group—but after my little speech, everyone seemed to settle down. Even Beverly backed off and let Murphy lead Giancarlo to the squad car. Murphy shoved Giancarlo onto the front seat, next to his partner. Then he lifted Patty out of the car and stood at the curb with his back to the rest of us.

The car's siren blared and it pulled away.

Within a few seconds a black station wagon pulled up. There was a woman at the wheel. Murphy and Patty got in.

I waved to them both. Nobody waved back.

FOURTEEN

A narrow, low heel, called "the kitten heel" was made popular by Audrey Hepburn.

"Tell your friend Murphy he's barking up the wrong tree, arresting that kid." My estranged husband Larry, the Loser instructed me, over the phone the next day. "This Giancarlo cat isn't the brightest bulb in the chandelier."

It annoyed me that he mixed metaphors up in that manner. Everything he did managed to irritate me. It was too bad I found he came in handy once in a while.

"So I suppose you've climbed that tree and looked into the window of the Precinct where they booked the kid."

I can never figure out how he knows so much about what is not his business. "I got a friend downtown."

"Yeah. Come to think of it, one of those women cops has big breasts. Just your type."

I heard the creak of his desk chair—never did get it fixed, the lazy bastard. "I'm not even going to honor that comment with a reply," he said to me. "I've called you up to do you a favor, not to be insulted."

Touché. Sometimes, although it is against my better judgment, I have to concede that he might have a point. "Okay. Hit me," I said.

"This Giancarlo kid is hardly Mafia. His father had some low-level position and went to jail for a couple of years for one of the big guys. In return, they occasionally use this kid to deliver messages from time to time. Messages—they don't trust him with 'merchandise.' Also, it's not Mafia style to kidnap kids. If—and that is a big if—this Giancarlo kid did take Murphy's little girl—it was some hair-brained idea of his own, or he was taking orders from someone else. I'd focus on this Bellini guy. He looks too good. No criminal record—but there's something fishy about him. According to Immigration, he came to America from Milan about ten years ago. But here's no record of any Bellini of his age living in Milan. Lived with his father here in the Bronx. They bought a small apartment building. Lived off the rents. But I checked immigration. There's no record of his father coming with him. No record of his father anywhere. Father died a couple of years ago."

I tapped my pencil on the pad next to the phone. Much of this I already knew—but the phony name. That was interesting. And that the father was probably already here, long before the son arrived. Seemed to confirm the idea of a desperate war-criminal, escaping to the U.S. and living all those years alone, under who knows what name.

"And, I checked into that Galina woman you told me about. Just to make sure The Russian Mafia wasn't involved. Those guys would kidnap a kid."

"Really! They are that bad! I t does my heart good to hear you concede something negative about your Russian friends." I couldn't stop myself. Every time the subject of Russians came up, I saw red.

"Yeah. Yeah. Your feelings about Russians are very well known to me. I try not to let them color my investigative skills. This Galina is a so-called model. Turns tricks on the side. Has some Russian pimp she runs around with. Nobody of any significance. They're in business for themselves. She might have something to do with laundering money for someone—or maybe she just found the jewels accidently, like that school teacher you told me about. Beverly Bernheart or whatever her name is. And that Tanya Solowitz? The one who's been bothering Shana? She's a cousin of this Galina. Could be how Galina started shopping at Emily's Place. Shana probably recommended you highly. Tanya must have thought you'd be as dumb as your sister. I'd threaten both of them with The Big I"

Frighten her! What a good idea! All we had to do was remember which letter would do the job.

"And, by the way, I had that mink cleaned up for you. Sent it to Saks for a "glazing" whatever that is. Want to have dinner next Friday?"

His pound of flesh. I can't say this comes as a surprise. "Sure," I told him. "Just give me a ring about the time and place."

I hung up the phone and looked down at my shoes. Red leather pumps. Ferragamo. I had been inspired by Giancarlo's red sneakers.

I hadn't been satisfied with the story Galina told me about selling the shoes to that guy in the Flea market. She only would have made a few dollars on the deal. I didn't think she was that hard-up. Putting pressure on her to scare off Shana's patient gave me a good excuse for a return visit.

"I don't understand," Galina clasped her hands together as if in prayer. Praying we would leave immediately was my guess. "I have no shoes. I have no jewels. This is big mistake."

She looked at Vladimir with round, frightened eyes.

For the first time in recent memory, my sister Shana seemed to have found some boyfriend who can do something right. Of course, he may also do a great deal wrong, which I strongly suspect, but I was not interested in that part of his personality for the moment.

He was Russian. He could speak Russian. And he was big and tall. These things could be very useful in our present situation which was somehow to scare Gallina into calling off her cousin Tanya who was threatening Shana with a law suit. And just in case she knew more than she let on about the shoes, we'd scare her into coming clean.

It had taken us a couple of hours of discussion to figure out how to dress Vladimir up in what we all thought was Russian-

Mafia high style. This was a problem because we all had a different opinion as to what this exactly was.

Tee shirt and jeans? Leisure style stretch pants and jacket? Double-breasted suit jacket over jeans? Wind-breaker over white shirt and fancy shoes?

Vladimir himself finally prevailed. He would 'borrow' a flashy suit from a 'relative' in the 'business.' Said relative also happened to have an expensive pair of cowboy boots, which, Vladimir swore to us, was an essential part of any Russian Mafia attire for anyone of real standing in the community. This outfit we could 'rent' for a very small fee of only $50.00 because we were friends.

So, okay. $50.00 was much too much to pay. For people who were not friends the fee would probably be little or nothing, but I had signed on for a confrontation with Galina and I wasn't going to let $50.00 stand in my way. Shana herself dressed in orange, which she claimed was the color best suited for attracting good karma, which, she assured me, we would need if we expected anything positive to occur. As for moi, I wore a black suit with my red pumps, to show that I, at least, was a legitimate business woman and representative of the American Establishment.

Galina's first mistake was to buzz us in. I had called to tell her I was bringing a friend who might be interested in buying one of her furs. This was not exactly a lie. Our visit had actually started in a very friendly manner. Galina had served us all tea and then marched out wearing a gorgeous, red fox coat. Shana nearly dropped her tea cup when she saw it.

"I love it!" she gushed.

Surprise! My baby sister, the Buddhist who wouldn't kill a cockroach, had fallen in love with a fur coat! How was this possible?

Vladimir's eyes opened wide.

Hello. This was clearly better quality stuff than he usually encountered. He crossed his legs and wiped a bit of dust off his alligator boots. He let out a stream of Russian that could have meant anything but seemed to please Galina. It was entirely possible he had asked for a cut of anything she made on the sale. Meanwhile, little sister had latched on to Galina's arm and was petting the coat as if it were her pet cat

I thought it was a good time for me to remind my colleagues that furs were not the real focus of our visit. "That coat is truly beautiful," I commented, "but we have more important matters to discuss first."

Shana looked just as disappointed as Galina at my little speech.

I motioned for them to sit down and I took the floor. "You remember I came here looking for a pair of shoes."

Galina nodded. "I tell you. I don't have shoes. I sell them to my friend at the flea market."

"I know. I bought them back at the flea market. But there is a problem."

Galina looked from me to Vladimir and back again. Vladimir scowled and uncrossed his legs. "Those shoes had diamonds hidden in the heels. And now they don't.!"

Galina jumped up from the couch.

"Diamonds! What you say diamonds! There was no diamonds. Only gold rings. I swear. I find only gold rings!"

Vladimir rose and walked over to her, letting loose a barrage of Russian than made her cringe and retreat quickly back to the chair.

I hugged myself and tried to bite my lip to keep still. This was even better than I could have hoped. Now Shana seemed to wake up. She walked over to Galina and shook her finger in her face.

"Shame on you!" she said. "You steal from Russian Mafia! You are in big trouble now."

That was when Galina folded her hands in the praying position.

"I know nothing!" She shook her head back and forth. "I buy the shoes at Emily's Place. I know nothing. I buy any kind of shoe I like. Shoe is good price. I buy it to wear. Then something feel funny. I shake the shoe and it make noise. Shoe doesn't make noise. I take off heel. Inside gold rings!"

I scowled at her. "Those gold rings belong to me. They belong to Vladimir. They do not belong to you."

Vladimir grabbed her shoulder and shook her. Then he let loose with another stream of Russian.

At that point Galina started to cry. Shana and I exchanged glances. It was difficult dealing with someone you really didn't trust who was speaking a language you didn't understand.

Shana put a restraining arm on Vladimir.

"I believe you," She said to Galina "but now you have to make it good."

Galina twisted her hands again. Then she addressed Vladimir in Russian.

"She says she will sell you the coat at half price. Only $1500."

Shana waved her hand. "Ridiculous. Tell her I'll give her $300 and save her from the Russian Mafia."

This was too much to bear. I stood up. Someone in this family had to have some principles.

Also, I wondered, where would Shana get an extra $300 she didn't need? Last time we spoke she hit me for her rent money.

Come to think of it, neither Vladimir nor Shana seemed the least surprised to learn that the shoes I was trying to recover had a treasure in the heels.

I took a deep breath. "We didn't come here to buy a fur coat. We want the jewels. You say you found gold rings. Bring them to me now."

Gallina chewed on a strand of her hair. "If you don't want fur, I have also camera and computer. Very good. From Israel. "

Vladimir followed this speech with one of his own rants in Russian. I could only hope he was not trying to cut his own deal. Galina rushed into one of her back rooms, as if she had just been sprung from jail. I wondered if she was actually going to climb out a back window but I figured we were up too high. A few minutes later she emerged with a cigar-box. She handed the box to Vladimir and sat back down on the sofa, her yellow hair now limp and disheveled.

I couldn't help feeling a little sorry for her.

Vladimir opened the box and took out a handful of gold rings. Then he handed the box to me. I glanced inside and then shut the box quickly. I felt a chill go through my body. It was one thing to read about Fascists, Nazis and Jews murdered in the Holocaust. It was another thing to hold in your hands the rings these poor murdered victims once wore.

There was no doubt now that there was a WWII connection, and Bellini was our man.

I put the cigar box into my large purse and looked sternly at Galina.

"There's one more thing. Do you know a woman named Tanya Solowitz?"

Galina looked from me to Vladimir. She was clearly deciding whether or not it was worthwhile to lie.

Shana moved closer to her. "This Tanya Solowitz? She's your cousin. She told you to go to Emily's Place for the best shoes in town, right?"

"Yes. I go for shoes. I know nothing about jewels. I sell furs. Tanya—Tanya sells paintings. She have a friend, makes paintings. She say Picasso, Matisse make them. She sell them, make big money."

Vladimir let loose his Russian invective again. I didn't know what he said but I knew it was powerful.

Shana put up her hand. "We don't like Tanya. You tell Tanya if she bothers Shana Levine, ever again, she will be cut up in little pieces and thrown into the Atlantic Ocean."

Vladimir nodded vigorously.

"Tell her, Ivan—The Big I—has ordered that this be done—unless she obeys immediately." I added.

I paused for a moment, but I was having too much fun to stop,

"Not to mention that what is left of her will be turned into the police and she will spend the rest of her life in jail."

Galina wrung her hands and nodded.

It was time to take our leave. We had received more than what we had come for.

Bellini shook his head and ground out his cigarette. "You are mistaken. You are all mistaken. The Italian government was mistaken. It was for this reason I came to America."

Murphy sat on a large, elaborately carved wooden chair that looked very uncomfortable. Very Italian Renaissance—or a good reproduction. The cushions of my own chair gave out a cloud of dust when I sat down, but it was comfortable enough. A big, overstuffed, Queen Anne's chair with the carving on the legs, not the back.

After my visit to Galina, and my repossession of the gold rings inside the shoe, I called Murphy to report developments. I told him again I didn't think the real criminal was Giancarlo, even if he did carry out some feeble kidnapping that even an eight-year-old could escape from. These gold rings proved some WWII criminal activity and Bellini was our man. But, of course Murphy, being a man who liked to think he was always right, could not give me the satisfaction of agreeing.

"Goin' to crucify that Bastard, put his hands on my baby girl. Tear his balls off, and don't tell me anything different."

He was truly like a dog with a bone. He just wasn't going to let it go.

"But what about the gold rings? They are old and worn. Many of them have initials. I even saw an inscription. That's got to be jewelry stripped from people those Fascists sent to the gas chambers!"

When I finally got up enough courage to open the cigar box and take a close look—I saw more than I had ever wanted to see. Rings with beautiful gothic engraved initials, intertwined. Hebrew lettering I couldn't understand, a heart with an arrow through it. Some were large and ornate; some were small and narrow. I could close my eyes and picture them all—shadows on the way to eternity.

But to Murphy, they were simply evidence. "Try to restrain yourself from messing up all the evidence—like handling it and trying on the rings. There could be some residual DNA. At least we could try to trace that Russian gal's prints."

Oops! I guess I did it again. I was beginning to think Murphy knew me as well as I was getting to know him.

"Want to come over and pick it up?" I offered.

He thought for a minute and then told me he'd pick it up later. It wasn't a bad idea, he conceded, to confront Bellini with this new evidence. He told me to bring the cigar box and he'd meet me at Bellini's apartment on Arthur Avenue.

Bellini paced the floor in front of us.

"An old, sick lady thinks I look like some Fascist she unfortunately encountered in her past. This is not evidence of anything. I simply came into a shoe store looking for a gift for my girlfriend."

Murphy sniffed and lit his own cigarette. "You don't seem to have a girlfriend," Murphy countered.

Bellini lit another cigarette and took a long drag. "This is somewhat embarrassing," he looked from me to Murphy and then back again. "but I have to admit that I sometimes like to dress-up in lady's shoes."

I shook my head. "Not in size 7's you don't."

Bellini sat down on the sofa and put down his cigarette. He held his head in his hands.

Murphy got up and walked over to him. "You asked for the exact size and style that concealed diamonds, rings stripped by Jews being deported to death camps, and assorted other precious stones. I don't believe that was a coincidence. We also have reason to believe that your father entered this country illegally, was named a war criminal by the Italian government, and was the notorious, Fotinni Fatale."

Murphy took out a photo from his breast pocket and threw it down on the coffee table in front of Bellini. Then he motioned for me to give him the cigar box. He put it down on the coffee table next to the photo. Bellini picked up the photo and looked at it silently. Then he kissed it and put it back down on the coffee table. He stared at the box for a minute and then he opened the lid.

I must say his reaction was very close to my own when I had first seen the rings. He gasped and closed the box quickly. "Where did you get this?"

"They were hidden in another pair of size 7 shoes, same style, bought by a Russian girl, named Galina Kaplankaya who lives in Brooklyn. A friend of yours?"

Bellini shook his head. "There were five pair of shoes, with jewels inside. I knew they were specially marked but I couldn't find the mark. I had to track down all the shoes that came to New York."

Murphy took out a pair of handcuffs. "I think we should continue this conversation downtown."

Bellini's eyes opened wide. "No! No!, You don't understand!" He tried to rise from the couch but Murphy pushed him back.

"I'm here to arrest you for the murder of Sophia Sarfatti, Freddie Baldino, known locally as Freddie-the-Fox, and the kidnapping of Patricia Murphy. You have a right to remain silent…"

Bellini kept shaking his head. "Listen to me! I only ask for you to listen to me!"

"I'll listen," I said.

Murphy gave me a nasty look but backed off and stood in front of the door in case Bellini decided to make a run for it.

Bellini took a deep breath. He took a drag on his cigarette and blew the smoke slowly out through his nose.

"That photo is a picture of the man they called "Fotinni Fatale," the man the Italian government said was guilty of war crimes and that man was my father." He crossed himself. "But he was not a war criminal. The war criminal is the man you and your friends call 'The Senator.' I have been trying to set the story straight my entire life. That is the reason I finally came to America ten years ago. I thought once I was here, it would be easy." He took another drag on his cigarette. "It has not been easy. It has only been recently—in the last few weeks, when I finally was able to come close…close to clearing my father's name."

He settled back against the cushions of the sofa. "Picture this is you can—you American woman and you American policeman who I fear could never really picture this. Two young policeman train together in the city of Milan in the 1940's. One of them is not Jewish. He is very ambitious and worships Mussolini. The other one is only half-Jewish, on his mother's side. His name is pure Italian. One night these two policeman drink too much wine together, and my father, half-Jewish on his mother's side, tells his secret to his 'friend.' Two weeks later, my father is promoted to Chief of Police for the city of Milan. The next morning, this man, the one you call 'the Senator,' tells my father he has a plan to make them rich. My father is to offer rich Jews a way out of the labor lamps. All they have to do is pay a fee—in diamonds or other jewelry, never in cash. They would later divide the money. The Jews would be gone, one way or another, and they would both prosper.

My father was appalled by this. He was an honest man, a compassionate man. Also, he was part Jewish. Under Jewish law, if your mother is Jewish, you are fully Jewish. Under Italian law, it depended on who was enforcing what, and when. Mussolini liked the Jews. He had a Jewish mistress and many of the rich Jews thought he was a much better choice than the communists. But the Italians never took orders well from anyone. If they knew you and liked you, they left you alone. If you were a problem, they could find some reason to lock you up.

My father said "no," to the plans of this other policeman. But the policeman would not take no as an answer. He threatened to tell others in Mussolini's gang that my father was really Jewish if he didn't cooperate."

Bellini looked again from me to Murphy and back again. He tapped the top of the cigar box. "My father began to ask the

Jews who came before him for money to ensure their escape. He gave all the money to the other policeman. He tried his best to honor the agreement. He helped many Jews escape to Switzerland, obtain forged papers and get passage to the U.S. It became more and more difficult to get people out. But the other policeman demanded his blood money. My father tried to honor his promise but sometimes it didn't work out. The Jews were transported despite his efforts. At the end of the war, he was known as Fotinni Fatale. And the other policeman? He became The Senator."

Was Bellini telling the truth? It was hard to tell.

"But your father sneaked into this country illegally. If he was innocent, why didn't he give himself up and stand trial. He could have told his story to the World Court."

Bellini covered his face with his hands once again. When he lifted his face, he turned to me. "Yes. This was probably his fatal mistake. He was afraid. He had some letters from Jews he had helped, but his name was on so many deportation documents. How could he make them understand? Right after the war everyone was out for blood. He had a wife, a baby—me. How could any of them bear the shame of a trial? And a possible death sentence at the end of it? He couldn't take the chance. He got hold of some forged papers and he sneaked into the U.S. He left me and my mother in the care of old friends who knew the true story. We didn't know what had happened to the other policeman until a couple of years ago. We found out he had left Italy shortly after the war and immigrated to the U.S."

I looked at Murphy and he looked at me. His eye-brow twitched, a sign that he really didn't buy it.

"How did 'the senator' get the jewels out of Italy if he was living here since the 1940's?" I asked him.

"The Senator had made several tries to get the money out of Italy. My friends and I had tracked these jewels for years. He had friends in the police department who covered for him, friends who hid the jewels for years until they thought everyone had lost interest. Once they tried to send them sewn in the linings of raincoats, shipped from a manufacturer in Italy, but my family has ties to the fashion industry in Italy and we tipped off the police. They recovered some jewels but never traced them further, back to the man behind it all. This time The Senator made contact with the son of an old friend who had a small shoe manufacturing company. He thought it was the perfect cover. He had made enough friends on this side of the Atlantic that he thought he could get away with it. They set up some store-front a few blocks from here to receive shipments. I've had my eye on that place. But something went wrong and they only got two or three pair, and none of them had any jewels hidden in the shoes."

Now it began to make sense to me. Murphy drew closer. "But how did you get to Emily's Place?"

Bellini smiled at me. "I figured the missing shoes must have been shipped to another store. Emily's Place is famous. Whenever I asked anyone I knew where I could buy a good pair of lady's shoes, everyone said, go to 'Emily's Place.'" Was this guy buttering me up or what? I wanted to believe he was telling the truth. He was a hell-of-a-lot more attractive in every way than The Senator.

"So far, so good, "I told him, "but just a few hours after poor Sophia Sarfatti saw you, and you learned she had bought the shoes you were interest in, she was found dead."

"Proverina!"Bellini met my gaze without flinching. "That must have been a coincidence." He threw up his hands. "What would I gain by murdering Signore Sarfatti? I knew she no longer had the shoes. You had them. But The Senator? He didn't know this."

I suddenly remembered what SuperMama had said about The Senator catching Sophia, as she was about to fall down the stairs of the front stoop—Sophia had blamed the shoes! He would have recognized them as soon as she said it! He would have thought for sure he'd find them in her apartment!

Bellini took a final drag on his cigarette and put it out. Murphy sat down on the couch next to him. He took the handcuffs out of his pocket.

"Wait!" I called out. "I think he is telling the truth!"

Murphy glared at me. "Sounds like it might be true," he said. "I don't make those kinds of decisions. I'm only a dumb policeman, got to bring in enough suspects so a judge and jury can figure it out."

He reached over and pulled Bellini's hands together. Then he snapped on the handcuffs.

He put his hand on Bellini's shoulder. "We may not be the World Court," he said, "But we can tell lies from the truth….if you give us a little help. Right now we don't have anything to connect The Senator to any of this."

He put his arm under Bellini's elbow and helped him to rise from the couch. Then he went to the hall closet and took out an overcoat. He threw the overcoat over the handcuffs so no one could see them. Then he took Bellini's arm and led us both out the door and down the steps.

When I got home that night, I couldn't sleep. The story Bellini told was so creepy, it had to be true. Every time I closed my eyes I pictured all those Jews, tall ones, short ones, skinny ones, fat ones, walking slowly towards me like the Zombies from The Night of the Living Dead. When they got close enough, they took off their gold rings from their stiff, bony fingers and dropped them one by one into a big, copper bowl that sat on top of my desk. I could actually hear the little 'bing!'sound each one made when they hit bottom.

I saw little children too, clinging to the dank rags of their dead parents. I saw the little sister of poor Sophia Sarfatti holding fast to the arm of her mother.

That was when I sat up in bed. Sophia Sarfatti's sister wasn't clinging to her mother's arm in the photo I had been given. The photo that rested in that safety deposit box Sammy had given to me. The photo showed two little girls holding on to each other.

It was the story I was remembering. The story Sophia had told Sammy who had told me. That her sister had grabbed hold of a button from the uniform of the policeman who was putting them on the train to the death camps. She had pulled that button off the uniform of that policeman right before he shot her dead.

I got up quickly from the bed and turned on the light. Then I went into the kitchen and opened the freezer door where I had stashed the safety deposit box.

I took the box out and sat down at the kitchen table and opened it. There before me was the photo I had seen so clearly in my mind's eye.

And there in front of me was the brass button with a crest engraved upon it, the button Sophia's sister had torn off the policeman's uniform. I picked it up and ran my finger over the crest.

Now I remembered why The Senator's cuff-links had looked so familiar to me.

They were an exact reproduction of this button.

When I told Murphy what I had discovered, he responded with a mixture of amazement and annoyance. "I can't believe you were withholding evidence from me," he said to me, cradling the brass button his big hands.

"I didn't know it was evidence. You and your boys haven't yet concluded that Sophia's death was murder, even though there was enough Coumadin in her tea canister to kill a cow. How am I supposed to think of something as 'evidence' when there may not have even been a crime committed? We were sitting on the island in the middle of Broadway, and Murphy threw a lighted cigarette into the traffic.

'That's why you sell shoes and I catch criminals. I know what evidence is long before there is a crime. I know what evidence is even before the criminal is thinking of his crime. I know what evidence is when there is a chance, in the future, that some crime will be committed."

What could I possibly say in answer that would not be a curse word? And so I said nothing. Instead I looked at his shoes. "You need a shine," I told him. "I can give you some free samples of a great new polish you might like."

He extended his leg and stared at his shoe. “I’m not allowed to accept gifts.”

I sighed. “Well, now that you have your ‘evidence’ I guess we can agree that Bellini was telling the truth and that the real criminal, both in Milan in 1940 and on Broadway in 2015 is The Senator.”

Murphy nodded. “Looks like we have some reason to suspect that’s true. It’s a start.”

A start and a finish as far as I was concerned, but I knew better than to try to overpower Murphy with reason. There was still an obstacle we had to clear up. Giancarlo.

“So, what do you think we should do about Giancarlo?” I asked him.

“Giancarlo? What about Giancarlo. He’s locked up where he belongs. Filthy Bastard! He’ll be lucky if he isn’t murdered in the holding cell.”

This was really more than I could bear. I jumped up from the bench. “Now you listen to me,” I said to him, “I’ve had enough of this Police Brutality business. If you have a problem controlling your violent nature, you should go into therapy. I’m not going to stand by and watch you or your crazy Right Wing companions beat up that boy. That boy didn’t do much more than entertain your kid with a mask and a few magic tricks. He never laid a finger on her.”

Murphy scowled and looked over the traffic. “In case you haven’t noticed, kidnapping is a felony.”

Here we go again. Murphy has never met a felony he didn’t love.

“If you don’t give that boy a chance to explain himself—without intimidation—I will file a suit against you for taking advantage of a person with limited intelligence!”

“He passed the IQ test. He’s perfectly normal.”

I pulled Murphy up from the bench and led him to the edge of the island. “Where’s your car?” I asked him.

He pointed to the hydrant in front of Emily's Place. One of his favorite parking spots.

"We are going to take a little ride down to the holding cell where Giancarlo is currently being mistreated," I informed him, "or else I am going to photograph your cop car and send the picture to the Daily News."

I'm not sure if he was just too tired to argue with me, or he really conceded in his own way that I had a point about Giancarlo. Whatever it was, we drove down Broadway and arrived at the holding cell very soon after.

"Are you okay?" I asked Giancarlo, when he finally lifted up his head. Kidnapper and thief he might be, but all I saw was a scared young man who hadn't had much sleep.

"I didn't hurt nobody. I swear, I never hurt nobody." It looked to me as if his lip was swollen but it could have been the light.

Murphy took a key out of his pocket and unlocked the handcuffs. Giancarlo pulled his arms in front of him and massaged his wrists.

"Did they make you wear that all night?" I asked him.

Murphy stood up in front of me, "I'm asking the questions here," he said, "Why did you kidnap my little girl?"

Giancarlo squinted up at us. "The Senator. He killed my friend Freddie. He told me he would blow my head off and stuff it down the toilet if I didn't get back those diamonds. He wanted all the jewels but the diamonds were the most important."

"Who put the diamonds in the shoes," Murphy asked him.

Giancarlo shrugged. "I don't know nothing about any diamonds. Me and Freddie, we do some odd jobs for The Senator. He tells us he has a friend, has a shoe company in Italy. Looking for someone to be their "International Agent." Freddie, he jumps at the idea. The Senator tell him he'll set him up all nice in an office and everything. All he have to do is sign some papers, supervise some shoes coming in from the airport. So Freddie ask me if I want to help. Sure, I tell him."

Giancarlo rubbed his wrist. "So we get some shoes, send them up to this store in the Bronx, nothing like Miss Emily's Place, just some hole in the wall place. Doesn't even have a name. But then Freddie, he say to me, 'what if a few of these shoes fall off the truck? The Senator, he don't need any money. He's an old guy. What difference would it make if a few pair of shoes don't go to that place in the Bronx. Maybe instead they go to Emily's Place. We like Emily, right?" Giancarlo looked at me and smiled. Yes—for sure his lip was swollen. "So yeah, we do something wrong. We take maybe ten boxes of shoes from the truck. Freddie-the-Fox sells them to Emily here. We don't know nothing about any diamonds until The Senator, he fly into a rage. He come over to my apartment and he start yelling "Where are my shoes! Who took my shoes! So me and Freddie we tell him, "it's ok. We sell a few to Miss Emily. She pay better than the man in the Bronx. We'll give you the money!"

But he don't care about that. Then he tell us there were diamonds in those shoes. Rubies, Emeralds, gold. We got to get them back. So me and Freddie, we break into Emily's Place and I hack into her computer. I see a bunch of names, people bought those shoes. The one on the top of the list is Sophia Sarfatti. We give that list to the Senator. Next thing I know, Sophia Sarfatti, she dead. Freddie the fox, he's dead. The Senator calls me. He says I got to get all those shoes back or he going to kill me." Giancarlo looked from me to Murphy and back again. "Geeze. Can I have a glass of water?"

Murphy nodded and yelled something to someone standing outside the room.

"So I get this idea. I'll take that little girl."

Giancarlo paused and looked up at Murphy. "Not really 'take' her. I'm going to 'borrow her', just overnight. Like a sleep-over. I even got her a doll. It would be like a game. I would do magic tricks. I think she won't be scared. And then I could get those diamonds back."

The water came and Giancarlo finished the glass in one gulp. I glared at Murphy.

"So I take this kid—real cute. But she starts to cry. Wants her daddy. I feel bad. I want to let her go, so I tell her I'm going out to get her a hamburger, and she should be a good girl and just sit on the couch and wait for me until I get back." He smiled up at me. "I figure no kid is going to do what a grown-up says. I leave the door unlocked. Sure enough, when I get back, she's gone!"

Murphy banged his fist down on the table. The glass fell to the floor and splattered glass is all directions.

"So you just let a kid, eight years old, out on the street, middle of the night? That was okay with you? "

Giancarlo looked down at the table. "She's just a little kid. People on the street will help a little kid."

I moved in front of Murphy. "There was someone else with you. A woman. A woman who picked up Patti from school."

Giancarlo looked down at the table and said nothing. "Naw" he said at last, "It was me. I got dressed up like a girl."

I wasn't buying that one. "I don't think so. The school would never have handed Patti over to a transvestite."

Giancarlo looked up at the ceiling. He was thinking hard. "I had a friend." He said at last. "She knows more about kids than me. She brought her a doll."

"Name?" Murphy barked out

Giancarlo laughed. 'I don't know no doll's name."

"Don't be cute," Murphy said, "the name of your friend is what I want."

Giancarlo took a deep breath. "I call her SoSo."

"So…So…What?"

"What?" Giancarlo asked, "So What?"

I tried to push Murphy aside. He was planted like a stone wall in front of Giancarlo.

"What's your friend's last name?" I asked him.

He shrugged. "I don't know. Always just called her SoSo."

Giancarlo looked out over the table at us. "SoSo and me, we know The Senator our whole lives. He is a scary guy. We once went to his house and he was all dressed up in some kind of old uniform. He had boots and a gun and everything. He killed Freddie. I know he will kill me, I don't get back those shoes. I tried to get the shoes back from some of the other customers but it was too hard. I tried to find your sister Shana but I took the wrong train. Brooklyn, man. Brooklyn is like another country. There was someone else lived in Brooklyn, some Russian but I figured that was hopeless. You can't steal nothing from a Russian. I even broke into Beverly Bernstein's house even though she is my friend, but there was nothing in her shoes." He shook his head back and forth. "Man—do you think I can get something to eat?"

I knew I had good reason not to like cops. Nothing much had changed since they set the dogs on innocent people protesting the Vietnam War in the 1970's.

Murphy put his hand on Giancarlo's shoulder. "Soon," he said. Murphy wouldn't even look in my direction—he was so ashamed. "Kidnapping is a serious crime, but if you work with us, maybe we can reduce the charges."

He walked me to the door of the cell.

"Ask the guard to come in, please," he said to me.

"This doll, Giancarlo talked about, what happened to it?"

"My girl Patti—she won't give it up. Sleeps with it every night. Don't know what is going on with her. "

"You told me it was 'a piece of shit.' Don't throw it away," I warned him. "It's evidence."

He gave me a nasty look and half pushed me out the door.

As I was leaving the holding area, I heard Murphy say, "So what kind of sandwich would you like?"

FIFTEEN

The corset-like lacing as well as "toe cleavage" in women's shoes emphasizes their erotic appeal.

Sammy clung to my arm. "How is Gianni? They didn't hurt him, did they? That big policeman—Murphy—He was real mad! But I know Gianni didn't hurt his kid. He wouldn't never hurt anybody!"

I looked over at SuperMama, sitting in her usual position on the top step of her brownstone.

"How about you? SoSo," I said to Sammy, "would you hurt anyone?"

SuperMama turned her big head. "I ain't never heard no person call Sammy that name 'cept Giancarlo when he a little kid."

I figured that was it. Giancarlo was not as dumb as he pretended to be. Child-like in some ways, but not dumb.

Sammy smiled. "Giancarlo and me. We've been friends ever since we were little kids. But he couldn't say "Samantha." So when he was little, he just called me "SoSo." Course when we grow up, he call me Sammy like the rest of them—cept sometimes, when he really upset 'bout something. Then he still call me SoSo like when we were kids."

I sat down next to SuperMama and pulled Sammy down next to me. "Well, I'd say he was pretty stressed out right now. Whatever made you think you could get away with kidnapping Murphy's little girl? Giancarlo, I can understand. He can be a little 'slow' about some things. But you? You must know that kidnapping is a serious crime."

SuperMama moved her big legs up and down. She shook her head from side to side.

"What you sayin, Missy Emily? My girl don't kidnap nobody! My girl never done anyone wrong!"

I put my hand on her shoulder. "Your girl sure do someone wrong now. Giancarlo, to name one. He's protecting her. Won't tell the police who was the woman who picked up Patti from school. Don't know how long we can keep this a secret. And, Giancarlo can go to jail for a long time. Sammy too if Murphy finds out she helped."

"But we never hurt the kid. We told her it was a game. A sleep-over. I even gave her a doll. Same doll Sophia Sarfatti gave me when I was a kid. I thought she would like it. And she did. Hugged it to her right off. When we see she scared, we let her go. Nothin' happen bad to that kid." Sammy took hold of my shirt. "Listen. That crazy guy—The Senator—he going to kill Giancarlo. He already kill Freddy. Isn't anyone can stop him. Giancarlo better off in jail than out on the street where that crazy guy will get him!"

What I really didn't understand about all this was why everyone was so afraid of The Senator. "We can stop The Senator. I've already got some evidence. Those gold cufflinks he wears—I think they are an exact duplicate of that brass button you gave me in Sophia Sarfatti's box. I think we can prove he's wanted for War Crimes in WWII. All we need is for you and Giancarlo to testify that he threatened you, to tell the cops about sending the diamonds through those shoes shipped from Italy. Don't you see? We've got him now!"

SuperMama took my arm and stared into my face. "That man. He, the Angel of Death. Ain't no person goin' to put him away. He comin' back for all of us we sittin' here!" She sat back and stared up at the sky. "Lordy, lordy. He comin' to get us all."

I stood up. "Nonsense! He's just an old man and we've got him now. He probably put Coumadin in Sophia Sarfatti's tea and murdered her. He's been killing people for years—you said it yourself. "

I bent over them. “There’s a poem by a 16th Century poet, name of John Donne, that says “Death, Thou Shalt Die.” The idea is that if we all stick together, and remember each other, we can defeat death. All we got to do is stick together and love each other. Death can’t kill love. If Donne could write about that in the 16th Century when everyone around him was dying of the Bubonic Plague, we can do it now.”

I hoped the Goddess of Poetry would forgive me for translating John Donne in a somewhat free manner for a contemporary audience. SuperMama put a heavy hand on my arm and slowly rose to her feet. She pulled Sammy up beside her.

“We got to do it girl,” she said to Sammy. “This dude, name of Donne, done show us the way!”

My next task was to get Murphy to cooperate. In other words, I had to yank that bone out of his jaws. “Here’s the thing,” I told him over the phone. “Sure, Giancarlo broke the law. Yes, he kidnapped Patti but he didn’t murder anyone. You have an opportunity here to make a real splash. Show up those Feds you are always complaining about. You can bring an international war criminal to justice. Plus, you can solve the murder of Freddie-the-fox and Sophia Sarfatti. But in order to do it, you’ve got to let Giancarlo out. We need him to help get the goods on The Senator.”

I waited while Murphy mulled this over.

“First off,” he said to me. “What is this ‘we’ you keep bringing up? I’m the cop, remember? You sell shoes. “

I bit my lip but remained silent.

Murphy continued. “Okay. I can bring in The Senator. What has that got to do with Giancarlo? And his mysterious friend SoSo? Kidnapping is still a felony. The way I see it, I get them all.”

I shook the phone. Why doesn’t he get it? “Life is more than a numbers game. Do you get a commission for the number of people you put behind bars? I certainly hope not. It’s not the number of criminals you catch who are important, it’s the importance of each criminal. If you make some kind of deal with

Giancarlo, in return for his help—forget about 'his friend' it's not worth it—he can help make the case against The Senator much stronger."

I heard Murphy taping his pen against his little pad. "I want This Senator guy's fingerprints. I want his DNA. I want to get him for Sophia Sarfatti's murder too."

"Now you're talking," I told him. "We'll get Giancarlo to set him up. I have an idea."

Was that a groan on the other side of the line?

"Remember your Hamlet?" I asked him.

"Holy, Mary, Mother of God, here we go again. I remember it better than The Merchant of Venice, mutilated by your friend, the kindergarten teacher."

"Funny you should mention her," I countered, "because I'm counting on her to help us out. Patti too."

Now he was really listening!

"Remember how Hamlet proves that the King killed his father?"

"That's an easy one. 'The play's the thing, to catch the conscience of the King!'"

"Right you are. Beverly Bernstein puts on a new play—just for Patti's Birthday. Special adaptation of Hamlet and Patti is one of the puppeteers."

Was that actually chuckling that I heard on the other side of the line? "You've done it now, me girl. You've got a deal!"

That actually, turned out to be the easy part. The next step was to convince Beverly Bernstein to do all the work necessary to create a whole new set of puppets. Not Martians this time but Jews, with yellow stars on their arms, an old lady who dies in her bedroom, and an unfortunate young man who is shot while sitting on a toilet.

First I had to listen to all her objections. "It's against my principles to show Jews as victims. That time is long gone. Also, I don't like to frighten the kids. We got to make it funny."

I couldn't quite figure out how we could make murder funny but I was willing to give Beverly Bernstein as much artistic license as she needed.

"And that Patti. How do we know she can work a puppet?"

"Patti can do anything," I assured her, hoping I was telling the truth.

"What about that cop? He's going to ruin my performance. Stop it in the middle!"

I shrugged. Murphy would do what Murphy would do. I couldn't guarantee anything in regard to Murphy.

"And where is this show going to be held?" she asked me.

I was ready for that one. "Emily's Place, of course. I might even give you a discount on a new pair of shoes if everything goes as well as I hope it will."

"What about the jewels I found in my shoes?

"What Jewels?" I asked her.

Then, I had to put the word out around the neighborhood that a new, original puppet show was being produced special for little Patti's birthday—the same Patti who had so miraculously escaped from her kidnappers. The whole neighborhood was invited to celebrate her good fortune. This part, I left to SuperMama, Sammy, Alec le Grand and my own Merissa .Murphy and I invited Bellini personally.

Beverly said her preparations would take two weeks. In the meantime, Murphy would put a tail on the Senator to be sure he couldn't knock off anyone else. There was plenty for all of us to do.

"Welcome," Murphy greeted The Senator. "Have a glass of wine. I don't know much about wine but Emily here, only buys the best."

The Senator sniffed the air, looked around and bowed slightly. "I come from a part of Italy that grows the most famous grapes." He nodded to me and extended his hand.

I shivered. I was glad it was Murphy and not me who greeted him. He seemed smaller, slighter, paler than when I had seen him a couple of weeks ago. He was carrying a cane. When he smiled, his skin stretched over his bony face, exposing a skull almost poking through his thin flesh. When he moved, I heard the rustle of wings. Surely this was the Angel of Death incarnate. With the help of Shakespeare and a little luck, today we would make the words of John Donne's poem come true.

I looked over Emily's Place. All decked out for a celebration. There were balloons filled with helium that had floated to the ceiling. There were bands of criss-crossed, crepe-paper in red, white and green, stretched across all the display cases. Tonight there would be no selling of shoes—only, the gathering of souls.

I had invited everyone on my customer list—more than three hundred people—from all over the city, including Brooklyn, Queens and The Bronx. Patti had invited her entire class. I had rented the empty space next door, as in Big Bingo, but tonight the only offering was an original adaptation of Hamlet, by Beverly Bernstein.

The wine was only for The Senator. Murphy wanted to capture his fingerprints and his DNA on the glass. For the other guests, Beverly, Sammy and I had made little Italian flags. I thought of tonight as not only a celebration of the return of Patti, but also a memorial service for my old friend Sophia Sarfatti, her sister, and all those dead souls whose jewels were secreted in the shoes that fell of the truck.

The Senator looked over the transformation of Emily's Place. On the far end was the stage, all the rest of the space, except for a small area near the entrance, was filled with chairs.

"Red, white and green," he said, "The colors of the Italian Flag."

I nodded. "A celebration of all our Italian friends."

The Senator shuffled his feet. "Where are the others?" he asked.

Murphy moved quickly to his side. "They'll be here, any minute now."

As if on cue, sure enough, there was Rachael Goldsmith, in her Prada four inch heels, coming through the door. "I came early to get a good seat," she told me, as she threw me a kiss.

And then there was Merissa, wearing a long, yellow taffeta dress with a yellow turban to match and red sequined Jimmy Choo sandals on her feet. She swept into the room, followed by her current sweetheart, our good friend, Alec le Grand. Even our dapper Alec was lost in the aura of Merissa's entrance, and he scurried to keep up with her as she moved quickly towards a seat in the sixth row—plunk in the middle of the seating arrangement.

I took a sip of my wine and held up my glass. "Centani!" the Senator said, the traditional Italian toast—100 years of life! But I couldn't bring myself to clink glasses with him. I pulled my glass back at the last moment, and turned away.

When I turned around again, I saw Murphy had a firm hold on his arm and was leading him to a seat, front row center, in row one in front of the stage. Murphy sat on one side of him, a young woman, who I recognized as Denise, a cop who worked in his precinct, sat on his other side.

I had left the play pretty much to Beverly and Sammy, but we had agreed on some of the scenes. There would be the transportation of the Jews. There would be a little girl clinging to the uniform of a police officer. There would be a tearing off of a button and then a shot. There would be a scene in which an old lady was given a glass of tea to drink and then she dropped dead. How exactly Beverly was going to turn this into a puppet show for kids, I left to her.

You have to trust someone.

Nevertheless, I had made my own back-up plans. Merissa was planted dead center in the audience. Giancarlo would be sitting three rows in back of her. Nancy the fence would be planted three rows in back of him. In the same row, on the right side would be seated my window-dresser Harold Shapiro. And at the very back would be my old friend, Angelina Grossi.

No one would be able to escape.

"Any wine for me?" my sister Shana planted a kiss on my cheek. She was dressed from head to toe in orange. Vladimir wore jeans and a dark blue windbreaker.

I hadn't assigned them any special seats. I loved my sister but her record of dependability was questionable. On the other hand, it occurred to me that Vladimir would be great at the door. Big and brawny as he was, he could certainly stop The Angel of Death from flying away. I stationed him there. I handed over my glass of wine to my sister. I had reserved a seat in the sixth row, near Merissa and Alec le Grand but I was too nervous to sit down. Shana downed the wine and roamed around the edges of the audience, calling greetings to people she knew.

They were all coming in now, one after another. I waved to Sally Henderson; I threw a kiss to Tiffany Brown; I nodded hello to Maria Ruiz and her friend Carlotta Sanchez. There was Nancy the fence; Jose the newspaper delivery guy.

And here was Massimo Bellini. His streaked gray hair combed back neatly. His face freshly shaven. He wore a double-breasted blue blazer, gray flannel trousers and a pair of elegant dark brown Italian shoes. On the lapel of his jacket was a brass insignia of some sort.

"What is that?" I asked, pointing to it.

Bellini bowed and kissed my hand. "It belonged to my father. It was the chief of police insignia he had once worn so proudly. He had to hide it in a drawer, but he took it to America."

Bellini's reserved seat was right behind The Senator's.

And then there was a bit of a tumult at the door and when I turned around, Vladimir was surrounded by a group of little kids and a very cute young teacher with short blond hair.

"The First Grade Class of St.Catherine's Church, I do believe," I greeted her.

"Andrew, stop that!" she pulled the sleeve of a little kid who had grabbed a hand-full of the little flags.

"We've saved the whole second row (except for one seat) for your class" I told her, and waved her in the right direction.

I looked around. Things were beginning to get a little wild. There seemed to be more people than seats and more seemed to be coming through the doors. Too late I realized I should have had some ushers or some people to try to check invitations.

Who were all these people?

And then I thought to myself, did it really matter? Let them all come. Let the whole neighborhood come. Let the whole of New York City come. We were here to celebrate life and put an end to The Angel of Death.

And then the lights dimmed. There was the mournful sound of a cow-bell and the curtains opened. A puff of smoke and there center stage was a small green figure, with giant ears, wearing a blue policeman's uniform, complete with brass buttons.

And emerging from the puff of smoke was another figure—bright blue—this one with white hair put up in a bun wearing a long, flowing nightgown and little glasses.

Ah oh—Beverly's Martians had returned to play Hamlet!

For a moment they circled each other, as the cow bell rang out.

"Wait! Wait! Wait!—what! What! What is this?" The Martian cop hopped around on stage. Could that be Beverly's hoarse voice spilling out his words?

"Boo!" cried out the old blue lady. She had the high-pitched voice of little Patti

The Martian cop fell down and the kids went wild with laughter. Then the old blue lady began to speak in a squeaky voice:

"I am the ghost of an old lady who once lived at 135 West 97th Street, in an old house."

The Green Cop quivered behind a cardboard box

"What? What? What?" he questioned the ghost, "Go away, go away."

He spit three times on the stage and then he made the sign of the cross. That really got the kids from St. Catherine's going. Little Andrew threw a couple of the flags he took on to the stage.

"You have to help me," the ghost implored, "A bad man put something bad in my tea and it made me very sick."

"What! What! What?" the green Cop seemed to gather his courage. "I'll get him! I'll get all the bad guys!"

Then he tripped over the box he was hiding behind. The entire audience roared.

"What did he put in your tea?" he asked, after he got up and brushed himself off.

"He put a whole lot of sugar in my tea!"

The Green Cop took off his hat and scratched his head.

"What! What! What? Sugar is good to put in tea."

He rubbed his stomach. "I love sugar!"

The old blue lady moaned and rubbed her tummy." But I have diabetes—I can get really sick from sugar. I can't even eat a cookie!"

And then she walked to the front of the stage and addressed the audience

"Any of you kids have Diabetes! You know you can't have regular cookies, Right?"

Three hands went up immediately. And then SuperMama rose up from one of the back seats and the spot-light lit up her huge form.

"Me!" she called out. "I's got diabetes. Can't hardly eat anything anymore. You got to watch out for sugar!"

I had forgotten all about SuperMama. There she was though—smack in the center of the last row, sitting right next to Angelina Grossi. Ready to deliver her message to all the young people in the neighborhood—and ready to help Vladimir block anyone's escape from the back door.

I tried to see how The Senator was taking all this but he was way in the front and that row was not in the spotlight. The play continued for a while. Instead of a kingdom being stolen, there was a toy shop, whose kindly owner—now the old blue ghost—had been robbed and cheated. I had to admit that Beverly had talent. She was wasting herself as a kindergarten teacher. Her sets were simple but very evocative. For the toy store, she had borrowed one of my shoe displays and filled it with some old toys—but front and center was a large doll with a porcelain face and long, curly blond hair. She came to life a couple of times, her blue-eyes flashing—to point the finger at the two bad boys who ran in and out of the store, stealing little balls and plastic cars. They ran rings around the old blue lady and elicited screams of laughter from all the kids. I figured Sammy was handling those puppets.

Then one of the bad boys took off the big doll's shoe. They huddled over it for a couple of minutes. Then one of them produced a box with the word SUGAR written on it. They chuckled to each other and then one of them poured it into the doll's shoe. They put the shoe back on the doll.

"Now her foot will get all sticky when she tries to walk," one of them said. And then the old blue lady chased them around the stage.

Suddenly the spot light began playing on the audience, it stopped here and there on the kids in row two, as Beverly's voice called out, "Who's a Bad Boy? Who's a Bad Girl?"

The kids yelled out "Not Me!" and pointed to one another.

Beverly was a whizz at eliciting audience participation.

And then the spotlight stopped on Giancarlo. Giancarlo rose slowly to his feet.

As if by magic, he took a toy truck out from under his cap. And then he lifted up a shoe—Sophia Sarfatti's shoe—and then he sat down.

There was some scuffling in the front row, near The Senator's Seat. I heard some loud phrases in Italian, but it was too dark to see. The spotlight returned to the stage, where the old blue lady was trying to figure out how she could trap these bad boys.

She decides to put on a play, to make the little boys sorry for their bad behavior.

And then the play within the play began to unfold.

There was the blue old lady climbing into her bed. Then—emerging from behind a curtain was a truly sinister figure—he was done up dark green and looked a lot like a vampire—with fangs and big black wings.

"Hello, my dear friend," he said approaching the old blue lady. The voice was Beverly's.

She screamed and pushed him away. "You're no friend of mine!" she yelled out.

"Oh yes, yes, yes… the vampire insisted.

He tried to hide his long black wings by sitting on them, but of course it was no-go. They filled up the chair and he toppled over. He tried to kiss her hand but his fangs got in the way and the old lady pulled her hand away, just in time.

Everyone in the audience was roaring with laughter. Then he picked up a tea kettle and poured something into a cup at the side of the bed. Then when the old blue lady turned her head, he poured a box of sugar into it. He handed it to the old lady. She picked up the cup.

"I'm so thirsty," she cried out.

"Don't drink it! No! no! No! the kids in the second row yelled to her. "It's poison!"

She lifted the cup once again.

The kids yelled again. "Don't do it!. No! it's bad!"

She lowered the cup.

The third time she put the cup to her lips and immediately, grabbed her stomach and fell off the bed.

And then the stage went black and the spotlight fell squarely on The Senator., sitting smack in the middle of the front row.

For a moment he looked dazed. Then he tried to rise. He was yelling something out in Italian and Murphy was trying to hold him still.

And then there was some noise coming from the back row

"WOOOOOOO….WOOOOO…"

Whoever was working the lights searched the audience and finally stopped at a figure all in black—her black wig tied up in a bun, black stockings and shoes.

And flying circles above her head—a dark feathered bird who crocked out the word: 'EVERMORE….EVERMORE….

My friend, Angelina Grossi and faithful companion, Henry, her gray Parrot. After all, Angelina already had the costume. As for Henry—she seemed to have managed to color his feathers black. As the spotlight followed her, she made her way out of the row and moved slowly towards the middle of row one.

"WOOOO…WOOOO…Centanni…Poverina…Centanni… Niente!…Centanni…Wooooooo." Swirling above her and accompanying her ever cry with cries of his own was Henry—now carrying his own message of doom.

The audience was absolutely stunned. Not a cough or a movement marred their performance. She even surprised me. I had planned for Angelina's appearance, but had forgotten completely about Henry. When she got to the Senator, she paused and let out one more "WOOOOOOOOOO" And then she fell to the ground. Henry seemed to make a head-long dive in the same direction. The lights went out.

Act One was over.

When the lights went back on—Angelina and her black feathered friend were gone. Only still floating this way and that on the air above row one, was a single, fluffy black feather.

The Senator was bent over in his seat with Murphy holding tightly to his arm. Others seemed to gather around him. I couldn't see much more. There was to be no intermission, but the lights stayed on for a few minutes as people gasped and questioned each other.

"Who was she? Where did she go? What will happen next?"

On stage there was some shuffling about. A couple of the kids needed to use the bathroom.

And then the lights dimmed again and Act Two began.

The little green boys who had been stealing toys now hung their heads. The doors to the toy store were locked. The sign said a " vegetable stand" was going to open there instead.

All the kids in the audience groaned.

The green cop arrived and chased the little green boys away. And then there was a puff of smoke and a little blue Martian with long, golden curls emerged. The Green Cop hid behind a cardboard water hydrant. "What? What? What? What do you want?" he stammered.

The little blue girl moved forward. On her arm was a red band with a large M. on it. "I am the ghost of that old lady you met in the first scene."

The green cop shivered. "But ….but….but…."

The little blue girl shook her finger at the green cop. "You didn't catch that bad man!" she admonished him.

"But! But! But… he's not a man. He's a Vampire. No one can catch him."

"Yes" She said. "Yes you can. You just need to believe you can." She walked closer to the green cop and held out her arm." Look what he did to me!

"What? What. What? That's an M. Why are you wearing a band with an M?"

"The M stands for 'Martian.'

The green cop shook his head. "I'm a Martian; you're a Martian; everybody here on Mars are Martians. What's the big deal?"

"The big deal is that I'm a blue Martian and the vampire is a green Martian. He wanted to send me to Saturn. He wanted to send all the blue Martians to Saturn. Saturn is very far away. Martians can't breathe on Saturn. My asthma would really be a problem. "

She approached the green cop and put her arms around him.

"He sent my sister to Saturn. She never came back. He sent hundreds of blue Martians to Saturn. You've got to punish him!"

The green cop marched forward. "I'll take care of him! Where is he! I'll get him now!"

While this little speech was going on, the vampire popped up and hid behind a tree. As the green cop went looking for him, the vampire hid behind a carton; then he hid behind the fire hydrant, always one step ahead of the green cop. The whole audience called out "Over There! No…over There!"

When the green cop finally got hold of the vampire, the vampire protested his innocence.

"Who me? I didn't do anything. This ghost is making it all up! Trust me! I wouldn't hurt a fly!"

With that a buzzing was heard and the vampire viciously stumped on something. "Let me go! Let me go!" he struggled with the green cop.

The ghost turned to the green cop, who now held tightly to the vampire's arm. "I'll have the players show you just what that bad vampire did!"

The lights went out for a couple of seconds. When they went on again, the scene had been changed to something that looked like a train station. Again, Beverly had managed the illusion with just a couple of props. There was a cardboard cut-out of a steam engine. There was a black and yellow railroad sign that is used at crossings. Fog bathed the stage.

Now there was another cop. This cop was wearing an old fashioned uniform, a darker green with bigger buttons. On his head he wore a cap with a brass coat of arms on it.

The little blue girl with the golden curls was carrying a small suitcase and a big doll. Two of the other blue players were dressed as adults, a man wearing a brown hat and brown coat; a woman wearing a red hat and red coat. The policeman gesticulated towards the train. The little girl clung to the hand of her mother. The policeman pulled her away from her mother and pushed her towards the train.

Then the little girl fell to her knees and clung to the uniform of the cop. The cop pulled away and the little girl fell on the ground, a brass button clutched in her hand.

The audience held its breath. There was absolute silence.

And then there a loud shout was heard—followed by a stream of words in Italian coming from the front row. The spotlight began panning the audience and lighted on The Senator.

He had risen from his seat and grabbed his cane. He approached the stage and shouted at the puppets. And then, while the entire audience watched, he grabbed his cane and began striking the puppets and pulling at the flimsy wooden rods and spokes that held up Beverly's puppet theater.

And there was Murphy trying to pull him back into his seat but the Senator pushed him away. He had summoned strength from somewhere. For a moment his dark shadow loomed large in the spotlight—his arms flailing like giant wings.

My breath caught in my throat. Had I really believed that I could capture The Angel of Death? In Dante's Hell one of the rings was reserved for those who committed the Sin of Pride—and I wasn't even Catholic.

Nonsense! I was beginning to be as superstitious as SuperMama. It was time for action.

I tried to make my way to the front row of chairs but everyone was up now and crowding the aisles. I grabbed a chair and climbed on top of it. I watched as the man we called The Senator and others called "The Angele of Death, tear wildly at the curtain with one hand; with the other he swung his cane hard against the structural walls. He made a few futile lunges for the puppets themselves. And then, in one final sweep of his cane, he brought the entire little theater tumbling down on top of him.

There, exposed to the light were little Patti, Beverly Bernstein and Sammy—the Puppeteers, They looked stunned—suddenly naked—exposed to the audience.

Suddenly, the spotlight went out and the houselights went on. I saw Murphy snap the handcuffs on The Senator.

Patti clung to his other arm. The audience swirled around me, swirled around them, everyone began yelling at once and at last, I saw Murphy and another policeman half carrying The Senator out the door. Patti following closely behind.

At that moment, SuperMama rose again.

I don't know how the crowd noticed her, but as she slowly struggled to her feet—it was as if the voice of a mountain—the

Blind Seer—was about to speak. Whatever it was, the crowd grew eerily quiet.

SuperMama moved her big head to the right and then to the left. And then she said: "The Angel of Death. He done died today!"

As if in unison, the entire audience began to cheer. They embraced one another, they kissed each other on both cheeks, they shouted "Hooray!" And then they began to make their way down the aisles, and through the door into the street.

Act Three was supposed to depict the murder of Frankie-the-Fox but we didn't need it. Murphy would surely have enough evidence to put The Angel of Death away forever. John Donne would have been proud!

SIXTEEN

Shopping for shoes is a fantasy for many women, who believe the right shoe can change them from an ordinary housewife into an exciting, exotic, sexual partner.

"So this is the famous Beverly Bernstein," Larry the loser said, "I've heard so much about you."

Was that a blush I saw rising from Beverly's neck and slowly spreading over her cheeks?

I never thought Beverly was the type to blush. But of course, Larry-the-Loser was capable of eliciting all kinds of unexpected responses from people. That is why he had been such an effective prosecutor. I busied myself by adjusting the napkin on my lap and tried hard to hold my tongue. It wouldn't do to try to spoil his sport. Not yet. After all, he was here at my invitation. To do me, and Beverly a favor.

He motioned to the waiter. "How about some Orzo? What do you two lovely ladies say?"

"Sure—why not? It's Sunday. Nobody's working." I answered for both of us.

We were sitting at a corner table at Niko's, a semi-upscale Greek restaurant in the neighborhood. It was semi-upscale in that it had tablecloths.

Larry looked over the menu. "I recommend the meat-balls and the Moussaka," he told her.

"I only eat fish," Beverly answered. "Better for the planet."

Larry threw me one of his, 'not another one of your nut-cases' kind of glance. I shrugged.

"I'll have the meat-balls," I said.

Beverly had a Bronzino fish, lightly grilled. "No sauce," she said. "I'll take a couple of wedges of lemon. Only grill one side. Don't put any vegetables on the plate with it. I'll take everything else on the side—separate plates." She leaned over the table. "I don't like the juices to run together."

Okay. So all my friends are a little strange. What can I tell you?

"Thanks for coming," I said to Larry when our drinks arrived. "We have something we'd like you to do for us."

"My pleasure," he beamed, downing his drink in one gulp.

A regular Zorba the Greek, is my estranged husband Larry-The-Loser. Always taking pleasure wherever he can find it. Had he taken to drink since I left him? He always liked a couple of scotches. I bit my lip. What Larry-the-Loser did or didn't do was no longer my business. But twenty years of living with him had left some habits hard to break.

"You ladies are to be congratulated. I read all about how you trapped that war criminal into convicting himself—in front of the entire neighborhood."

Beverly beamed. "There will be plenty of witnesses. Son-of-a-Bitch, piece of Shit."

I smiled at Larry. "Here's the thing. Beverly and I have some extra money and, this year, Big Bingo didn't bring in as much money as usual. There's a recession going on. Lots of people out of work."

Larry chuckled. "Seems to me, in your neighborhood, there are always people out of work."

Beverly shook her head. "They all work—just not at conventional jobs. Take Giancarlo, for example. That young man is very talented. He can do anything with his hands. Unfortunately, he tends to pick locks and hack into computers. Maybe you know someone, could use his talents? "

Larry looked down at his plate. "I'll give it some serious thought."

Translation: "What…are you crazy? All I need is some psychopathic kid on my hands. It's enough I'm still saddled with Shana." That's one of the consequences of being married for twenty years. I can always tell what Larry is thinking.

The waiter arrived and put down our plates.

"So, as I was saying, Beverly and I have some extra cash and we thought of making up the deficit by trying to set up some kind of annuity for the school."

Larry chewed thoughtfully. "Nice gesture, but you'd need quite a bit of cash for something like that."

Beverly bent over the table. "We've got about $100,000." she whispered. "That ought to be enough to buy some crayons, don't you think?"

Larry coughed and dropped his fork. I thought I'd have to give him the Heimlich maneuver. He took a gulp of water from his glass.

"That's a lot of money," he conceded. "I think I could work with that. I'd need a list of your bonds and securities."

"It's all cash," I remarked casually, reaching for a piece of pita bread. I dipped it into the olive oil and avoided looking at Larry.

Larry coughed again and cleared his throat. He looked at Beverly and then he looked at me. "If you don't mind my asking, where did you two ladies come up with all that cash?"

"Careful planning," Beverly quipped.

I nodded.

Larry scowled. "The IRS will want to know where the money came from. Better you should tell me than have to tell them."

"Reparations." Beverly said, "I had some relatives murdered by the Nazi's in Germany. Someone in the family found my address and sent me some jewelry that had been buried in the backyard."

Larry speared a meatball. "Do you have any letters attesting to this?"

"I can get some," she said. "I know a guy with magic in his fingers."

Larry shook his head. "I didn't hear that," he said, turning to me. "And you, where did your windfall come from?"

"I inherited it. I sold a diamond. It was in a safety deposit box left to me by Sophia Sarfatti."

Larry rolled his eyes. "You'll have to pay some kind of tax on that. Did you have it appraised?"

I was way ahead of him on that one. I had sold it to Nancy for $30,000 but he gave me an appraisal for $40,000. Since Sophia's entire estate was only worth about $75,000—she had left various bequests to different charities, there wouldn't be much tax to pay anyway—but at least I had a cushion. The full $30,000 could go into the annuity plan.

I had carried that diamond around with me for weeks. For a while it felt like a pebble from Hell, bringing only bad luck. But ever since The Senator had been caught, I had some warmer feelings towards it. I liked the feel of it. I liked the way it caught the light when I took it out to look at it. But the truth was, I really didn't have much use for a diamond like that. It would look out of place at Nino's, the pizza parlor on the corner of my street, the Three Brothers Diner around the block or even here at Niko's.

And, after I had seen that heel full of wedding rings, it made the fate of those lost people so vivid, I couldn't look at the stone again without thinking of them.

Ghosts, Zombies, like those from The Night of the Living Dead, stalking me night after night. No. Much better to give the diamond away—to transform it into an engine of good.

For a while, we all chewed our food in silence.

"Ok. I'll draw something up for you two ladies to sign. We'll have to discuss how you want to invest the money. I can make a few suggestions."

We shook hands all around. Larry motioned for the waiter.

"How about some dessert? "They have a lovely yogurt and honey dessert here. Very traditional."

After dessert, Larry looked at his watch.

"Got a date with a football game," he said to us. He shook hands with Beverly and gave me a kiss on the cheek.

"I'll see you next Friday night" he said to me. "We have a number of things to talk about."

I nodded. I had promised to go out with him next Friday. His pound of flesh. I had gotten rid of the diamond but now would have to take delivery of a mink coat. What was I thinking?

Beverly and I lingered over coffee.

"Nice guy, Larry," she said to me. "So what is it with you? You always refer to him as 'your estranged husband.' What does that mean?"

"It means we're estranged, as in strangers. We see each other occasionally but we don't live together."

Beverly seemed to mull this over. "But you are still legally married?"

"There is a piece of paper, says we are married. I say we are not. I live alone."

Beverly shrugged. "So Larry, your estranged husband, is, shall we say, up for grabs?"

This was annoying. What could Beverly be thinking? Larry was certainly not her type!

"He's not worth your time," I told her. "There's some Russian slut he's been screwing for years."

Beverly fiddled with her spoon. "I'm not worried about any Russian slut. I can do anything they can do better."

Here was a side of Beverly I hadn't seen before—and I didn't like it.

On the other hand, if I didn't want Larry, why was I still so annoyed when anyone else showed any interest? I had never really looked at Beverly before. I mean really looked—like maybe a guy would look at her. She was younger than me—probably not more than forty. She had wild, curly dark hair that defied the clips she was always sticking in. Her clothes always looked a little too tight to me—as if all of her was barely under control and ready to burst out at any moment. Some men would surely find this sexy.

"I think we need a couple more meetings with him to get this Annuity business straightened out. Did he say something about next Friday night?"

I shook my head. 'That's just for him and me. We've got family business to discuss."

Beverly looked up at me. "I thought you had no family."

"There's Shana," I told her. "My sister has a few legal problems we've got to sort out."

It was, after all, the truth.

Beverly sighed. I motioned for the check. "Let's split it," I suggested.

And we did.

Patti chewed contentedly on a chicken nugget and hugged her doll.

"Me girl—eat up! Eat up! Detective Little Belly needs all her strength to help Big Belly catch the bad guys!" Murphy's whole face lit up when he was with Patti. It was awesome to see. He offered her a bite of his Big Mac but she made a face and went back to her nuggets.

I reached over for the doll. "You wouldn't want to get your greasy finger marks all over her dress," I warned.

But Patti held tight to the doll.

"Don't know why you want anything to do with an old doll like that. She smells. I'll buy you a new Barbie. Any one you want—the one with a motorcycle. Remember you wanted that motorcycle for Christmas, right?"

Patti shook her head. Murphy had made that offer half a dozen times just during this lunch with the same result. Patti ignored him completely.

"So what is it about this particular doll that you like so much?" I asked her.

We waited while Patti gobbled up a French Fry.

"I like that the pumpkin head lady gave her to me. She is special. She can talk. She can be a detective too." She gave her a kiss. "I like her smell. She smells like mommy's closet."

Murphy mumbled something that sounded like "Piece of shit doll" under his breath. "The pumpkin head lady broke the law. I could put her in jail. She scared you and made you cry!"

Patti reached for another French fry and chewed contentedly.

I thought that Patti would go far in this world. She seemed to have the capacity to answer only those questions she felt like answering, engaging with only those people who interested her at the moment.

I chewed on my own Big Mac. It wasn't half bad. I removed the top of the roll to try to save a few calories. "I think your doll has been through a lot of stress—a kidnapping—catching a bad man. Maybe we can give her a little examination."

I reached for the doll, but Patti held her firm.

"Ok. Let's do it this way. I will call out a part of the doll, and you do an examination—that way if any part of her is broken, we can find out and fix it up."

This seemed to be an idea that Patti could live with. She put down her French fry and lifted up the skirt of the doll.

"Two legs, made of leather" I called out.

Patti felt the legs. "OK!" she said.

"Face made of china!"

Patti looked closely at the face. "Right!"

"Eyes that open and close!"

Patti moved the doll's head up and down. "Right!"

"Old fashioned Dress and shoes!"

Patti picked up the dress. She took off and replaced each shoe. In one of them, there was still a little sugar from the puppet show. She carefully spilled it out onto the table.

"Right!" she called out.

"Well then. I think all is in order." I reached into my pocketbook and took out a print-out from my computer.

"I'd take care of that doll, if I were you," I said to Murphy. "It won't pay for her first year of college, but maybe if you invest the money wisely now—you'll have a head start." I handed the print-out to Murphy. It was the record of a German made doll from the 1860's, that showed up for an appraisal recently on the Antique Road Show. The photo was a dead-ringer for the doll Patti now held in her greasy fingers. It had been appraised for $8,000.

"That doll was given to Sammy as a gift by Sophia Sarfatti. She had brought it with her when she came from Germany all those years ago. It had probably once belonged to Sophia's mother."

Murphy looked over the print-out, folded it and put it in his pocket.

"That doll is evidence," he said. "Got to take it down to the station one of these days."

Patti held the doll close and turned away.

"I don't think so." I told him. "The doll is a gift from the lady in the pumpkin mask. She's already pleaded guilty to a misdemeanor. The doll isn't evidence of anything except Sammy's good nature."

Murphy stared at Patti. "Evidence is Evidence."

Patti stood up and stamped her foot. "Okay," Murphy conceded. "I'll think about it."

I took a sip of my soda. It felt good to be with Patti and Murphy. They were beginning to feel more and more like family. I began to wonder about getting a bigger apartment. If I had a two-bedroom apartment, one above ground with windows in all the rooms—would Murphy bring Patti to visit me? Would they ever stay for a weekend? I made a note to myself to check the real estate section in the New York Times when I got home later. There was still a recession going on and the prices of rentals were falling. Also, if I had to say so myself, Emily's Place was thriving. This was a plan I would need to think about more seriously. For the moment though, I needed to turn my attention to the here and now.

"Patti and the doll did help you catch The Senator, remember. Patti deserves some kind of reward."

Murphy raised one of his eye-brows and stared at me. "The Senator surely did bring down the house, now didn't he?"

We all laughed at that one.

"And of course I did help a little," I reminded Murphy. "You found a match between The Senator's fingerprints I got from his wine glass and those mixed-up shoes in Sophia's apartment."

Murphy nodded. "Don't forget the tea canister. His prints were all over the tea canister. 'course he could have claimed that he visited her frequently and made her tea. The really damming evidence was the WWII revolver and policeman's uniform we found in his apartment."

I wondered if I should remind Murphy that I had first put the finger on The Senator when I recognized those cufflinks he had been wearing. I decided to hold my tongue. Take a page out of Patti's book. I couldn't help shivering though, every time I thought of what kind of creature could murder innocent people in that way—and then memorialize the events by casting his uniform buttons into 14k gold. And the more I thought about Sophia Sarfatti, the more I admired her courage—and her intelligence.

She had kept that brass button her murdered sister had torn from the uniform of that Fascist policeman; she had kept the photo of herself and her sister; and she had left the contents of that safety deposit box to me, because she knew I was clever enough to figure out how to use them.

"In fact, lots of people helped finally capture The Senator. Beverly Bernstein and her wonderful Martian puppets; Sammy and Patti here as brilliant puppeteers. Giancarlo confessed he had been threatened by him—made to break into my computer. And that he was the one who had been sending the shoes from Italy. When The Senator saw him stand up during The Puppet show, he must have realized his game was up." I hoped that Murphy would cut some kind of decent deal with Giancarlo so he wouldn't have to do much jail time.

Murphy laughed. "I'd say so. I had to hold him down. He wanted to destroy him with his cane."

"And then there was Angelina Grossi. She really sent him over the edge."

Even Patti laughed now. 'The lady who kept saying WOOOOO! She scared me. Beverly didn't know who she was."

Angelina. My insurance that everything would work out the way it actually did. We had all been very lucky.

"And of course, we need to give credit to SuperMama, William Shakespeare and my old friend John Donne."

Murphy crossed himself. "Let's hope The Angel of Death stays dead. Looks as if he was preparing to return. Used some of his loot to build a fancy tomb for himself. Staked out a nice plot in that cemetery in Westchester. Rose marble and stained glass windows. I had wondered what the old guy would do with the money if he had been able to lay his hands on it. Too bad—he only got the tomb half finished. Probably drove him nuts."

"Nuttier." I commented. "Do you think that Bellini will ever be able to clear his father's name?"

Murphy shrugged. "Who knows? I think it will still be tough. He was, after all, The Chief of Police in Milan, who signed most of the deportation papers. He's not here to profess his innocence. An international court might still find him guilty of collaboration. I guess Bellini will have to be satisfied that at least he was able to bring down the monster behind the acts of destruction. If you ask me, none of those people were lily-white."

I nodded. I wondered where Bellini and his father had gotten the money to buy an apartment building in the U.S. I wondered too what the ordinary person, living back in those times, would do to save themselves and their families.

Murphy's thoughts seemed to run alongside of mine. "Wonder how many of those stones Bellini found in the heels of those shoes he kept for himself. We know he had bought one pair from me; he had tracked down a few more at that store on Arthur Avenue. He claimed to have turned over whatever he found—an assortment of diamonds, rubies, and sapphires, worth several hundreds of thousands of dollars."

Murphy yawned. "Temptation. Temptation is a terrible thing. Take your friend Beverly Bernstein, for example. Sure—she gave me back a handful of stones—but how many did she put in her own pocket? And then there's that Gallina—the Russian girl. How many rings did she keep for herself? I guess we'll never know. And then there is your little sister Shana."

He took a sip of his soda and looked at me.

"What about my sister Shana?" I had my own suspicions about my baby sister—but I wasn't about to squeal on her to Murphy the Cop.

"She told me there was nothing in the heels she left in the cab. Vladimir found the shoes and tracked down the owner. Does that seem like a realistic scenario to you?"

Now it was my turn to yawn. "Shana doesn't go by the rules of reality. She lives in her own universe. I don't know what to say about Vladimir."

"I would suggest a scenario in which either your pretty little sister discovers a treasure in the shoes and decides to dump the shoes in a cab after she cleans them out, thinking that would be the end of them—or she really does forget them in the cab and this fellow Vladimir, who figures he'll sell the shoes to his friend at the flea market, jiggles them around, hears some clinking noises and pries off the heels. Lo and behold, he finds a fortune in precious stones and he thinks there may be more where those came from, so he tracks down the pretty little owner of the shoes to find his fortune."

"I guess we'll never know. Neither one of them is likely to confess to me."

Murphy smiled. "And then there are the diamonds that you found in the heels of Sophia Sarfatti's shoes. You never mentioned she had left you one in that safety deposit box."

"Oops. Guess it slipped my mind."

Murphy leaned over the table. 'Temptation. It's how the Devil works."

"How would you know?" I asked him. "Don't think you've ever experienced it."

Murphy chuckled. "You're only half right. Money? Jewels? No. They don't tempt me. Now, but …." he fell silent.

"That's only half a sentence," I told him.

"Well, me girl. That's all I'm offering."

Devil's work, he called it. Temptation. What were his temptations? And how hard did he fall? He might have used that old Brooklyn saying, if he knew it: That's for me to know and for you to find out.

Patti had finally finished all her food and literally licked her fingers clean.

I picked up the dirty napkins and empty paper cups and dumped them into a garbage can.

Patti reached up for my hand; the other was held firmly in Murphy's and we walked out into the Spring sunshine.

"it's such a fine day, my lovelies," Murphy said. "How about maybe we go on a Ferry Boat Ride to Staten island?"

Patti literally jumped up and down. "I love the Ferry Ride! I want to see the Boats! I want to see The Statue of Liberty!"

I thought it was a fine idea myself. It had been years since I had been on The Staten Island Ferry. About ten years to be exact when my friend Rita Kamorofsky visited from San Francisco.

And then there was that hated little ding-a-ling.

Murphy let go of Patti's hand and reached into his breast pocket where he kept the phone with his private number.

"Yeah! Well…I've still got a couple of hours. It's only 3:00 O'clock! So…she can be a little late for the birthday party. Come on!" And then he turned his back and I didn't hear the rest of the conversation. When he turned around again, I could tell from his face what he was about to say. "Well—my lovelies—looks like we have a little conflict of events here." He knelt down to Patti's level. "it seems you have a birthday party to go to at 4:00 and we've got to get moving or you'll miss the cake and ice cream!"

Patti stamped her foot. "I want to go to Staten Island."

Murphy lifted her up. ‘Hey Little Belly. You know what happens when you get orders from The General. Sometimes even Big Belly’s got to listen up. The General says the Birthday party is for Timmy Daley who is your very special friend. If you don’t show up, he will feel real bad.”

Patti clutched her doll and said nothing—but she didn’t struggle either.

Murphy turned to look at me. “Sorry about this. Another time. I promise.” His arms were full so he couldn’t even shake my hand. He nodded in my direction. “I’ll be in touch,” he said, and he set off down the block without a backward glance.

I stared after him for a minute or two.

No. That wasn’t my family and it never would be. I would need to stop thinking about getting a bigger apartment.

I looked up and down the block—Sancho’s Grocery; Nina’s Beauty Salon; Patty Palomino’s Bar.

I didn’t have much of a family but I did have a neighborhood.

My store, Emily’s Place, was right around the corner. I decided then and there to expand my store instead of my apartment.